A WHISPER IN THE WILD

A KINGDOM OF ANIMAL NOVEL

ALLYSA SALENA

SUNSHINE HOUSE

DISCLAIMER:

This is a work of fiction. Names, characters, places, and incidents either are the product of the author's imagination or are used fictitiously. Any resemblance to actual persons, living or dead, events or locales, is entirely coincidental.

TRIGGER WARNINGS:

A Whisper in the Wild is an action-packed fantasy novel in a world where herbivores and carnivores live harmoniously. Despite their peaceful coexistence, the animal spirits are still human and, as we know, humans can be the most violent creatures of all. Throughout the novel, readers can expect battle scenes with hand-to-hand combat, bloodshed, violence, and brutal injuries, threats of kidnapping, discussion of mental health issues including depression and anxiety, and minor uses of graphic language.

For a comprehensive list of triggers, please visit the author's website:

www.allysasalenawrites.com

PREFACE

This is a novel for readers who love fast-paced high fantasy, animals, and otherworldly kingdoms. While the animals and some aspects of the novel were inspired by Africa and African culture, the world that exists in *A Whisper in the Wild* is fictional and entirely separate from the world we live in. As a lover of Disney's *The Lion King* and Marvel's *Black Panther*, author Allysa Salena created a diverse kingdom of animal shifters featuring a diverse cast of characters. Readers can expect a strong female main character, family and found family, chosen one/prophecy elements, and a coming-of-age story with romance, nature-based magic, and epic adventures. Immerse yourself in the vibrant Kingdom of Animalia as you explore the jungles, plains, and deserts in, *A Whisper in the Wild*.

GLOSSARY

Please see the glossary in the back of this novel for further information about the animals featured in this book. There you can learn about each species' endangerment status and how you can help with animal and wildlife conservation.

KINGDOM OF ANIMALIA

TUNDRE
ZALAN
Isle of Zwolfa
SANDSTONE
CHAHINI DESERT
GEON MAJIK
UMAN
Poacher's Land

CONTENTS

PART I | CHAPTER 1

EVERYTHING YOU SEE EXISTS TOGETHER IN A DELICATE
BALANCE. AS KING, YOU NEED TO UNDERSTAND THAT
BALANCE AND RESPECT ALL THE CREATURES, FROM
THE CRAWLING ANT TO THE LEAPING ANTELOPE.
- MUFASA, DISNEY'S THE LION KING

"Stop hesitating. You gotta aim to kill."

Kat sharpened her focus and tightened her grip. With powerful strength, she pulled back the bowstring and watched as the arrow missed the target and crackled into an old hazelwood tree.

The faceless lump of hay stared at her mockingly. Repositioning, Kat tried to strike the scarecrow again, but the combination of shaky hands and an uneven breath caused her to miss for the eighth time in a row.

"Come on, you can do much better than that. You didn't miss a single one last week," Amos said, yanking the missed arrows out with an inhuman-like ease.

The wood crackled and split upon their release, spewing chunks of bark and wood splinters against his forearm.

Kat hesitated to declare that her brother had matured. Physically, he had a faint line of stubble, yet yesterday, the pair spent the afternoon hiding in the barn instead of tending to the fields of their family's tea and spice farm.

Mature. She didn't think so. He was just different, like a raging ball of hormones with a need to cause trouble.

Kat took the arrow from Amos's grasp and lined herself in front of the target. Her brother's golden eyes surveyed her footing, the position of her shoulders, and how high she held her head.

"No, no, no. Take a deep breath."

Grabbing the top of her shoulders, Amos used his body weight to push them down. A breath she didn't know she was holding released and worried frown lines plastered across her brother's face.

"Sounds like ya been holding that in for a while. You alright?" He carefully pulled the bow from her unsteady hands.

These panicked moments of chaos and impending doom had become an unwelcome part of her personality. It crept in like a beetle through the door cracks and when she least expected, it rattled against her ear drums like the fluttering buzz of wings.

"Nothing. I'm *fine*." Kat lied through seething teeth.

"Yeah, I'm sure you're *fine*." Amos gave her a skeptical look paired with an eye roll. "Let's just call it a day. Tomorrow's storms are coming a bit early. I can smell the must of it in the air."

She couldn't smell the rain. Never could until the clouds were hovering, pouring droplets on her skin. To Kat, the sky was clear as day, but who was she to argue with someone with senses twice as strong as her own?

Amos headed toward the boat and as he walked across the clearing, she could only picture him walking out of her life. She tried to move. Her mind willed it, but her body kept her frozen. There was a disconnect between the two. Spiraling thoughts combined with an increased heart rate caused her to lock up around a solemn heart.

Alone.

That's what she would be when her brother left to join the king's guard.

She spent her whole life surrounded by shifters who thought her hopes and dreams were forged with the webs of a vague and unsound prophecy. Her only reprieve was the support of her brother, the power of a weapon, and a scarecrow to take the blunt force of her anger.

Noticing she hadn't moved, Amos stopped in his path. "What's wrong, Wild Kat?"

The childhood nickname stirred at a small flutter in her heart. The golden glow of his eyes narrowed, and he held her gaze until she was no longer trembling. This made her wonder, how many times had he pulled her from this darkness and how was she to do this on her own?

"It's just I—I'll never be able to get this much practice without you."

It was a poor excuse that failed to mask the truth behind her words.

Without you.

His supportive gaze faltered but quickly flashed into a toothy grin. "You'll do just fine. You're strong, Kat. Stronger than any girl I know, and determined, too. You just gotta build that confidence and you'll be the toughest carnivore in all of Tulamund."

Fighting is for the boys. Her father's words were a constant echo that played on repeat every time she picked up a sword. Sometimes she found her target would take on the face of her father with narrowed eyes radiating his disappointment. Often it hindered her abilities, other times it fueled it.

"I'm not strong, Amos. I don't have any muscles. All I am is *beauty and birthing hips*," Kat said, rolling her eyes.

It was, as the women in their tribe often said, the only requirement for a young girl growing up in the heart of the kingdom.

"Oh, come on, look! Don't you see?"

He moved his fingertips to the small, barely visible bump on her gangly arms. With no warning, she was sucked into his wicked trap as his wiggling fingers dropped below her armpits. Her body reacted of its own accord, kicking him hard in the center of his shin. Hard enough for Amos to draw his hands away from her.

"You're wicked strong, you know that?" Amos dramatically rubbed his shin.

Normally, the element of surprise was how she stood a fighting chance against him, but as a young man coming into his Animalia abilities, he could hear, smell, and track her every movement.

"I didn't even mean to do that. I don't have it in me to fight and you know it," Kat argued.

His voice was coated with kindness as he pulled her into a hug.

"No one, and I mean no one, has your fire. The goddesses see it, I see it, and it's about time you did too."

With her eyes wandering across his freckled skin, she pictured him as a child, nearly as small as she felt. High dimples with a wide toothy grin and a full mane of chestnut curls sitting low on his shoulders.

Amos wasn't a liar, but Kat had a hard time opening herself up to the belief that she was destined for anything more than working on their family's farm. Even though she tried to ignore the curious gazes of the kingdom's shifters, the words of her prophecy played in her mind like the cadence of an echo.

Protect the child of the night.
Secure her tribe. Stake her claim.
Protect the child of the night.

Vague in its meaning and vague in its direction. It led their king to believe that a girl born to a herbivore tribe was destined to be a carnivore instead. Most days, it haunted her. She'd compare herself to anyone and everyone, and all the shifters she compared herself to shared the same question.

What made Katariya Abara so special?

Kat offered Amos a soft smile, as reassuring as she could make it. She *wanted* to believe him. It wasn't her fault that the voice in her head wasn't in agreement.

Sweeping her into his arms, Amos flung Kat over his shoulder like a defiant child. Laughter and screams echoed off the treetops as they approached the boat, where their sister Sade sat reading a book. Despite the curdling screams, Sade barely lifted her eyes to acknowledge their childish antics.

"Let me down!" Kat yelled, kicking her feet. "Let me down now!"

"No! Not until you make me a promise."

Tickling her side, she squealed and hollered like a wild boar.

"A promise?" she asked.

"I need you to follow your heart. Promise me you won't give up this part of yourself. Tell me you will keep practicing when I leave."

Holding onto her feet, Amos shook her side to side until Kat was a trembling mess filled with blind rage and violent laughter.

"Okay. Okay." Her laugh settled into shallow coughs. "I promise to keep practicing."

Jostling her once more, he pressed. "*And?*"

"I promise to follow my heart."

The words came out so quickly that Kat feared she'd have to say them again, but somehow, he took her rushed answer as the truth.

"Look." Amos leaned down to help her stand. "I know, and you know, that if we lived in an outside tribe, we would've been trained to use a weapon way before now. You'd have muscles on those gangly arms and be the toughest warrior in the city."

Although she had made promises, Kat wasn't entirely sure if his confidence in her held any truth. Even if she trained all day and night and started lifting extra crates of mangoes, women weren't allowed in the king's army. She'd never have the chance to show anyone but Amos the skills they had been practicing.

Often, she daydreamed of a life absent of countless rules, surrounded by spacious plains where she could wander and roam freely with no constraints. No longer bound by the mountains or the tightly packed streets of Tulamund, she'd have the freedom to fight, the power to defend herself, and the skills to squash anyone or anything that stood in the way of her dreams. That's what they were though.

Dreams. Wishes and wills that were cause for exile.

Their sister, Sade, peeked her nose up from the thin pages of her book.

"If you two lived outside the city, you would be fighting for your life. The lack of food and water should be enough to shut down that idea. Let alone the violence, thievery, and don't forget the *murder*! I'd rather catch these slimy fish than hunt for rabbits. Or better yet, we'd be savages forced to hunt one another."

Sade's typical bird song voice was filled with disgust.

"And what do you know, Sade? All the answers of the outside clans and tribes in those little books of yours," Amos grumbled as he untied the boat.

Sade scoffed. "These books contain knowledge that is far beyond your understanding. Knowledge that can cure illnesses—*save lives*. Answers that have helped our kingdom break from the reigns of violence and terror." She tilted her chin and stared directly into Amos's eyes. "You don't know what it's actually like to fight in a war. All you have are your fantasies and that stupid bow."

The pair argued back and forth until a buzzing tension grew between them. It wasn't anything new. Sade used her words as a weapon, while Amos fought back with mischief.

"I think we all need a cool down!"

His hand swept below the river's surface, and a spray of water splashed Kat.

"Amos!"

A high-pitched scream left her mouth as the cold rush shocked her system, shivering up and down her spine. Water droplets fluttered in between her eyelashes as Amos boomed with laughter.

Even though she didn't get hit, Sade's dramatic squeals were twice as loud, spooking a family of birds in the treetops. Her squeals only fueled their brother, turning the façade of a man into a playful child.

"Oh no, don't you dare! You can't get this dress wet!" Sade shrieked, backing up as far away from him as she could.

A mischievous look passed between Kat and her brother before a fit of laughter fell out of their mouth like a pair of cackling hyenas.

Amos cupped his hands below the water, and a wave twice as big as the first covered their entire frames.

No longer thrown off by the shocking surprise, Kat welcomed the refreshing cool down on a hot summer day. A rumbling giggle vibrated through her whole body as she listened to her sister's cries.

"I swear to the goddess, you both are going to regret this!" Sade screamed, ringing the water off her dress.

With her straight hair transforming into wavy curls, Sade no longer held any reservations about staying dry. Fueled by their brother's carelessness, Kat gasped as Sade splashed him directly in the face. Without a care in the world, the two sisters flung sprays of water until Amos was covered from head to toe.

Upon his beg for mercy, they settled back into their seats. Kat noted their reddened cheeks, wild eyes, and wide stretched grins.

There was nothing in this world she wanted more than to bottle up this feeling and hold on to it forever.

If she had a bottle, she would open up the cap and fill the air with the sound of their laughter, the soft hum of their favorite song, or even the chaos of their banter. Open up the cap and bask in the fonder memories where the burdens of growing older and meeting expectations withered, then melted away.

CHAPTER 2

STORMS MAKE TREES TAKE DEEPER ROOTS.
- DOLLY PARTON, AMERICA SINGER, SONGWRITER,
ACTRESS & PHILANTHROPIST

"What species do you think will be at the ceremony tomorrow?" Sade asked, flipping her species guide open to a tattered page.

Pictured was a detailed drawing of an Orangutan with rusted ginger fur, wide stretched arms and sand sunken eyes. The beast was a flanged male with big, padded cheeks and a thick flabby neck. Their neck pouches attracted the attention of females, but Kat could never see the appeal. All she could think about was how heavy the beast's head must be with all that excess fat.

"Well, I've heard talk of a redheaded girl from the Tiger clan. They say she's a real beaut, but her Pa has no interest in a union with a herbivore tribe." Amos's eyes danced while he drifted into a daydream about a girl he could never be with.

Under no real obligation or pressure, Amos signed away the next five years of his life to train as one of the king's fearsome warriors. He would no longer have time for her or their family, let alone a potential mate.

"I have to be prepared, Kat. I can't truly protect you if I don't have a warrior's training."

Regardless of his presence, Kat knew her safety was nothing to be concerned about. She had an overwhelming shield of cousins, uncles and an entire kingdom commanded by the goddesses and the king to protect her. Her brother didn't *need* to become a warrior to lead the tribe. The prophecy's call for her protection, some unnerving level of pride, and an unnecessary drive to be like their father, fueled Amos's interest.

"You never know. When the time comes, I can see Pa offering the girl's father all the vanilla and saffron his heart desires." Sade gave Amos a reassuring smile.

Stirred by a wicked idea, Kat turned to Sade giggling. "We'll have to look for her tomorrow! Maybe mention a few things about our dear brother."

Mischief mirrored on both their faces and Amos's cheeks turned bright red. Too stunned by the rare truce between the two sisters, he had to clear his throat three times before he could speak again.

"You two will do no such thing. Sade, you know better than to meddle in other shifter's affairs."

He redirected his gaze toward Kat and slammed a pointed finger at her chest. "And *you* won't say a word because after tomorrow I will live under the same roof as the prince. Just imagine all the embarrassing stories I could tell him in passing."

"Ohh, ohh! What about the time she thought that poor hippopotamus fella was just a large rock floating in the river?" Sade laughed, excited at the idea of torturing her little sister.

"That's not even fair! I swear he was completely covered in dirt. How—how was I supposed to know that the brown blob was a shifter?" Kat stuttered, mortified by the lingering embarrassment she felt when the poor fella kindly asked her to get off his back.

If it had happened to Amos, Kat would have brought the story up a few times to have a good laugh. If it happened to Sade, Kat would have made her sister relive the moment every single day of her life just to torture her. Her siblings were nicer than her. Well, they were until they plotted against her with plans on how they could embarrass her in front of the prince.

As they neared the shore, Kat could make out the faint outline of their father, Reevus Abara. His impala antelope spirit was aged from the hardships of not only being a respected war hero, but the stress that came with leading one of the largest tribes in Tulamund. With dark brown skin and a thick graying beard, his hazel eyes were reminiscent of hers, but were filled with stories and a legacy that Kat could only dream of fulfilling.

Now, as they drifted closer to the shore, their faces began to sweat, and their heartbeats quickened. Reevus Abara was an inspiration for many, but he was also a strict father. Each of their eyes darted to the back of the boat. Under Sade's seat were two swords, a bow, and several arrows.

Looking back and forth between her siblings and their father, Kat could already feel the swell of a red bottom. Haunted by the scoldings that would follow the punishment if he were to find out why she was so keen to join Amos on his fishing trips.

"Oh goddess, Pa's at the dock. Hurry up! Hide the bow," Amos begged, shooting Sade a pleading look.

Sade's eyes grew wide with fear as she stared down at the weapon.

"No, no way. I accompany you so that you two fools don't get hurt. I am not about to hide your antics from our father. No way. I'll never hear the end of it."

"Please, Sade. He'll punish all three of us if he finds out you have been keeping a secret." Amos held his hands together pleading.

"That *I've* been keeping a secret?" Sade raised her eyebrows.

To avoid drawing their father's attention, Kat sent him a friendly wave and plugged a strained smile onto her face. Through her tightly snapped teeth, she said, "Sade, you have known of my lessons since the beginning. What do you think Pa's gonna do when he finds out his perfect daughter has been lying to him?"

A shiver ran up Sade's spine. "Fine, but you both owe me. I mean it."

Shoving the bow under the seat, Sade used her foot to kick the arrows as far back as possible. Within moments to spare, the bow was concealed, but they continued to hold their breaths. Almost nothing went unnoticed by their father.

"Oh, my sweet children, what did you bring back for us to cook?" Their father asked, reaching out a hand to help the girls off the boat.

"Papa! Look how many crawdads we have!" Kat exclaimed.

Using all her might, she pulled out the bucket of fish. The water splashed off the rim, and a crawdad made a swift escape onto the docks.

"Crawdads, those slick little fellas. It's been a while since we've received a bundle. How far down the river did you go?" Her father asked, helping Sade from the boat.

Kat didn't miss the side eye he gave her brother. He said nothing yet, but from the corner of Kat's eye, she could see an arrowhead. Not only had it been sticking out, but it somehow rolled to the front of the boat. Right in front of Kat's seat.

"Pa, you know me. Sometimes the river just gets going and the next thing you know you've been talking to Atlaua, and she's answering all your prayers with your favorite last meal," Amos chuckled.

He reached down to pick up the floundering crawdad. Without a second thought, he ripped off the head of the crustacean before taking a crunching bite into its hard, shelled flesh.

It wasn't uncommon for Animalia to eat their fish raw, whole, and filled with shells and bones. Except that was the way of life for most carnivorous tribes, not herbivores.

"Yuck, you are disgusting!" Sade screamed in horror. Quickly, she snatched her satchel and made a swift exit up the stone pathway and into their family home.

Contrary to her sister, Kat and her father let out boisterous, full-bellied laughs.

"You're not dying, sweet boy! The king's warriors receive our spices almost daily. You should know that yourself. You have made plenty of trips up that mountain. There will be no talk of a so-called last meal," their father scolded, shaking his head.

"Pa, there's no doubt in the world that catching your own fish is the greatest gift of them all. I know there will be spices, but will we get crawdads on the daily? I highly doubt that all the king's warriors are as lucky and blessed as me," Amos said proudly with high, upturned cheeks.

"You won't be feeling blessed if you don't get that fish to your mother soon."

Kat and Amos's eyes swiftly shifted toward the boat, before silently exchanging a worried glance with one another. Their father's footsteps lagged behind them, and the sibling's anticipation grew.

They walked up the pathway until they reached their family's ancestral home. Thick shards of lapis lazuli and jagged cuts of raw quartz stuck out of the clay and mud. The gold flecks in the blue crystals shimmered like little specks of magic glistening in the sunlight, reminiscent of the magic that lived and breathed in the world around them.

Walking through the entryway, they passed carvings, paintings and stone statues of the ancestors that came before them. Everyone said a silent prayer as they shuffled past the memories of the deceased. Along with the standard prayer for health and safety, Kat didn't forget to silently pray for her soon-to-be sore behind.

The beady eyes of Gaya, a female Gazelle, stared back at her from the painting. Gaya lived long before the birth of Tulamund and well before the attacks from the poachers of Uman. A thousand years ago, her Animalia spirit roamed freely in the land before greed, the birth of kings and queens, and unnecessary wars. Animals only took what they *needed* from the land; it was humans who took what they *wanted,* and they always wanted more.

"Amos, come inside please. Even from across the hall, I can tell that you look a little pale. Are you feeling alright?"

Their mother's voice was a soft blanket, encasing them in a layer of comfort. She was a worrier, but for once she had good reason.

"I'm fine, Ma. The rain is just hitting me hard today. Does it always smell so—*damp*?" Amos wrinkled his nose.

"Oh, you'll eventually get used to the smells. The senses in my nose were so strong the first few weeks that every smell made me nauseous. Cinnamon, nausea. Catfish, nausea. Your father's breath after eating a half dozen crawdads. Straight vomit," her mother joked, keeling over with laughter.

Their father gave their mother a stern but playful look. "Hey now! I didn't even start courting you until two months after your ceremony, Sabine. Don't go telling the children lies."

"Yeah, well, you never really get used to the smell with or without the extra senses." Their mother squeezed in the last remark and the room filled with their laughter as they traveled down the hall.

When they settled inside the kitchen, Kat sat down at the nook and dumped her satchel on the wooden table. Without instruction, Sade sorted through their collection of berries and handed them off to their mother to be washed in the basin. While the woman prepped the dishes, the men fired up the wood stove and gutted the fish. The process was seamless as they all worked together.

As the minutes passed, the aroma of cloves, garlic, paprika, and cayenne floated from the steaming crawdads, mingling with the fragrant sweetness of their freshly brewed tea. With each sip, she could taste the perfect balance of imported Assam from the Isles of Beruk, and the aromatic blend of rosehip, mint, and jasmine cultivated from their family farm.

This was a typical day for the family, aside from the lingering silence. A silence that was loud, reminding them that the sacred day would be the start of many changes.

When the meal was done, her father started his prayers to their blessed goddesses, but Kat was too distracted to hear his every word.

"—may you bless him with the spirit of the Impala. May his horns be tough, his hooves be strong, and let the strength of his legs allow him to travel among the joyous lands of Tulamund and serve our king as a—"

Amos licked his lips in anticipation. Hunger had him drooling from the corner of his lips, and the gurgling sound of his stomach made Kat chuckle. Immediately, the silence grew uncomfortably loud. The prayer stopped, and a lack of respect was noted.

Bubbling steam drifted from their father and his voice boomed.

"First, I find a bow and *several* arrows in the back of the boat. Now, I hear laughter during the song of prayer. Do you wish to feel the rage of our goddess? Tell me, daughter, why would your brother bring along his bow and arrow?"

The anger in her father's voice made Kat shiver. However, his eyes weren't directed at her but rather his pointed look was focused on Sade. Her sister wasn't one to bend the rules, unlike Kat and Amos, who sought to break them. It didn't take more than a few seconds before Sade crumbled, spilling the secrets of their river trips. The archery, the swordplay, and the fights in the mud.

Their father's face flashed from wide eyes to furrowed brows, then settled into a thin line. He was not only mad, but incredibly disappointed.

Fighting is for the boys, not for young girls with beauty and birthing hips.

"What were you thinking? What if someone had seen your sister?" He pushed his plate away and the thunderous motion caused his teacup to rattle. "I know we led you to believe that Tulamund is safe, but the prophecy still lingers. Kat's safety was demanded by the goddesses themselves and the future of our tribe is threatened by our king."

As her parents' eyes locked onto Kat, a flicker of anger passed through them before settling on Amos as the target of their blame. Once again, he would bear the brunt of the punishment.

Typically, Amos would melt under their father's pressure, but tonight he feigned composure as he spun a web of lies.

"It was harmless, Pa. We never left the Antelope land, and I was careful. No one saw us, I swear."

Even though Amos was a trickster, their father could see right through his lies. In his anger, his Animalia spirit flashed to the forefront of his mind. Their fathers' hazel eyes darkened to the deep beady stare of an impala antelope.

"Do not lie to me. Atlaua can see the contents of your heart. This prophecy, this gift, whatever the goddess has seen in your sister, has brought this family security. She is to climb the highest ranks, but she cannot do so if her reputation is ruined."

Kat let his words slither off her back, determined to keep the hurt from settling into her spirit. While the prophecy brought their tribe security and gained the king's favoritism, the lingering threat of the goddess's words continued to torment her.

It had been fifteen years since war and death plague the Kingdom of Animalia. Most shifters feared that Kat's prophecy was a warning for the next Red War, yet King Cairo held a different belief. Out of all the creatures, it was a young herbivore girl that the goddesses singled out. A herbivore who wasn't dainty and graceful like the rest of the women in her tribe. One who frequently got scolded by not only her parents but by the priests and priestesses for her loud mouth and strong opinions. Said to be a child of the night, Kat was believed to embody the spirit of the rare black jaguar. Her new responsibility to the kingdom was the continuation of a pure and powerful jaguar dynasty.

"You want to lead this tribe one day, know that you will need to make *impossible* decisions. Our tribe's success depends on the safety and purity of her spirit. Why would you risk that?" Their father slammed his fist on the table.

Amos's golden eyes narrowed as a fire ignited inside him. Rising from his seat, he turned to address the entire family.

"This prophecy. These rules. The expectations. Every single day, Kat bends to the will of others and the entire tribe bends to the wills of the king. She needs to learn to defend herself. I do not care that you disagree. I do not trust the carnivores' intentions." He violently shook his head. "No, not when it comes to my sister. I promise you this, King Cairo will ruin her, and then he will stake claim over our tribe."

Amos snarled as foam coated the corner of his lips. Hysteric cries sounded from both ends of the dinner table and their mother began her prayers, begging for the sanctity of her children's souls.

They were stunned by Amos's words, but his growls were expected on the night before his ceremony. That could be forgiven, but his words and their intent would not be forgotten. Their father observed him for a few moments. An alpha and an alpha's son facing off head-to-head.

A beastly huff ruptured from deep inside her father's chest. As the tribe leader, he was typically level-headed in his actions and decisions, but Amos was pushing him to an unexpected breaking point.

"Amos, I want you to think hard about your accusations and be smart about what you say in the king's presence. I can't protect you in the palace. Just like I won't be able to protect your sister when she marries the prince." He turned to stare at Kat, his eyes were less angry, and his voice was pleading. "You must learn to behave, Katariya. Do as the king commands and you will receive the goddess's blessing. That is how we keep you safe."

Kat couldn't argue. There was no room, no air, not even an inch of space to whisper a rebuttal, nor an apology between the jarring aura of despair.

An understanding would not come on a night filled with so many emotions. Kat saw the defeat settle as her father sunk further into his chair and his head turned toward the heavens. Her mother's sobs became silent tears, while Sade trembled, and Amos quickly retreated to his room.

The remaining tension was broken by the crackle of lightning as the yearly flood poured from the heavens. The abrupt change in the weather meant that the sacred day was now upon them.

CHAPTER 3

WISDOM IS LIKE A BAOBAB TREE;
NO ONE INDIVIDUAL CAN EMBRACE IT.
- AFRICAN PROVERB

A sanctified mountain graced the northernmost peak of Tulamund, its shadow stretching over the entire city. During the last week of summer, the rain poured from the heavens and down the waterfalls, flowing with the essence of their mother creator, Atlaua, who nourished the fruitful land and blessed them with the Animalia spirit.

Concealed amongst the sea of clouds was a grand palace, so immense it could be mistaken for its own bustling city. On a rare adventure, Amos and Kat scaled the tallest tree to witness the palace gleaming in gold. Because of this, Kat grew up thinking that King Cairo was a god. He commanded himself as though he were a member of the divine, living in the celestial home of their ancient gods and goddesses.

Throughout history, humans from every corner of the world relocated to their sacred city to receive to Atlaua's magic. In Tulamund and Tolego, they found shelter within their mother's mountainous shield and gained the protection of the jaguar king and his army.

Shifters in and out of their animal forms crowded the streets to show their appreciation of the goddesses' blessing. Rhinos chatted with antelope, wildebeest mingled with leopards, and ostriches gallivanted with painted dogs. In a rare moment of unity, Animalia shifters of all different cultures, colors, shapes, and species set aside their disputes and differences to celebrate the Animalia gift.

King Cairo's fascination with Kat's prophecy led to Amos's invitation to celebrate his first transformation among the rich and royal. While it was considered an exclusive invitation, Kat would have preferred to remain at home, away from the curious looks and low murmurs.

The antelope tribe held ceremonies that involved long days of food preparation, hair braiding, and hours of song and prayer. Throughout the morning, the women cooked, and the men spent their days scouting the newest shifters for potential mates. In the evenings, the women gossiped while the men butted horns to see who would be the first to stake their claim. There were no elaborate palace parties, lavish gowns, or heavy jewels, just family and good food.

Attending the royal ceremony meant that Kat couldn't spend the day lounging around with her grandparents, aunts, and cousins. It also meant that her household, along with her protective uncles, were forced to wear tight, vibrant gowns and full-length robes.

In order to impress the king, her father traded a season's worth of saffron for the imported silk from the Isle of Beruk. Using great skill, her mother transformed the fabric into stunning designs, while Kat and Sade adorned them with embroidered leaping antelopes.

Her family appeared as though they fit among the royal tribes, but there were very few herbivores among the greats. Even though teas, herbs, and spices were considered luxurious, they paled in comparison to the sheer might of carnivores and the wealth of silver, gold, rubies, and diamonds.

Grateful for the rain's early morning halt, Kat's father and uncles used the two-hour hike to talk about their preparations for the next harvest while her mother considered potential mate matches for Sade. As they climbed higher, Kat and Amos became increasingly overwhelmed, their voices fading into an unexpected silence.

Amos's body perspired and his breaths became heavy as his inner beast began to reveal itself. The bright glow of his golden eyes grew hazy, and a distance spread between the present and his wandering mind.

For Kat, being in a crowd increased the threat of the prophecy. She seldom went beyond the farmlands except for river trips and supervised visits to the city market. With the tension between her family, the prophecy, and the impending farewell to her brother, she felt on edge.

The tremor of drums and the rush of the falls bounced against both the walls of the cave and the walls of her mind. Ape shifters used their fists to pound the steel bowls with an aggressive beat. Any human within two miles and any shifter within twenty could hear the music welcoming them to the start of the sacred day.

As they rose the steepest slope, strong vibrations rumbled below Kat's feet. A gust of wind grazed her cheekbones like a whisper of breath from the goddess that lived in the air, water, and dirt around them. The tension in her shoulders evaporated as the chill washed over her, dusting her skin with bumps.

Taking shelter inside the ceremonial caves, several prominent tribes rushed to greet their family. While they were wary of Kat, her father gained widespread recognition for his efforts in the Red War. In the fight against the poachers, he was one of the few herbivores to join the big cats, wild dogs, and ape shifters. Despite the foreboding threat of his daughter's prophecy, shifters admired him.

The tribe leaders competed for the opportunity to shake her father's hand. They shared their excitement about her brother's ceremony and sent praises to both her mother and sister. Only the bravest dared to meet Kat's gaze.

Hearing compliments about Sade made Kat more aware of their contrasting features. Her thick, curly chestnut hair was much harder to maintain than her sister's dark, wavy tresses. Kat's mother braided her curls into a tight spiral bun and decorated the layers with charms made from the same lapis lazuli that was embedded in the clay of their family home. The ochre face paint blended in with the freckled patterns of her golden skin, making her full-faced nose look even bigger.

Although Sade and Kat had similar curves, Kat's muscular arms and thighs were noticeably different from those of an antelope girl. In fact, if Kat didn't look exactly like her brother, she would have wondered if she and Sade were related at all.

"Lovely, isn't it?" her mother remarked, admiring the creatures, both big and small.

That wasn't how Kat would have described it.

"It's quite marvelous, don't you think?" Sade tilted her head upward, acting as though she were royalty.

"It's *something*," Kat mumbled, looking around to see a combination of orange, yellow and silver eyes surveying her family's every move.

Her heart pounded, unsure if it was their predatory gazes, the anticipation of the ceremony, or nerves about seeing King Cairo and Prince Zahir. One thing she was certain of was that at least half of the shifters in the room could hear the panicked thumps.

The weight of her father's disappointment had time to fester, and while she wanted to support her brother, she couldn't help but think about the consequences that the goddesses might bestow upon her. Kat wasn't the only one affected. All throughout the morning, Amos avoided her, and now he stood with dead eyes and a brow pulled with sweat.

Reaching out slowly, Kat lightly touched her palm to the small of his back. On contact, his face paled, and he pulled away with a jolt.

Troubled. Worried. Scared. She was too familiar with his panic.

Attempting to force a smile over a deep ingrained frown, Kat failed to hide the hurt from his actions. The pain decreased as Amos searched her form as though he could barely make out the shape of her body. Kat tried to comfort him again, but he pulled away as though her touch burned him.

"I'm fine, Kat. Just leave me alone."

Amos sank even further into his chair, like he was trying to make himself small and unseen. Just like the lies she told him the day before, his words slipped through his teeth effortlessly, forcing her to accept them as the truth.

Suddenly, the drums grew louder, pounding a beat that echoed off the walls. The whispers and gossip came to a halt. It was time. Straightening her back, Kat put on her bravest smile and moved into a reverent bow to welcome the royal family.

As soon as they rounded the corner, she felt breathless. The aura surrounding them was bold, and the bright red robes that laid over their shoulders captured the power of their Animalia spirits.

Zahir stood out to her the most. *Of course he did.* The rumors of their future betrothal had reached the mountains, farmlands, and the jungles of Tolego. There were nerves Kat wouldn't quite classify as butterflies, but he did have a tendency to make her lose her words.

His tight, coily hair was done in elaborately designed braids, and his dark brown skin glowed against the brightness of his robe. The embroidered design of a jaguar stood in an attack stance, emulating the beast under his thick skin. His presence alone sucked the little confidence she had completely dry. He was as arrogant as any carnivore could be, but Kat couldn't deny he was effortlessly handsome.

As though he could feel her thoughts and wandering eyes, Zahir abruptly turned toward her. His caramel-colored gaze narrowed as he gave her an appreciative look from head to toe. Under his careful observation, Kat's temperature rose, and her cheeks developed a pinkish glow. The glimmer in his eyes reminded her of a mischievous little boy. What wicked games did he have up his sleeve, and why did that fill her with excitement?

Holding her gaze, Zahir took her hand in his and lifted it to his lips. The action was slow. So slow, that she barely noticed that she was holding her breath. It was soft too, like the touch of a feather. A wisp of wind against her sensitive skin.

It was pleasant until suddenly, it wasn't. He stuck his tongue out at a slight point, and Kat felt the tiniest lick dampen the top of her hand. From afar, the action would look innocent, but there was no denying that Zahir licked her. When she pulled away, Kat caught a glint of fire in his daunting smirk.

It was clear he was trying to stir a reaction from her, but they were no longer children. She couldn't afford to risk the success of her tribe with a hasty remark. Instead, Kat gave him a menacing smile and in a sultry voice said, "You look quite dashing, my prince."

Shocked by her praise, Zahir pulled his hand away, and his dark skin glowed. He adjusted his robe before pushing his shoulders back, taking a moment to collect himself.

Smiling wider, Kat used her dramatically upturned cheeks to hide a chuckle, and Zahir quickly caught on to her idea of a challenge.

When he turned to her mother and sister, Kat took note of their wide, curious eyes. It was then she remembered how exposed their interaction was. Her cheeks flushed, and his smile grew wicked.

"By the heavens, you look absolutely gorgeous in that dress, Mrs. Abara. And you, it's Sade, isn't it? Absolutely *ravishing*."

Kat wanted to roll her eyes as he stressed the last word. She imagined the harem of women that followed him around the palace swooning over every little thing he said, much like her own sister was doing now. It was pathetic, really. *She was pathetic.* Almost falling victim to his charms the second his lips grazed her hand.

Sade's jaw dropped in awe. He gave her a long, drawn-out kiss on the top of her hand, skipping out on the mischievous lick. When Zahir pulled away, Sade held her hand to her chest as though she were cherishing it.

Kat couldn't help herself this time. Her eyes rolled involuntarily as her face contorted in disgust. It was impossible to ignore the cheeky grin Zahir flashed her, as he reveled in both of the sister's reactions.

"Thank you, our prince. We are most excited to be here today. Katariya has been looking forward to seeing you, haven't you, dear?" her mother asked.

No matter how quickly Kat tried to cover up her mistake, her mother did not miss the eye roll. She forcefully tugged on her arm, silently begging her to behave.

Kat wanted to roll her eyes once again but forced out a smile.

"Yes, very much so."

Zahir chuckled.

"It has been written in the stars, wouldn't you say?"

Handsome? *Yes.* Trustworthy? *No.* Kat knew Zahir cared even less about their union. He cared more about the possibility she could be a powerful Animalia than he cared about them being a perfect match. It was a game of power and the shuffling of status. She was to be a jewel on his arm, just as the queen was to King Cairo. A rarity, a gem worth protecting. It was a reminder that Tulamund was not a kingdom made for love nor the dreams and wishes of the heart.

Clearing his throat, Kat's father said, "Indeed. It is an honor to be in your presence, Prince Zahir. We are very thankful, not only for Katariya's protection, but for allowing our son to celebrate with you today."

Zahir gave Amos a pat on the shoulder and, just as when Kat touched him, Amos jerked away.

"Amos Abara. My apologies. I am sure you are on edge." Zahir smirked. "I'd say this is the hardest part, but as a herbivore shifter, your years as a warrior will be the most challenging time of your life. You're a tough man, though. I'm sure you'll be fine."

"Good. To. Know."

Every word was an animalistic snarl that had even the prideful prince too stunned to say anything more.

Everyone knew that as a carnivore himself, the king favored the wild cats and dogs over herbivores, but it mostly came down to strength and size. As an antelope, Amos would have a lot to prove, but that was the thing; her brother always felt like he had something to prove.

Amos was strong and daring, even if he lacked the physical appearance of a fierce predator. He could keep up with the best of the best and was impressive with a bow and arrow, but Amos would never have the same prey drive that big cats and wild dogs did. That never seemed to bother him before, yet he seemed riled by the prince's display of power.

Zahir lifted his head high, pretending as though her brother's snarls didn't faze him. He started to walk away, but then abruptly turned back, his eyes fixed on Kat.

"I almost forgot. I have a gift for you."

Waving his hand, a small servant woman rushed toward her. Coming up from behind, she draped a matching red robe over her blue dress.

Zahir's mischievous glow turned sinful. He leaned forward, and he whispered, "A perfect gift for the *jaguar* princess."

With the slight shimmy of her shoulders, the fabrics moved together, creating an image of a jaguar attacking the leaping antelope. A herbivore devoured by a ferocious beast.

Zahir gave her a seemingly earnest smile as he once again gave her a look from head to toe. Despite the unsettling feeling the jaguar spirit gave her, Kat knew it was an honor to receive a gift with the royal family's emblem.

"Thank you, my prince."

He leaned forward and lightly cupped her cheek. The same lips that tickled her hand softly grazed her ear.

Kat shivered with a soothing purr as Zahir whispered, "The spirit of the jaguar flows between you and me. Can't you feel it?"

CHAPTER 4

LIONS MAKE LEOPARDS TAME.
- WILLIAM SHAKESPEARE, RICHARD II

T he melodic hymns of the choir fluctuated to a low ethe-
real pitch as Tulamund's most respected priests and
priestesses entered the cave. Out of all of the unique and rare
species, one stood out to Kat the most. Priestess Osha—the
okapi shifter.

As the secret giraffe of the jungle, her elusive species dwelled
in the southern marshes of Tolego and, despite their incredible size, only the truly blessed would see her animal form. Kat
had only ever seen tattered drawings of the species with slick
brown fur and a small set of horns.

Not only was her animal a spirit of mystique, but she had
also been blessed with the ability to speak to the goddesses
since childhood. It was Priestess Osha who called for Kat's
protection, and it was King Cairo who bowed to the will

of her decree, forcing the entire kingdom to keep Kat under their watchful eyes.

Along with the okapi shifter were an elder chimpanzee, an anteater, an aardvark, a sloth, and the orangutan shifter from last year's ceremony. There were no rules as to which species could commune with the goddesses. It was the practice of patience. The ability to slow down life and listen to the call of nature. Very few could master the whispers in the winds and the secrets flowing through the river's currents, but those who could carried the highest titles in the kingdom.

For some, the gift came naturally, like elephants, who were known for their wisdom. For others, like the elder chimpanzee, it wasn't until the woman was old and gray before she heard the divine wishes from above. Kat always wondered what it would be like to talk to the mulberry trees in her backyard, to discover what secrets they held in the history of their roots. Were they happy to provide her family with their berries, or was it a tiresome obligation?

Priestess Osha greeted the royal family with nothing more than a slight smile before King Cairo rose to address the waiting crowd. Not a single word, snort, huff or roar was heard. His aura demanded their full attention.

"My brothers. My sisters. My children. Thank you for joining us to celebrate these young men and women as they welcome their Animalia spirits. Without the gift, the poachers, these *slavers*, would have destroyed every bit of good from this land. No matter the species, no human or animal has been spared from their violence and greed."

The thunderous boom of his voice was so loud it echoed off of every surface of the cave walls. A tremble of excitement flared inside Kat as she felt the power of his command.

"It is because of our goddesses that we now see the way. With good faith, they share with us the balance of the human body with the animal spirit. I, too, had once walked under the waterfall and became a new man, a jaguar, fit to lead Tulamund. We have fought the poachers, and with the Animalia gift, we fear them no more!"

King Cairo walked back and forth across the room. The orange hued gaze of his inner beast focused on every tribe leader he passed.

"Today, I have called for the antelope tribe to join us. We welcome Reevus Abara's son, Amos Abara, to convene with the goddesses through the magic of our sacred water."

King Cairo stood in front of their family. The corner of his lips turned upward, reminiscent of Zahir's devious grin.

He stared down at Kat as he said, "Priestess Osha heard the whispers in the winds. Katariya Abara, of the antelope tribe, requires our protection. The threat and promise of the prophecy have made me believe that the goddesses see something in this child, a powerful spirit that you and I cannot."

His words gripped tight around her throat, confirming what Kat had already known. She piqued the interests of the king, but no one could see or understand why.

He held out his hand toward Kat's father.

"Katariya Abara, your king and the goddesses command it. Upon receiving your gift, you shall be wed to my son, Prince Zahir Olani II, born to the jaguar tribe, future leader of Tulamund."

Kat's father shook the king's hand with no hesitation, not even a glance in her direction. Marriage to the prince was how she stayed safe. Marriage to the prince would bless their entire tribe. Kat had known of the rumors, nearly everyone in the kingdom had, but hearing the decree aloud made her feel the weight of chains. All of her freedoms were sucked away as the king's boisterous voice staked his claim in front of the other tribe leaders.

The crowd cheered, while those in their animal forms boomed with the cackles of hyenas, brays from zebras, bleats from the antelope, and the roars of big cats. Hooves and paws thumped on the ground, and those in the gorilla tribe, whether in human or animal form, beat their hands against their chests, pounding out the sounds of joyous celebration.

Priestess Osha bowed to the king before standing tall beside him, her dark hair shining under the water's majestic glow.

"It is true. The current's whispers echoed in my ears, crashing against the base of the waterfall. The union between our prince and Katariya Abara shall keep her safe."

Priestess Osha stopped in front of Kat, flashing her a warm smile and a soft gaze. She then gestured toward Kat's father and affirmed, "I have known Katariya for her entire life. The antelope shifters are a formidable tribe blessed with both inward and outward grace and beauty. We can only imagine what a great Animalia shifter Katariya shall become."

Priestess Osha gestured toward Kat while pointing her other hand at Prince Zahir. She finished her proclamation with a shout.

"To Princess Katariya and Prince Zahir!"

Kat knew that prophecies and whispers from the goddesses weren't rare, especially when the water that they bathed in, drank, and fished from came directly from the heavens. What was rare was an Animalia shifter so easily climbing status within the animal kingdom. The ceremonial shift from a herbivore to a carnivore wasn't impossible, but it was uncommon. Kat didn't believe she had proven herself or was deserving of such a sought-after gift.

Last summer, a young man from the zebra tribe saved a child drowning in the swift currents of the Tulamund River. The heroic act may have gained him the favor he needed because at the end of the summer, he transformed into a cheetah. The whispers around the village declared that the young man had acted with the speed of a wild cat, risking his own life to save a helpless child.

It was a common belief in all tribes that if a shifter did good, good would come back their way. Kat couldn't comprehend that a goddess had seen something special in her from the moment of her birth. She was humbled by the blessing but felt a lump in her throat as she held back the words to tell them they were wrong.

"Of course, even on Amos's special day, all the attention is on you," Sade said in a harsh whisper that burned against her ear.

Jealousy flashed in her sister's eyes, and the spiteful words that followed were like a heavy weight on Kat's shoulders. Without saying a word, she did the only thing she could think of. An impulsive and childish act, but one that got her point across.

Forcefully, she stepped on Sade's toes. Sade squealed loud enough to draw the attention of her mother and her brother away from the ceremony.

"Girls! For goddess's sake, we're in the presence of the almighty. Priestess Osha is already conversing with the goddesses as we speak. They are watching this behavior, and I know they are just as disappointed as I am." Their mother placed a firm hand on each of their backs, her nails digging into their skin.

"She started it!" Kat hissed, leaning away from Sade.

Amos, who sat two chairs down from Kat, barked through seething teeth. "I don't think Ma cares who started it. You're a future princess now, Kat. You can't act this way in front of the entire kingdom, especially not in the presence of our king."

Surprised by his sternness, Kat shriveled in her seat. Amos had never scolded her before. In fact, he usually didn't like to acknowledge her role as a child of prophecy. Above everyone, he knew how much Kat hated the prospect of her future.

Rolling back her shoulders, Kat tried her best to ignore the bite of his words, but she always took everything Amos said to heart. He kept her safe but pushed their father's boundaries. With her brother, it felt like a collar and a loose lead, but under their father's watch, she was shackled in heavy weighted chains. As a future princess, she could only imagine that along with the shackles, they'd give her a muzzle, put her in an extravagant gown, and mold her into a well-behaved queen.

Amid their foolery, Kat failed to notice the shift of magic in the room. The water from the falls came rushing down even faster. Priestess Osha waved her arms and chanted prayers, drawing in a mist of magic that flowed down the waterfall. The white glow emanating from the water made it difficult for Kat to keep her eyes open, and those without the Animalia gift had to squint in order to make out anything beyond the blinding light.

Amos rose from his seat and turned around to receive wishes of good luck from their cousins and uncles. He placed a kiss on their mother's cheek, and as he turned to their father, the whole family was pulled into a group hug. Here and now was where Kat felt the safest, in the warmth of her family's embrace.

When it was time for her brother to pull away, their father yanked on his arms and uttered the words that muddled Amos's frown lines.

"Do not be nervous, son. You will always belong with us and to the antelope tribe."

CHAPTER 5

WHEN TWO ELEPHANTS MEET ON A NARROW
BRIDGE, THEY GET NOWHERE UNTIL ONE
OF THEM BACKS DOWN OR LIES DOWN.
- A SOUTH AFRICAN PROVERB

An alluring young woman eagerly stepped forward, ready to take part in the ceremony. Her bronze skin contrasted against her bright red tresses, and the luminescent glow of her yellow-green eyes was predatory. This gallant woman was the redheaded girl from the tiger clan.

Breathtaking, brazen, and born from status. As apex predators, tigers could take down prey twice as large as their colossal, agile bodies. The immense size of a tiger, combined with their natural ability for camouflage, made them nearly unstoppable. Kat could see why Amos was nervous to make an attempt to gain the tigress's attention.

Dropping her robe, the redheaded woman presented herself to the awaiting tribes. There were no tells to show if she was scared. Nothing more than the roar of pain as it rang against the cave walls. With the sound of bones crushing and skin tearing, thick paws and magnificent stripes emerged from thin skin, fingers, and toes. Shaking out her silky fur, the tigress stretched her legs to become familiar with her four-legged form. Her eyes flickered a bright yellow glow, and with a confident roar, she respectfully bowed to the king.

"A tigress! Just as fierce as the brothers and sisters before her. A magnificent start to the ceremony!" Priestess Osha declared.

Following her announcement, the tiger tribe, a wild and boisterous bunch, hollered their praises and pounded their staffs against the rocky terrain below.

"A great start indeed! Strong genes that will birth even stronger warriors." King Cairo nodded his approval.

While the tigress's father soaked up the king's awe, her brothers shot menacing looks at the other men. It was a rational defense to protect their sister from the lustful gazes. A young woman from a remarkable family and of an alluring species. It wouldn't be long before her father found someone worthy of his daughter's hand. Kat could see the desire in the prince's eyes, a gleam that made her realize that if Zahir was older, he would abandon his father's wishes for the tigress. He would be a fool not to.

The next man to undergo the shifting ceremony was a rugged, broad chested tank. He towered above the others, standing at the miraculous height of a large brown bear. There was a palpable aura to the power emanating from him, and Kat knew without a doubt that he was destined to become one of the largest beasts in the animal kingdom.

Visible steam developed from his widespread nostrils as he walked under the glistening water. Glowing sparks of light trickled down his head, arms, and legs. This time, the surrounding water created a dome around his frame.

Deep, painful grunts rumbled from his body. As his screams got quieter, the crowd's whispers grew louder. A spray of water burst through the air, drenching their forms as the spirit cascaded down the falls.

Kat heard the gasps before she could see what had caused such a startled reaction. Past the balls of light dancing across her vision came a behemoth of a creature that towered over every shifter in the cave. In the man's place was an elephant with magnificent tusks, deep gray skin, fanned out ears, and a talented trunk. With instinct, he let out a trumpet from the long, flailing appendage. Its short but powerful burst rumbled the walls and the stones beneath her feet.

After another quivering shake, the elephant forced himself back into a man. He shifted for the second time with ease, as if he had been doing it for years. As the magic shimmered against his body, his animal form receded into the heavens, leaving behind a dusted trail of mystical light. The crowd was in awe. Their eyes flashed between the elephant man and King Cairo.

Skipping the king's inspection, the enormous man squeezed back into his robe and rushed over to a crying woman. Beside them stood a tapir. Similar in shape and size to a large pig, but with a long snout and an even split of black and white fur. They lived in the southern jungles and had no claim within the royal court. It was rare to see them in the northern region, but regardless of the reason, Kat was comforted to see other herbivore tribes among the renowned carnivores.

While the woman dwarfed him in size, her curly blonde hair and bright blue eyes were identical to the man's human form. Her cries turned into wails, then silent sobs, but no matter how silent they were, Kat could feel the pain of a mother saying goodbye to her son. In their embrace, it was as though the elephant was etching their touch and scent to memory. The rise and fall of his chest synchronized with each painful cry.

There was an eerie silence as the kingdom watched on, but they allowed the colossal beast to feel his sorrows. He gave his family a tight squeeze before fixing a strained but brave smile on his face. With his head held high, he presented himself to the king.

"What happens now?" Kat asked her father.

"As customs states, he joins the elephants. That is, only if King Cairo doesn't convince him to join the army first. If the elephants haven't already received word of his spirit, then they will travel to Tulamund and bring him back to their territory." His eyes flashed to the priestesses and priests. "Although it is a curiosity that his arrival was unforeseeable in the whispers."

As if her father knew his intentions, King Cairo joined the elephant shifter alongside his tapir parents.

"What a rarity he is. You should be proud to have birthed and raised a son that is so worthy of this spirit. A force to be reckoned with in his human form, but even more impressive is the mass and strength of an elephant. You will be a fine warrior, Bron."

King Cairo's eyes brightened as he admired the future warrior. It didn't take long for Bron to be introduced to every important tribe leader and nearly every captain in his army. When the day started, Kat thought that King Cairo viewed her as a prized jewel, but if Kat was a ruby, then Bron was a precious diamond.

CHAPTER 6

NATURE ALWAYS WEARS THE COLORS OF THE SPIRIT.
- RALPH WALDO EMERSON, AMERICAN POET AND
PHILOSOPHER

The next two ceremonies went by swiftly. The first was a scrawny shifter with deep black eyes. He cried incoherently and cackled all the way back to his hyena tribe.

The nervous shifter was a man of lean stature, slightly shorter than Kat's brother. He had tan skin, facial piercings, and two tattooed lines next to his right eye. The man was a leopard shifter through and through.

He wore his tribe's mark proudly, a symbol of his loyalty that he would carry with him forever. Perhaps that was what made him so nervous. The mark of the leopard, but the scent of another species would be socially unacceptable among other tribes. If he, by gift of the goddesses, transformed into another species, they would feel disrespected that he would wear the mark of another clan. Their leader would more than likely sear the tattooed flesh from his skin.

Most tribes waited until after the ceremony to adorn any tribal markings. Tattoos, piercing, branding, were among some of the physical alterations that differed from tribe to tribe. Hippo and wildebeest tribes wore piercings on not only their faces, but some of them also had gold and silver hoops decorating the entire length of their spines. Gorillas and painted dogs were covered in tattoos, and rhinos didn't dare to leave an inch of bare skin visible. Panthers carved notches in the skin right below their cheeks, and jaguars never left home without wearing red ruby rings, necklaces, and bracelets.

The antelope tribe was similar to the jaguar tribe in their use of gemstones. They mined the Azul blue of the lapis lazuli stone that dazzled through the upturned soil of their farmlands, and they wore it often. All the time, really. Seeing the red robe against her blue dress showed the difference between who she was and who they wanted her to be. A blazing fire against the calming sea.

After Priestess Osha stated her blessing, the leopard shifter walked under the water where he was washed, bathed, and blessed by the goddess Atlaua. He, just like his ancestors before him, shifted into the golden glowing beast decorated with black rosettes. All the leopards shouted and roared in delight. King Cairo gave his assessment, and while he was more than happy to add another member to his army, his praise was short.

As the line grew shorter, Kat's heartbeat grew faster. Amos bowed his head, presenting himself to the blessings of the goddess, and the faces of the crowd blurred behind him.

He was nervous. Pale and panting, Amos didn't bother to wipe at the sweat dripping from his forehead. His eyes darted across the room, almost as though he couldn't focus. As Amos stumbled forward, Kat jumped up from her seat to steady his quaking form.

There was no fear of consequence or reminders of mindful decisions. Not when it came to her brother.

"Ah yes, Amos Abara, descendant of the impala antelope, sister to our future princess," Priestess Osha said, her eyes drifting from the hugging siblings to the surprised crowd.

Placing a soft, reassuring hand on both of their shoulders, Priestess Osha said, "Do not worry your heart, sweet girl. I am positive that your brother will make you very proud."

Amos was her kindred spirit. The sea that put out the roaring flames. Kat wasn't worried about the contents of his soul. She was worried about the animal spirit and the toll it was taking on his body, affecting him more than any other shifter in the cave.

Pulling away with a feigned smile, Amos searched her hazel eyes. "It's going to be fine, Kat. Priestess Osha said it will be alright."

He spoke the words as though he were trying to convince himself more than he was trying to convince Kat. She wanted to pull him away from the watchful eyes of the kingdom. It wasn't too late. They could go home and have a traditional ceremony. With the help of her family, she would support his body as they submerged him into the river. Together, they would recite the blessing by heart, a call to Atlaua. The birthright of the Animalia gift.

The ceremonial rains lasted an entire week, but Kat didn't think Amos could last more than a few days without transforming. The beast inside him was on the surface, and his human body was suffering from the effects. If they left now, they would make it home before sunset and could celebrate with their entire tribe, in the comfort of their ancestral lands.

"I love you," Kat whispered into the fabric of his robe, his scent rich with cinnamon.

Amos's pupils softened as her comfort soaked up his fear. His mouth opened, but with a harsh tug, Kat was pulled from her brother's arms and spun into her father's firm grasp.

"I am sorry, my priestess. My king." Her father's eyes lowered. "Katariya should know better than this."

His grip didn't lessen until she was firmly planted in her seat. Hushed whispers of the crowd caused her cheeks to redden, but Priestess Osha wasted no time to start the ceremony again.

"Amos, please bare yourself to the goddesses. Let them soothe your soul and bless you with the breath of Atlaua."

Priestess Osha began the prayers, speaking the words of their ancient language, the call to their mother creator.

As soon as the robe was off his shoulders, Kat redirected her gaze from her brother's naked form. Even though she couldn't look, Kat joined the priestess in the prayer to their goddess. The sound of water hitting a hard surface signaled that Amos was under the falls. She shivered with anticipation, but her heart dropped at the clash of thunder crashing beyond the cave. The goddesses resounded, and rocks came tumbling down as the ground shifted from above.

The speed of the water rumbled faster as the cave filled with the crowd's murmurs. The spirit was palpable, strong, moving through each human and every animal. Stronger than the tigress. Stronger than the miraculous elephant.

Light enveloped his body, and Kat covered her eyes. It was the sound of his screams that let her know Amos had begun his first shift.

It was a powerful gift. A blessing that made the pain worth it. One day, it would be worth it to Kat, yet the bloodcurdling sound of his screams made her sick to her stomach. Somehow, her sweaty palm found her sister's, and Sade held her hand in a tight grasp.

Suddenly, as quickly as it formed, the bright light that enveloped Amos burst. The spirit caressed her skin before dissipating back into the falls. Breath-catching gasps embraced her before a ground-shattering roar pushed her body to the ground. As though under a spell, every shifter in the cave dropped to their knees in submission.

The gasps and whispers were no more. The only sound was the echo of the roar and the heavy stream of water crashing down the mountain. Unable to make use of her limbs, Kat forced her eyes downward, and panic rose in her chest.

What was that? She had never heard a roar so powerful before. Sure, King Cairo could control his warriors with a deep command, but full, immobile submission was nothing she had ever experienced before.

Kat was stuck, trembling in the presence of the roaring predator.

The patter of large footsteps crept closer, thick claws scraping against the cave floors. No one made a sound, but she wasn't entirely sure they could even if they wanted to.

Kat tried to raise her head but couldn't. This was not fear, nerves, or her uncontrolled anxiety getting the best of her. This was the powerful command of a superior beast.

When two tan colored paws stood in front of her, Kat's heart jumped. Those were not hooves, and that was not her brother.

The hairs stood up on the back of her neck as a large, furred snout nudged the side of her head. She looked up to see a full chestnut colored mane, sharp jagged teeth, with a lean muscular body and golden colored eyes. A spirit of myths and legends, marked by violence and bloodshed. *The lion.* Dictators, damned by the goddesses and destroyed by the jaguar tribe.

A silent scream caught in the back of her throat. Fear fluttered in her stomach. With her head raised, Kat suddenly felt mobile, but she was too stricken by fear to push herself away. One small move, and he could have her head.

Kat's eyes darted from left to right, but she couldn't see Amos anywhere. What she saw was the royal family and the king's guards with their heads down, shaking with the fear of an unsuspecting herbivore caught by a wild cat. Never had she seen such a display of power. Gorillas, tigers, jaguars, and even the elephant were subject to the lion's commanding roar.

The beast had a fire in his eyes, speckles in the irises that danced like little wildfires. There was a tinge of anger in them, but staring closely at the flames, she could see a worrisome soul settling into an awakening fear.

The beast held his mouth open as if he wanted to say something. A small chuff, trailed into a heart aching whine. Without the Animalia gift, Kat was clueless as to the words of his distressed cries.

He loomed over her, and she shivered at the sight of his beastly jaw and deadly sharp teeth. His breath was hot and sticky but wafted a faint hint of cinnamon. A low chuff re-sounded from deep within his chest.

A long, drawn-out moment passed as the beast studied her, taking his time to decide which of her gangly arms he would tear off first. He made slow, calculated movements. So slow that she wondered if the person whose spirit was lying beneath the lion was present at all. If the rumors were true, the stain of blood would soon taint the cave walls.

Fifteen years ago, the goddesses called for Kat's protection. The weight of the potential danger loomed, but never did she suspect that the King of the Jungle would make a return. He came for her. Determined to slaughter her people and destroy the kingdom that King Cairo tried so hard to secure. The evidence of his power was in his roar.

On their knees and powerless, the antelopes would be one of the first to go. Her uncles. Her parents. Sade and Amos.

Nowhere could she see her brother's patterned freckles. Nor could she see the distinct glow of their matching chest-nut hair. There were no impalas in sight, and all the antelopes were cowering behind her. Desperate tears streamed down Kat's cheeks.

Where was Amos?

A sob broke from across the room. No one dared to move, but the sound meant that one of two things: their bodies could no longer hold in their fearful cries, or the lion's power was dissipating. The sudden sound disturbed the beast, his mane shuffling left and right as he searched for the noise.

It could be Amos. Those cries could be Amos.

Kat trembled, cracked and broken. A sound she had never made before slipped from her lips. Unfocused, spiraling, and on the brink of a hazy darkness, Kat stiffened as the lion licked her cheek. Not a bite, but a sandpaper tongue that ran from the bottom of her chin to the side of her forehead. It was like a bucket of water to the face, a punch in the gut as the breath she was holding escaped, pulling her out of the panicked daze.

An unnecessary, almost manic giggle slipped from her lips as a second lick ran up the length of her nose. Was he playing with his food? A slow, torturous death. Her laughs mixed with her sobs as the beast ruffled his mane against her long, braided tresses.

No longer able to keep herself up, Kat fell into the lion as though she were a gift being presented to his awaiting jaws. Upon contact, she felt her frigid muscles loosen, but she didn't dare to move.

It was then, curled into the lion's mane, that she heard a soft purr. A smooth whisper that instantly pulled at her heart like a bowstring.

With his jaws, he grasped her hand, cradling it in between his deadly canines. Slowly, Kat released her hand, and his purrs encouraged an ease in her panicked state. Driven by an unexplained feeling, Kat cupped the beast's tan furred snout.

She stared into his golden cat eyes, and the almond-shaped glow flickered to a familiar gaze.

"Amos."

CHAPTER 7

MADNESS IS THE MOST DISGRACEFUL THING
THAT CAN OVERTAKE A WILD CREATURE.
- RUDYARD KIPLING, THE JUNGLE BOOK

A melodic cadence echoed through the cave, resounding over low whimpers and bleats as Priestess Osha said her brother's name.

No. That could not be Amos. The beast couldn't be the same boy who fought off her bullies. The playful soul who taught her how to catch lightning bugs and told made-up stories about the stars.

Under all the mass and fur was the young man who said it was her *right* to learn to defend herself. The realist who saw Kat's potential for more than just an empty prophecy.

It was then that the fear for her own life transitioned into a fear for her brother's fate. With her arms stretched wide, Kat moved in closer, but her embrace was abruptly interrupted. A brush of cool air, a snarl, and a roar. Within seconds, a jaguar forcefully tackled Amos to the ground.

The jaguar and the lion fought for dominance. Teeth clashed and beasts snarled, and the onlookers geared themselves up for a fight, ready to defend their king.

Kat ran toward the fight, making it just past her parents before Prince Zahir snatched her into his arms.

"No, please no! That is my brother! You have to stop him! Please, please, stop!" Kat screamed at the top of her lungs. Violent tears streamed down her cheeks, dampening Zahir's chest as he tried to redirect her gaze.

The king growled loudly in Amos's face, just inches away from his neck. One powerful bite from the world's strongest jaw and he would be dead.

King Cairo's growl made Amos's beast complacent, and instead of fighting, he shook under the king's deadly grip. Rolling to the side, the lion turned over to display his belly in an act of submission, but that did nothing to stop the jaguar.

Kat tried to break from the prince's hold, but her efforts were futile. Her stick sword fights did not compare to the boy trained by his father's warriors.

All the jaguar could see was red. It was the need to protect his kingdom, to display his status as the ruler of Tulamund's largest and most powerful beasts. Beasts as strong as gorillas and as large as elephants bowed to the king with respect and mercy. His beast could not fathom the idea that someone would challenge him.

The jaguar held himself above Amos, orange eyes darting back and forth across the lion's face in predation and disbelief. He was arguing with the beast inside him.

It was the jaguar that wanted to protect his kingdom, but it was the man inside that saw through the eyes of the lion and could see the face of an innocent young man. King Cairo's jaguar growled even louder. His teeth were bared while foam and spit fumbled from his mouth.

Suddenly, Zahir pushed Kat into her parents' arms. It wasn't her tears and tireless begging that made the king see reason, nor was it her mother's soft wails or the ragged breath that huffed out of her father's chest. It was Prince Zahir who braved the beast, grabbing his father by the scruff of his neck.

The anger behind the king's eyes seemed to lessen as Zahir stared deeply into the blazing fire. In a cautious plea, he said, "Papa, please, we beg of you to think of what you are doing. Not in front of his family."

As the fire dwindled, his hold on Amos eased. The lion transformed back into a human, and horrid cries accompanied the crackling bones of his reformed limbs.

He was left naked, shaking violently beneath the jaguar. Upon seeing the human body, the king transformed. Instead of jaws, enormous hands wrapped themselves tightly around Amos's neck.

"Please, no! Please make it stop!" Amos cried out.

Mumbles and nonsense fell from his lips. The king made no movements as he watched Kat's brother lose himself to an invisible entity, fighting off the beast that wanted to take over his mind. As eerie as his cries resounded, they were pitiful pleas rather than snarling threats.

Priestess Osha ran to King Cairo, her voice rattled in distress. "My king, please let the boy go! He is a generational child of the antelope tribe. Brother to our future princess. You cannot argue with the goddesses, my king. Send the boy away. Spare his life and send him to Sandstone."

King Cairo's eyes darted back and forth between the priestess and his own son and wife, and then landed on Kat's pleading eyes. He saw the desperation and took a deep, huffing breath.

"Send the boy away! I want him escorted all the way to the desert, not just lingering outside this city. I want him gone!" King Cairo demanded of his guards and the entire kingdom.

Somehow, the unknown of Sandstone could be seen as a worse fate than death. The place where traitors were sent to die. A desert without rain or any form of life. A lawless and cannibalistic land.

"Sandstone? M-m-my king, please! That will send him straight to his deathbed," Kat's father cried.

"Would you rather I kill him, Reevus? Do you want me to show you how easy it would be to rip his head from his throat?" His snarls sent a chill down Kat's spine. "Our ancestors banished the lion two hundred years ago, and I will do the same."

King Cairo motioned for his guards to come take Amos from his lethal grip. A gorilla shifter grabbed him and tied his hands behind his back with rope. His eyes were bloodshot, and his teeth clashed together, grinding the canines.

"Don't you hear him? The lion is unstable, and he is bound to go mad. I will not let this monster remain in my city!"

Amos wept, cried, and thrashed in the guard's arms. Kat could not believe her eyes. A young, stoic man with a spirit that bounced and filled the room with laughter was now broken. Ruined by the spirit and destroyed by the threat of her own prophecy.

"Please no, not my son!" A crumbling mess that struggled to stand on her own, Kat's mother held on to her as though every one of her children would suddenly vanish.

The king dashed across the room and stood over her father, but his eyes focused on Kat.

"I will not have history repeating itself. I only spare him for the sake of my future daughter." King Cairo smiled at her, but there was no kindness in his eyes. No hope in his words.

Shivering under his eerie gaze, Kat looked to Amos for support, but the image of her brother only brought her more discomfort. Any color that was left had drained from his face.

Sweat poured down his brow, and his golden eyes were wild with fire.

"Our king, he—" her father tried to reason but was cut off by King Cairo's hands against his throat. Wheezing coughs fell from his mouth as the king ignored her breathless pleas for mercy. His terror didn't stop until her father turned blue.

"Your son is an abomination. A mistake and an insult to Tulamund and to our ancestors. I will not cower in fear of the lion's madness, violence, and dictatorship. I banished Amos Abara to Sandstone! If I hear another word, you will soon find me holding the boy's head *in my hand*," King Cairo sneered.

Growling in his face, the king broke the remaining threads of her father's spirit. His word was final, and her father was no match for the jaguar king.

"Take him away before his beast takes over and slaughters us all!"

The kingdom's most powerful shifters escorted Amos down the mountain. His blood curdling screams gradually quieted, and the crowd's shock turned into an eerie silence.

As much as Kat wished to remember her brother with bright eyes and a toothy grin, her mind wouldn't allow her to block out this memory. Defeated and crazed with the spirit of the lion, the bloodthirsty beast would take Amos's humanity.

Kat cried until her sobs were silent. Begged until her voice was gone. Thrashed until her body felt beaten. Prayed until she passed out.

PART II | CHAPTER 8

OUT OF THE ASHES OF THIS TRAGEDY, WE SHALL
RISE TO GREET THE DAWNING OF A NEW ERA.
- SCAR, DISNEY'S THE LION KING

"Hurry Katariya, you are letting the flies in."

Shutting the door behind her, Katariya walked through her family's home, saying a silent prayer as she passed tokens of their tribe's ancestral history. Crystals, paintings, and golden trinkets. In between it all was a new oil painting of her family, a portrait without her brother's crooked smile.

Down the hallway, Sade sifted through the oak wood cabinets, searching for herbs to craft their afternoon cup of tea. This time, she was in search of a combination to calm the nerves and ease the pains of Katariya's spiritual and physical shift.

The past three years had been tiresome, but the last few weeks had been draining. Cravings for fish and crawdads, burning sensations running up and down her back, and mood swings that kept getting Katariya in trouble.

The worst of it was the compulsion. The need to twist and untwist her braids, the tip-tapping of her foot, and a habit that had her brow furrowed and her body frozen as she stood in the kitchen doorway.

There was a chip on the bench. A chip that gave her splinters and caused her nails to bleed. The same chip that reappeared no matter how many times her mother sanded it down and re-stained it.

Through countless breakfasts, lunches, and dinners, Katariya sat, enduring fruitless conversations, reminders of her duties, and the hurtful shame of her brother's ceremony.

She found herself *chip, chip, chipping away* at the wood, as her mother and father turned every nostalgic moment into tarnished memories.

For a while, Katariya kicked the habit, not so much because she successfully managed her nerves, but, in time, her brother's name disappeared from conversations at meals and teatime.

Days before her own Animalia ceremony, the chip was bigger than ever.

It was only a matter of time before her mother would notice the rough edges of the bench. For once, Katariya would escape her wrath, but she would be trading it for the daunting reality of living with the man responsible for her brother's uncertain fate. The dread she felt in the king's presence almost had her willing to endure the extra chores and a sore behind.

Sade walked across her line of vision, pulling Katariya out of her muddled mind. She had been staring so hard at the chip that she hadn't noticed their tea set on the table.

Two distinct scents wafted from the steaming cups. Two different flavors for two very different sisters. Butterfly pea flower, ginger, jasmine, and honey— an overly sweet cup of tea for her seemingly sweet sister. While Katariya's cup seeped a blend of lemongrass, assam, oil of bergamot, and devil's claw— it was delicious, but the bitter taste wasn't for everyone.

With Sade, the compliments flowed out of the mouths of the merchants, dockmen, and on-duty warriors. On the other hand, Katariya's interactions with boys were marked by uncomfortable silences and side glances. The threat of the prophecy and her unusual appearance had boys fleeing long before her engagement to the prince.

When Amos was around, he kept the kingdom's opinions from picking apart pieces of her soul. Now alone in her battles, her heart had grown frigid.

How much more could they take away from her? Time and time again, they had proven that Katariya's life was not her own.

Even if she transformed into a jaguar, the kingdom's fear would never waver. Golden, freckled skin, high cheekbones, and curly chestnut hair. There were times when her ever-changing hazels mirrored the luminescent glow of her brother's eyes. She saw him in herself. The entire kingdom did, too.

Taking a seat at the table, she perused through the newly replenished basket of fruits and vegetables. With greedy fingers, she picked up a fresh apricot, taking in the tart taste and crisp texture. The delicious fruit alone proved the existence of their all-powerful goddesses.

"Are you nervous about the ceremony?" Sade asked, placing a cup of tea in front of her.

Her eyes crinkled at Katariya, but the stress lines across her brow showed more than disgust over the improperly disposed apricot pit sitting on the table.

Upon welcoming her Animalia gift, Sade transformed into an antelope. Much to Sade's disappointment, her ceremony was at home, but it helped ease the minds of a fearful kingdom.

Even with Sade's successful transformation, their fear remained, and because of that, she had received no marriage proposals. It took years of rejection before Sade's spirit broke. No longer distracted by boys, she shoved her nose even further into her love of books. A year ago, she took over their mother's role as their tribe's healer and now, she almost never left the shop.

The entire family handled their brother's loss differently, but Sade's grief transitioned into a deep-rooted anger that wedged an even larger gap in their strained relationship. While Katariya saw their brother as a victim, Sade argued he was a violent monster.

It was rare to see them having civil conversations, but her know-it-all sister had the answers Katariya needed.

Rising from her seat, Sade picked up the apricot and discarded it in the wooden bin. Spinning around, she sucked in her teeth.

"I don't get why you asked me here. You clearly just have plans to waste my time."

Katariya blinked out of her thoughts but searched her brain for Sade's question. Further testing her sister's patience, she took a long sip of her lemongrass tea before letting out a groan.

"I was going to throw the fruit away when I got up."

Sade rolled her eyes and bit her lip as though she had something smart to say. Instead, she let out a slow breath and said, "Seriously, Katariya, I canceled two patients to be here today. Did you at least go see Priestess Osha?"

"In fact, I did. Papa got me up bright and early for a blessing. You think he would even risk it? I remember the weeks leading up to your ceremony. They almost drowned you during a cleansing."

That wasn't an exaggeration. The entire summer leading up to the ceremony, Sade started her mornings gasping under the rushing falls. Prayers, chants, and songs. Katariya's blessings were weekly rather than daily and being reminded weekly that her brother suffered because of her was more than anyone deserved.

"Oh, good. That puts my heart at ease. You should be more excited about it then. So go on, tell me. What are you so worried about?" Sade hummed as she finished her sweet tea.

"What if they interpreted it wrong? What if what happened to him—" Katariya shook her head. "What will happen to me when I don't transform into a jaguar? Will the prince still accept me as his bride, and what will become of our tribe?"

Never had she expressed such concerns before. Ultimately, it was wrong to question the will of the priestess, let alone the will of the king, but Katariya couldn't deny it. She felt anything and everything but great. She was not a magnificent beast worth protecting.

Since birth, Katariya had been told she had a greater calling. There were those who believed her life held as much weight as King Cairo's, cherishing it above all others. Atlaua saw something in Katariya that others could not see. What she failed to see herself.

Katariya was a decent swimmer and a newly taught seamstress. An exceptional tea and spice cultivator like her mother and sister, and with good luck and many secrets, she was confident with a sword and a bow.

None of those things made her worthy of the goddesses' protection. That meant it came down to the beast that was bubbling beneath her skin.

Ever since her brother's banishment, there had been a hole growing inside her heart. A deep, dark pit that sucked the life out of her and everyone around her. That darkness kept her in bed, took her appetite away, and filled her with habits that ruined her parents' furniture.

Years of trials had tested her faith. The only prayers sent to the heavens were for the safe return of her brother. There were no whispers in the winds or decrees flowing from the waterfall. No reason for the lion's return.

The Animalia were taught that life and death were a delicate balance. Light cannot exist without dark. Good cannot exist without evil.

Katariya had no choice but to believe that in the creation of her so-called protection, the goddesses plagued her brother with the mark of death.

CHAPTER 9

TIME IS A MONSTER THAT CANNOT BE
REASONED WITH. IT RESPONDS LIKE A SNAIL
TO OUR IMPATIENCE, THEN IT RACES LIKE A
GAZELLE WHEN YOU CAN'T CATCH A BREATH.
- JIM CARREY IN THE FILM SIMON BIRCH

Sade let out a deep sigh, pulling at a strand of her soft black curls. "You are about as stubborn as an elephant. Embrace this Katariya. This could be good for you, good for everyone."

Katariya rolled her eyes. The tribe benefited from the marriage, the protection, and the king's keen interest in her. It eased their fears and filled their pockets with riches. It was good for everyone—everyone except Amos—and the weight of that truth made it even harder to accept her fate.

"Every tribesman's daughter dreams that their father possesses enough riches to entice the prince. Your role is to be our queen, surrounded by the blessings of our sacred lands. Why do you have to be so miserable?" Sade asked.

Was her sister truly this jealous? Sade had always been indifferent, quiet unless provoked. Committed to her studies and too concerned about how the world perceived her. She desired to be poised, polished, and knowledgeable in all species and important topics of conversations. *A good wife.* That's what Sade wanted to be.

At least her sister knew what she wanted out of life. Katariya couldn't have wants, desires, or dreams. No one gave her any choices. Atlaua's prophecy forced her into a collar, and the priestess who heard the goddess's whispers handed King Cairo the lead.

Katariya took another bite of the sweet apricot. With a mouthful, she said, "I would gladly swap places with you, Sade. I know that's what you truly desire."

Rather than responding to her claims, Sade's eyes followed Katariya's open mouth, and her nose crinkled in disgust. "Are you going to eat like that in front of the prince?"

She continued to take big juicy bites. "I'm pretty sure Zahir has already seen me eat like this. I know he's to be my husband and our future king, but the prince is just as vile as I am, if not more."

Sade gasped, removing her hand from Katariya's to place it over her mouth. "Hold your tongue! You can't speak that way about the prince. If Ma heard you, she'd whip you until you were crimson."

Katariya was familiar with the belt. Classically trained in royal etiquette, she had perfect posture. She could name every tribe and explain each of their traditions and customs. Even though she had two left feet, she knew every step to the tiresome dances. Her mouth, however, had very little filter and was her greatest fault.

"You don't even know him, Sade, so don't act like you do," she snarled, her voice more animalistic than before.

It was the truth. Shortly after her brother's death, Katariya found his sword nestled away in the corner of the barn. Her father took away the bow and arrow, but she never gave up practicing her swordplay. After taking the time to re-stuff the scarecrow, she found that fighting gave her the escape she needed.

On days when she was supposed to be fishing, Katariya would see the kingdom's golden prince swinging from the top of the tallest hazelwood tree, sipping out of an amber bottle. Prince Zahir was battling his own troubles, and he dealt with it by wrongfully stealing, flirting with salacious women, and drinking away his sorrows.

Katariya couldn't judge him, not when he was the one who spared her and her family from witnessing Amos's gruesome death. Zahir wasn't her favorite person, but she wouldn't go as far as calling him heartless like she would his father.

"I know what they say about the prince. I have heard the rumors, but Katariya, you must take your role as a princess seriously. It is a decree from Atlaua. The goddess that brought you into this world is a sister to the goddess of death. If prompted to do so, she will take you out of this world just as quickly as she brought you in it."

"I promise I will be a doting wife, Sade, but I have to get through this ceremony first," Katariya pleaded.

Contrary to Sade's belief, there was some truth to her words. Being in the palace meant she could do some snooping. A team of warriors had escorted her brother to Sandstone. While there was no word of his survival, there was also no confirmation of his death.

In time, Katariya could make a friend in one of the king's warriors. Perhaps charm or entice him with gifts. Gold, crystals, jewelry... anything the prince would give her, Katariya would use as a bribe to discover her brother's whereabouts. There would be no relief from the madness until she knew whether her brother was dead or alive.

It was so important that Katariya would bide her time and wait until she was queen. She would study Queen Cherise until she knew how to wrap a man around her finger. Please, beg and plead, whatever she had to do to make sure they returned Amos back to the kingdom.

"I'm not sure if I believe that, but seriously, Katariya, I know you have genuine concerns. You haven't stopped picking at the bench."

Ugh, she was doing it again. Her mind was suddenly aware of her unconscious actions, and a stinging pain radiated from her raw fingertips.

Taking a deep breath, Katariya asked, "Is the pain really as intense as it sounds?"

She had witnessed shifters transform into animals her entire life. Their bones broke, ligaments shifted, and their skin shed, while fur and feathers replaced the exposed flesh. It only took a second, but a second too long.

"It's different. I'll be honest, Katariya, it hurts the first time. You're coming into an entirely new body." Sade's eyes flickered to that of a dark brown doe, emulating the antelope beneath her skin. "It burns through you until, suddenly, it doesn't."

Despite the king's rule of no more than six hours a day in their shifter forms, Sade opted for below the minimum. The shifters in Tulamund lived in constant fear of succumbing to madness, aware that prolonged stays in their animal forms could strip away their humanity. The unfortunate souls were left to die in the barren deserts of Sandstone, where their rage and a lack of resources forced them to turn against one another.

Sade took two shallow breaths before her beast settled, and her eyes returned to their vibrant green glow. "The sights and smells are overwhelming for a moment. All the air escapes your lungs, and for a second, it's no longer you, it's just them. The animal spirit."

"Do you ever feel separate, the two of you?" Katariya took the last sip of her tea. The combination of her sister's reassurance and the calming effects of the herbs slowly made her itching nerves settle down.

"It may only seem like the shifters are underwater for a few seconds, but it doesn't feel like that. Time slows down, and the life of the animal is playing like a daydream in your head. When we merged, we became one."

That was the exact feeling that Katariya longed for. The feeling of being whole, feeling like she belonged.

A tribe was supposed to do that for you, but from the beginning, the goddesses determined she would not fit in with the antelope tribe. They labeled her as a carnivore, as an almighty jaguar.

Amos had never seen her as such. He viewed her as an extension of himself, and Katariya felt the same. If the Animalia gift gave the feeling of unity, was it possible it could fill the hole in her heart? Was it fair that she felt a sense of relief in thinking that the spirit of an animal could replace her brother's love?

Sade gently placed a hand on Katariya's shoulder. "I know you are thinking about him, but the prophecy had nothing to do with our brother's demise. Amos rarely ever prayed and was too consumed with becoming a warrior. He was not quiet about his fascination with the Outlands." Sade's hatred seethed through every word. "He wanted to leave, and that's what he got. A way out."

Katariya's eyes grew wide at the sound of her brother's name. How could her sister say such hurtful things? Despite everything, Amos was family—*blood and spirit.*

Their brother had normal desires for a young antelope. He felt the urge to run and roam. A thousand years ago, animals moved in large herds, running through tall grasses and fields of wildflowers. Today, they were Animalia, caged within the mountainous walls and stone-laid streets of the city. No longer constricted by the tall mountains, shifters in the Outlands could truly be at one with their animal spirits. Was it so wrong of her brother to want more than what was expected?

"Sade, you are wicked to think that our brother deserved what happened to him. There are clans that are filled with violent thieves and murderers." She threw her hands up, shaking the basket on the table. "How dare you say his exile was justifiable! He was anything but a savage. He was our protector, Sade. He loved us."

The kingdom had no qualms about hurling insults about her brother. *Unworthy, a disgrace, an abomination.*

Katariya refused to believe that the insults were true. If anything, they were speaking more about the lion than they were about her brother.

Sade could call him names, but to hear her say that Amos deserved the cruel fate felt like a knife churning at an already open wound.

Unable to look her sister in the eye, Katariya grabbed her satchel and left. Sprinting away from the house, she pushed the boat away from the docks and let the current propel her down the river.

CHAPTER 10

WE HAVE A CALLING: A NEED TO BE CLOSE TO
NATURE, WHERE SHE MAY CLEANSE OUR SOULS AND
WASH AWAY THE STRESSES OF YESTERDAY. IT IS
EMOTIONAL RECOMPENSE FOR THE COST OF LIVING.
- FENNEL HUDSON, WILD CARP

Katariya's blood boiled as her sister's wicked words repeated in her head.

He wanted to leave and that's what he got. A way out.

Traveling up the river, away from the city's markets, she
allowed the sounds of nature to soothe her soul. The current
was steady but alive with the spirit of Atlaua. The inviting
energy tempted Katariya to paddle upstream, seeking relief
with the sword shoved under her seat.

Halfway to her usual hiding spot, an unexpected thump
pounded against the side of her boat. Heavy oranges splattered fruit juices across the wooden vessel.

Sitting in the treetops, with an orange in one hand and an
amber bottle in the other, was Prince Zahir. It was a little

early for the prince to be out on the river, but there was no mistaking the sweet vibrations of his voice when he butchered her name.

"Katara—Kataraeha—Kataris, Kataree, Katar, Katariya!"

Against her better judgment, Katariya redirected the boat to the river's edge. She had no expectations, but a lot of curiosity regarding what was on the prince's mind.

With wobbly legs, she climbed the tree. As she gained height, the world grew smaller, and her mind flashed to a memory of her brother searching for the goddesses in the stars. Summer air, joyful laughter. She could almost hear his chuckle like a whisper in her ear. Once she reached the top, Katariya swung her feet onto the branch, steading herself against the trunk. She scooted close enough for conversation, but far enough away from the edge.

"Did you steal that bottle from another poor merchant boy?" Katariya questioned, pulling an orange from a low-hanging branch.

She wasn't hungry. The crisp, sweet taste of the apricots remained on her tongue, but she needed something else to fidget with. Her raw fingertips couldn't handle the rough, serrated edges of the tree bark.

"My soul is bound to the stealth of a jaguar stalking its prey. No one would ever think to look at me for taking this. In and out, without a trace," Zahir said with a chuckle.

Taking another swig from the bottle, he wiggled his eyebrows and extended the glass bottle out to her. Sharp canines taunted Katariya as he gave her a lopsided grin.

She studied him, and the bottle, before her lack of morals settled below her ambition. Just one sip wouldn't hurt.

Zahir wore a plain black shirt and matching trousers. The vision of a thief lurking in the shadows. The casual outfit was a pleasant surprise, considering his usual choice of a traditional kaftan or robe. The dark complexion of his skin glowed under the sunset's waning light, and his naturally brown hair darkened just as a cub's fur darkens with age. His coily hair bounced freely in its lush, natural state. Tight curls that reached just below the bottoms of his ears. It was a stark contrast to the intricate braids he typically adorned.

A mischievous smile exposed sharp canines, and the flicker in his caramel gaze mirrored the eerie glow of a cat's eyes in the moonlight.

Katariya wasn't looking to hand out compliments, but if he asked, she wouldn't be able to deny that she quite liked him like this. At ease, dressed in comfortable clothes, curls flowing in the light breeze.

The sight could almost fool her into thinking that he was a normal boy, and she was an ordinary girl.

"I'm sure you weren't that sneaky. No doubt that your father's warriors pay off the merchants just to keep the rumors at bay. The better question is, *how* did you sneak out?"

Katariya asked, picking apart the orange peel, letting the scraps drop from the tree to nourish the fertile soil below.

There was more than curiosity in her question. She planned to devise a strategy, knowing that one day an opportunity to search for her brother would arise, and when it did, she would be ready.

"Oh, you think I can't be sneaky? Not one of my father's guards caught me walking down the mountain. Mindless fools think I'm in my room reciting my bloody prayers. I rarely sneak out this early, but I needed to snag a bottle from the market," he admitted, taking another big sip. "Do you want some more?"

Katariya stared wide eyed as he pushed the bottle into her hand. Rarely did the men in her tribe indulge in more than just a glass of ale. Never did they drink straight from the bottle. Katariya's decision to abstain from drinking had nothing to do with her youth. It was a slippery slope, where overindulgence could send her tumbling into despair. On the rare occasions that someone had one too many, Katariya learned that the amber liquid made men loud and loose.

With unwavering determination, she had every intention of figuring out the true nature of their kingdom's beloved prince. Katariya would indulge him to receive the answers she needed.

Motioning toward the bottle, he said, "Go on, drink it. I know your mind is filled with just as much chaos as mine."

She took a big sip and allowed it to burn down her chest. *Chaos.* Zahir was right. Her mind filled with chaos as the amber liquid burned right through the unnerving thoughts, stinging the hole in her heart.

With another sip, she passed the bottle back to him and muttered a quiet thanks. In return, Zahir gave her a soft smile.

Their eyes drifted to the peaceful view, and a comforting silence fell between them. The pair came to the river for some time alone, yet the goddesses seemed to have other plans. Who better to suffer with than the person who understood what she was going through the most?

Katariya knew that Zahir wouldn't feel the same about her brother's loss, but they were on the cusp of welcoming their animal spirits, dealing with the changes of the Animalia shift. If their ceremony went as smoothly as everyone believed, they would be married later in the week. Katariya was barely ready to accept her spirit, let alone come to terms with the fact that she was marrying a pompous prince.

It wasn't just him, though; he was—*tolerable.* It was the gut-wrenching reminder that in a few days, she would have to reluctantly submit to all the king's demands. There was no escaping him or the reminder of the cruel fate he set for Amos.

Turning away from the prince, Katariya turned to the breathtaking view from above. From the treetops, the sacred river appeared as though it went on forever, and maybe it did. Katariya had never traveled far enough south to find out. From this view, she could see hundreds of homes, little blazing fires and lanterns glowing as the sun set into a deep, hazy gray. A hundred different species lurked beneath the forest's coverage, hiding in the mountain's crevices and scurrying through the busy market streets.

From the trees, Katariya couldn't tell which shifters were herbivores and who was a carnivore. This view gave her a different perspective, one that allowed her to see the city how it should be—unified.

"It's quite beautiful from up here, isn't it?" she asked, breaking the silence, suddenly feeling the heat of his gaze.

"I am looking at something that is quite beautiful, but it's not this view," Zahir mumbled, his words slurring.

He rapidly shook his head before she could react. "Sorry, that was sappy, wasn't it?"

"Very." Katariya rolled her eyes and snickered.

He gave her a sheepish smile as his cat-eyes glowed. Sade was likely to fall for his charms, but this pathetic attempt would never work on Katariya, and he knew it.

While his compliment didn't win her over, there was a faint flustered glow in his cheeks that had her own cheeks reddening. For once, she was grateful for her cascading curls, her hair providing a shield from his surveying gaze.

"So why are you out here?" Zahir asked, barely making a face as he took two big sips.

"Fishing," Katariya said dryly.

He didn't need to know the rest. *Her secrets.* Despite having the threat of the prophecy looming over her, Katariya would continuously risk punishment just so she could spend a few hours on the river. He certainly didn't need to know about the serenity she felt when she took back her power and violently stuck her sword against a dusty scarecrow.

A prince and a princess sneaking out, hiding from their duties, just within the safety of Tulamund's sacred grounds but far enough away from the eyes and ears of other Animalia shifters. The coincidence of this moment had Katariya wondering why the goddesses brought them together.

"Fishing?" His eyebrows raised. "At this hour? Come on, what were you running from? Who were you running from?" He paused for a moment, turned toward her, and let out a fake gasp. "You weren't running from me, were you?"

Needing another drink to continue the conversation, Katariya grabbed the bottle. "Running from you? Never." She gave him a soft, cheeky smile, one that he returned.

With a groan, she said, "Sade and I had a fight."

"Oh well, that's nothing new." Zahir waved a hand in dismissal. "You Abara sisters are always butting heads. I don't even want to know what your home life is like."

Her blush deepened as she remembered the dozens of scoldings they received for fighting in front of others.

Katariya stuffed her mouth with an orange, munching away until she noticed him staring at her with a pointed look.

With a mouthful of food, the words fumbled out of her mouth. "You're right. It's not that we got into a fight. It's about who."

Zahir's brows crinkled, transitioned into a flat line, then somehow crinkled even further. Katariya thought he was going to say something about her manners, but his eyes widened as he made the realization.

She passed the bottle back, and he didn't hesitate to take another drink. His eyes lingered on hers before he whispered, "I'm sorry."

Katariya shook her head, surprised by his apology. "It's not your fault."

"Still, it must hurt to lose a brother. To be reminded of him, to be in that cave. I'm so sorry, Katariya. No one should have to go through that."

His eyes were intent, as though he were gazing into her soul. It may have been the drinks making her see more than sympathy in his eyes, and if it was, it would also explain the soft flutter she felt as his words registered as a solemn truth.

He was right. No one should have gone through that. He was talking about the pain of losing a brother, but she was referring to their all-knowing goddesses choosing to praise her and punish Amos.

Without an orange in her hand, Katariya chipped at the bark. The dryness of the wood was much easier to pick than she expected. Easier than the smooth edges of her parents' furniture.

"You're right. No one should have suffered the way my brother did. He didn't ask to be some wretched beast."

Her bottom lip quivered even though she was painfully biting on the corners to still them. There was no way that he didn't see her shaking. With her eager shifter abilities, Katariya could see and smell the faint whiff of sweat wafting from not only his underarms, but from the thin layer that was sparkling against his forehead.

In between it all, there was a slight trace of juniper berries. A unique pine scent that was a part of his natural pheromones. Then there was the tiniest movement she found herself focusing on. The distant look in his eye combined with the slow taps of his fingers against the side of the glass bottle. Zahir could see right through her, just as Katariya could see through him.

"You're right. I—I don't know, Katariya. None of it makes sense. I never thought the lion would return. They became a myth, a legend, like old bedtime stories. I mean, you saw him. He was mumbling to himself, vicious, wild, and foaming at the mouth. Then when I saw him try to eat you. I—I was so scared."

There were two splinters in her right pointer finger. Chipping past the first layer of bark, the pain of her deeply wedged splinters was nothing compared to the pain as his words shattered through her.

"He was confused, Zahir. We all were confused." There was the faint sound of wood cracking as her fingers dug deeper. "The lion may be vicious, but I could see my brother in the beast's eyes! He wasn't trying to eat me, he licked me. He licked me to let me know that Amos was there!"

A chunk of bark fell off, flying through the air. Katariya shrieked, feeling the burn of a slice along the length of her finger.

Zahir's eyes dropped down to her wound before meeting her gaze. She refused to look away, staring at him with fire blazing in her wild eyes.

"Let me see your hand," he demanded.

"No!" Katariya snarled as he reached for her. Holding her hands in clenched fists, she placed them in her lap, hiding the broken nails, splinters, and raw, reddened tips.

Refusing to listen, Zahir seethed. "Give me your hand, Katariya."

He pulled her fist away from her lap and inspected the bleeding finger. With the digit now overly sensitive to touch, the slightest graze had her wincing.

"How long have you been doing this? This extends beyond this evening. Are you hurting so badly that you feel the need to hurt yourself?" His voice was barely a whisper.

Shying away from the pitiful look in his eyes, Katariya transitioned into defense mode. Squaring her shoulders and locking her emotions in, she refused to show any sign of vulnerability.

"Hurting myself? You're the one hurting, wallowing in the treetops, drinking every night. I've seen you. When I row down the river, *I see you*." No matter how tightly Katariya clenched her eyes shut, angry tears spilled over. "Is marrying me so bad that you have to drink your life away? I didn't ask for this prophecy. I never asked for any of this!"

Her tears were violent streams. Uncontrolled and unable to hide her spiral, she scrambled to make her escape. With her hands struggling to grip the tree's trunk, Zahir abruptly whisked her around, bringing them face-to-face.

His eyes held a deep pain. That was clear. The amber liquid was loose in his system, and there was a slight dampness in the corner of his eyes. He said nothing for a while, just stared at her, his eyes never straying to the soft freckles that decorated her face or her untamed mass of curls.

Slowly, as though scared to spook her, Zahir clasped their hands together. In an uncharacteristic display of caution, he handled her aching fingers with care and calmness.

"The prophecy changed things for me too. It may be your name, but that threat, that pressure you feel, it also falls on me. There's this expectation that once we rise together, I'll be able to defeat the lion."

Words continued to fumble out of his mouth, voicing all his concerns to Katariya. As he spoke his truths, the weight fell from his shoulders.

"I—I just don't think I have it in me to fight. I never thought there would be another battle like this in our lifetime, yet the goddesses bring back our kingdom's greatest threat and they want to throw that on me. It's not just the lion. Herbivores are getting antsy, and carnivores are fighting one another to be on my father's court."

Nearly breathless, Zahir continued, "And my Ma, don't even get me started on her. She thinks just because you grew up in a herbivore tribe that the goddesses have stripped me of a powerful mate. You have the promise of greatness. Worthy of prophecy and protection. How much more does she truly expect?"

Zahir's hopeful eyes were gleaming, but quickly fell as he saw Katariya clench her fists. He didn't need another drink, but he put the bottle to his lips, taking tiny sips just to fill the awkward silence.

Why did her mind do this? A descending spiral down an empty hole. She wanted to care. They had so much they could relate to. The expectations, snide comments, and incredibly unhelpful advice. Under different circumstances, Katariya could imagine a playful banter between the two.

With the lion's return, it rumored her prophecy to be the beginning of her brother's downfall. It was just a rumor, but in rumors, there was a twisted version of the truth wedged between slivers of lies.

"You speak of the lion as though he is not dead."

She spoke carefully, as though the storms of their sacred day would roll in early and smite her down with a strike of lightning. The twisted truth of his rambling was giving her a tiny glimpse of hope. The only hope she needed to peacefully get through the ceremony.

Zahir stilled and said nothing for a few moments, but Katariya refused to back down. Staring into his deep caramel gaze, she said, "You need to tell me, and you need to tell me now. Is my brother alive?"

He looked to the sky, as though he were asking the goddesses for forgiveness before he turned back to her. "There have been whispers, whispers from the Outlands of shifters banding together in Sandstone. There is word of an army, far bigger than my father's, growing stronger every day."

"And you think my brother is what? Their ruler? Their king?"

He gave her a shrug of his shoulders as he said, "Who better to lead the monstrous beasts than the King of the Jungle?"

The lion. The King of the Jungle.

A glimmer of hope that her brother was still alive.

Katariya expected to hear that her brother had been driven to madness by the instability of his Animalia spirit. She never expected to learn that he was creating an army of murderers and thieves. Amos? *Her Amos.* Had his beast pulled him so far from himself that he too was as murderous and vengeful as the shifters in Sandstone?

"Who has seen this lion, and when did you last hear word of this discovery?" she asked, shoving away her fear of the goddess's wrath.

Zahir hesitated, staring deep into her hooded, flickering gaze. The wind filled with quiet whispers as it howled and rustled the leaves, but in between it all, there was a faint rattle of wind chimes that reminded her of the world around them. A reminder that they couldn't just drink and wallow in the treetops. No matter how desperately they wanted to.

"Honestly, Katariya, I'm not sure. My father keeps this to himself and his trusted court. I hear bits and pieces, but nothing that would ease or hurt your mind. All I know is that someone, somebody powerful, is keeping the savages of Sandstone in line. They aren't tearing themselves apart anymore. They are banding together, building cities, and creating an army. It has never been like that before, but there has also not been a lion shifter in over two hundred years."

His fingers thrummed against the glass, and he sighed deeply. "I'm only telling you this because I fear that my father's actions have already put a wedge between us. We have never been a perfect match, but how are you to learn to love me when my father expects me to kill your brother?"

Zahir's head and gaze were pointed downward, as though he were ashamed by the scar of a wound that would always fester between them. Her mouth parted as her mind swirled with unanswered questions, but no words came out as she clenched her fists tighter.

Love? Katariya had never imagined that there would be love between them. Not many shifters married for anything other than a partner with strong genes and a powerful spirit, but he was right. She would never forgive him if he killed Amos.

"I know you have questions. Your thoughts are rather loud, but I can't tell you anything more. I shouldn't have said anything at all, but if I had a sibling, I would want to know their fate." He gave her a soft smile before turning his attention back to the nearly empty bottle.

The silence between them filled with the sounds of crickets and the deep croaks of frogs. The soft flicker of lightning bugs signaled it was time to make her way home, but she hesitated to leave. There were so many questions on the tip of her tongue that she had to bite it to keep them from fumbling out of her mouth.

How long had Amos been a threat? Where was he located, and how likely was it that she would survive the journey? Questions like that made her frustrated. Frustrated because any chance she had to save her brother was in the hands of a horrible, vengeful king and his slightly less arrogant son.

Mindlessly, her nails bit into the wood again. The crackling sound made Zahir's ears perk, drawing his attention toward her. It didn't take long for him to bring up the topic that she thought she had successfully avoided.

"Does anything help with the uhh, hand thing?"

A ragged breath escaped as Katariya prepared herself for an unfortunate conversation. Their relationship would become way more personal once she started spilling her secrets.

In a voice barely above a whisper, she said, "Fighting."

Choking, Zahir spit out his drink and fluttered into a fit of coughs.

"Excuse me? What did you say?"

"Swordplay. Archery. Hand-to-hand combat."

His eyes widened as he misinterpreted her words. "So, the bruises are from fighting? Who would be dumb enough to fight the princess? Do they wish to feel my wrath?"

His response didn't faze her. It was expected. With a soft chuckle, she said, "No one. Not anymore at least. The scarecrow doesn't really hold firm like a human body."

Looking off in the distance, she shivered under his intense gaze. Admitting to breaking an old-line law was easier than what she had to say next.

"It's not just my hands, though. It's my—*everything*. My hands, my mind, my entire body. I don't really know when it started. Maybe I was just born like this, but my mind doesn't stop, so my body won't stop. When the world won't stop screaming, it's the only thing I can do to make it silent."

Katariya didn't need him to understand. Amos never did, but he did his best to ease her pain. She needed this weight off of her chest, and while it wasn't gone, there was a small sense of relief. Sometimes she needed talks with no judgments. Along with the fighting lessons, all Amos did was sit and listen.

"I can't change the laws overnight, but if it helps, I'll spar with you from time to time. I have a few guards that are good at keeping secrets, and who knows, maybe it'll keep me from this." He gestured toward the empty bottle with a soft lopsided grin.

Slowly, he took her hand in his. This time, he wedged his fingers between hers, careful to avoid her bruises and bleeding nails. The matching calluses on their thumbs came from wielding a sword, and she found comfort in the similarity.

The sun disappeared behind the heavenly mountains, and a sheet of darkness began to take its place. It was time for her to go. If she waited any longer, she would miss dinner, and she refused to disrobe at her ceremony with the display of her punishment decorating her behind.

Katariya pulled her hand from his and said, "I have to go. My Pa will have my head if I'm out after dark."

Zahir moved closer as she carefully maneuvered her body to the base of the tree. Before starting her descent, she felt a rough, guiding hand graze the small of her back.

Her breath quickened as he pulled her closer. The caramel gaze of his catlike eyes flashed to an orange-hued glow. With unwavering attention, he watched her like a big cat stalking its prey. It left her motionless, as though one wrong move would prompt him to devour her.

The beating of her heart fluttered at the speed of a hummingbird's wings. Zahir would hear it just as easily as she could. The creep of a pink blush covered her cheeks.

His eyes dropped, lips hovering just above hers, hesitating to close the distance between them. A low gasp escaped her as his tongue licked his bottom lip. Cupping the side of her cheek, Zahir let out a raspy breath.

"I'll see you tomorrow, little cub."

Katariya slipped from his tight grip and scrambled down the tree. As she paddled home, the rhythmic sound of her oars cutting through the water matched the beat of her racing thoughts. With one heated gaze, her contempt for the pretentious prince morphed into a desire to explore the softness of his plump lips.

CHAPTER 11

WHAT YOU DO MAKES A DIFFERENCE,
AND YOU HAVE TO DECIDE WHAT KIND

OF DIFFERENCE YOU WANT TO MAKE.
- JANE GOODALL, ENGLISH PRIMATOLOGIST AND
ANTHROPOLOGIST

Katariya had a lot to contemplate. There was a warmth in her chest when she thought about Zahir's large hands wrapped around her waist. It was unexpectedly tender, but it did not compare to the news about her brother.

The prince had more than hinted that Amos was the lion. He had to be. There hadn't been a lion in over two hundred years. If any shifter could survive the dangers of Sandstone, it would be Amos, wouldn't it?

Somehow, she made it just in time for dinner. Sade was setting the table while her mother and father moved through the kitchen, carrying a variety of dishes. Katariya spotted fresh fish covered with lemon slices, doused in pepper and garnished with a strip of thyme. Her growling stomach alerted them to her presence.

"Sorry, I'm late. I wanted to get another prayer session in with Priestess Osha, ya know, just for good measure," she lied, repeating the same excuse she always used.

With her heavy breath infused with spiced amber, she explained, "I-ugh, also had a drink after. The urges were becoming unbearable."

Taking a bowl of rice and plum spiced pineapple from her father, Katariya tried to make herself useful to distract them from her current state of being. They said nothing for a few moments. Frozen in place, they observed her every move while she continued to work.

As carefully as she could, Katariya placed the side dishes next to the perfectly spiced fish and patiently waited for whatever criticism they had to share.

Her mother was the one to break the silence, swooping in front of her with a pitcher of water. "It's fine, Katariya. I know you are under a lot of stress. I hope the goddesses have eased your mind some, and the drink, too."

"Yeah, I feel more at ease," Katariya said with a shifty smile.

She didn't feel at ease. If anything, she had more to think about. Thankfully, her mother didn't mention how strongly she smelled of the amber liquid. Instead, she gave a sympathetic and knowing smile before turning to Katariya's father.

After a prayer, they passed around each dish, but there was a lingering silence that had her picking at her plate. Waiting for the sound of yelling, Katariya froze, expecting a blow. She was late, and even if they bought her excuse, she had been drinking. Disheveled hair and red-rimmed eyes. Katariya was a mess. Knowing her family, they were waiting for the right moment to bombard her with questions. It was only a matter of seconds before they would explode.

"We have good news to share," her father announced.

She shook her head at the surprise and took a wary glance around the table. Everyone had smiles on their faces. Sade's smile was so wide that she was surprised her sister hadn't already blurted out the news.

"Oh goddess, I hope this isn't about me," Katariya groaned.

Sade's saucer eyes tightened.

"Good things can happen to me too, *princess*."

Katariya had been used to the double-edged sword. Throughout the years, she heard her title as a compliment, but also as a mocking insult. Oftentimes, Sade used it to fuel the fire when they found themselves in a sibling squabble.

"You're right. I'm sorry; I shouldn't just assume that the girl who spends her free time practicing her prayers and reading books would have anything interesting to share with the table. Please, Pa, go ahead and tell us. It seems like everyone else already knows anyway," Katariya replied with just as much attitude as Sade had.

In frustration, Sade threw a piece of bread across the table. With a splat, it slapped against Katariya's forehead. There was no hesitation. Katariya grabbed her dirty napkin and tossed it directly onto her sister's plate. Sade shrieked loudly, and in return, she howled in laughter at the disgust written across her sister's face.

"Hey, hey now! This is not the type of behavior I expect from two girls who are soon to be wives. You are both women now. I expect more from you than childish actions," their father scolded.

Frowning, Katariya's eyes widened and darted across the table, landing on each of their faces. Sade giggled at their father's words.

Did he just say *wives*?

As in her and the prince, and Sade and another man?

"Sade, has someone asked for your hand in marriage?"

The air was thick but dazzled with the vibrant energy that funneled out of her sister.

"Not quite, but soon. Oh, I really think it will happen this time, Katariya."

Sade reached for the gold chain dangling from her neck.

How had she not noticed it until now? The necklace was bold. A small sliver of ivory carved down to a sharp point. It hung in the middle of her chest and sparkled brightly under the candlelight.

"Who is he? Is he from the warthog or the hippo tribe?" Katariya asked, bewildered, inspecting the small chunk of tooth.

When did this happen? Had she been so blind with her own concerns that she didn't even notice that someone had been courting her sister?

Her mother beamed with excitement. "You remember the elephant boy, the one from the southern tapir village? Bron."

Of course, she remembered. Katariya remembered everything about that day. Enormous man. Blond hair, blue eyes towering over his heartbroken mother. The sparkle in the king's eyes as he surveyed his new prized warrior.

"How did this come about?" Katariya narrowed her eyes.

Sade was all smiles. The face of a love-stricken fool with pink dusted cheeks and bright eyes.

"We haven't formally met, but we will tomorrow."

"Tomorrow?"

"The king plans to give Bron and me his blessing," Sade giggled, bouncing with excitement.

With a mouth full of food, Katariya nearly choked, fluttering into a fit of coughs. The night's endeavors and unexpected news had displaced Katariya's manners and her willingness to care about her family's displeased looks.

Dumbfounded, she asked, "At the palace?"

"Yes!" Sade was giddy, filled with a level of happiness that had become foreign in their household.

There was a buzzing beneath her fingertips, different from the sensation of dread she normally felt. If her mind had been clear, she might have been able to distinguish the feeling of happiness. Under the weight of the amber liquid overstimulating her brain, Katariya could feel her heartbeat rapidly increasing. Her hands slipped down to the notch in the bench, slowly rubbing her fingers over the jagged edges of the chipped wood.

"Papa and the king have a plan to bless us in front of the entire court. You, of course, will be married first, but my ceremony will be shortly after."

Sade was glowing, like *really* glowing with a warmth that Katariya could barely remember.

She wanted to be happy for her older sister. If Amos were here, there would be a boisterous celebration. Drinks and a room filled with song and laughter. No matter how joyous the news, it didn't feel right to be excited without her brother here to celebrate.

"And have we heard good things about *Bron*?"

Despite the constant arguments between them, she was still fiercely protective of her older sister. They were a tribe. A family. Only Katariya had the right to be mean to Sade. No one else, especially not some boy.

Squealing, Sade nearly dropped her fork. "I have only stolen glimpses, but he is quite handsome in his armor and, oh, so very strong. A little boorish perhaps, but that's to be expected of such a massive beast." Her voice was lighthearted, and her eyes melted into a pool of affection as she spoke of him. With an earnest expression, Sade's green eyes locked on Katariya's as she said, "I think I'm going to like him, Katariya, and I hope you do too."

She was happy for her older sister, but there was a pit in her stomach. Guilt that crept up her spine, knowing that there was a wedge between them that felt as though they were miles apart rather than a seat away.

With her thoughts consumed by the prophecy and the idea of finding her brother, Katariya had left no room in her heart to care about anything else. Putting aside the fact that she was going through the hormonal changes of the shift, she felt displaced in a room full of shifters that loved her. A stranger looking in on a life she had once thrived in.

Would she have enough time to find Bron and intimidate him? That was her job as a sister, and Katariya would gladly toughen him up to guarantee that Sade's future husband would never cause her harm.

While she couldn't battle an elephant, she knew how to create at least one deadly herbal blend. It would be rather *unfortunate* if she swapped out his morning cup with something that would slowly poison him with every sip.

"Why wasn't this news brought to my attention sooner?" Katariya exclaimed, carelessly picking at the food on her plate.

"Well, you've had a lot on your mind recently. I didn't want your sister's engagement to distract you when you should be worried about your studies and, uhh, we—we didn't want the news to upset you," her father said, taking a sip of his water. He avoided her gaze.

"Why would the news make me upset? Sure, I'd like to have known sooner, but he seems like a fine enough man, and the elephants have great wealth. Sade is clearly happy with this decision." Katariya gestured toward her sister's sappy face. "Now, I can't imagine she'll be so happy when she has to push out elephant sized babies, but still, she seems excited."

Sade was love stricken, so stricken that she didn't have any shame when she said, "When we are married, Bron and I will make this our family home. I am to run the shop, and Bron will be in charge of the harvest."

Katariya now understood why they kept Sade's engagement a secret. That pit in her stomach was no longer coated with guilt but drenched in anger. She could imagine no one other than her brother inheriting the family farm. Once or twice, the dreadful thought had slithered across her mind, but she thought that the goddesses would see to her true desires and let the two sisters lead the harvest.

This land was a part of them. There was a lot of care that went into crafting everything they made. Sade loved precision, gaining knowledge and learning about the benefits of each herb. Katariya felt warmth in the alluring aromas and enjoyed pairing scents and creating delicate palates. Amos was the one who fell in love with the harvest, fueled by the feeling of loose soil and the gritty seeds. Never had she known anyone else to be so impressed by nature, captivated by the magic of a plant's growth.

Together, they would have made the perfect team. Now they wanted *Bron*, an elephant with fingers too fat to pinch a blueberry, to run the tribe's farm? None of this made any sense.

"And the other antelope shifters are okay with an elephant running the most profitable trade within our tribe?" Katariya asked, her voice laced with disbelief.

"I know you must be surprised considering how exclusive our species can be, but it is ultimately my business that makes our tribe as successful as it is, therefore I will have the final say. The king requested this union, and shortly after you are married, Sade will have her own ceremony." Her father's tone expressed that his word was final.

"Why would the king stake claim over the elephant boy?" Katariya pressed.

"If you must know, the elephants refused to accept Bron after his ceremony. You should know they aren't very fond of outsiders."

Elephants weren't keen on strangers, but they were gentle and had a close-knit herd.

"But he is of their own kind? How could they turn him away?"

If the elephant's shifting ceremony had differed from her brother's, the story would have been more memorable to her and the city. His ceremony couldn't contend with that of a near public death and an exile.

"The elephants are worried there has been a bad omen attached that day and truthfully, they haven't been quiet about it. The king, of course, was thrilled to add the elephant to his collection of warriors," her father said, halfheartedly.

His distant eyes suggested that he was lost in the tragic memory. She recognized the look immediately. A quirked lip, flat-lined by a despair that forced them to confront the memories of the past, both good and bad.

"Bron has been an incredible addition to the army and has become a close companion to the king. In fact, the king treats the boy as if he were his own son. Who better to run the farm than someone who has the full support of the entire kingdom?"

Sade's joy had her oblivious to the hurt written across Katariya's face. The idea was sobering. Did no one else remember that the king almost killed Amos right in front of them?

Rather than reminding them, she said, "I always imagined that another antelope would run the farm, or even Sade; surely Sade can be entrusted with the task. Most days, she runs the shop all by herself, anyway."

Her father scoffed, pushing his plate away. The rattling dishes were high pitched and sensitive against her new shifter ears.

"I can promise you this, Katariya. The kingdom will have a much easier time accepting an outsider to our species than to see a woman lead."

Her father's response suggested that Sade leading their tribe was the most preposterous thing he ever heard of, yet it was mostly women who ran the tea and spice shop. While the antelope tribe didn't have many qualms about women being in charge, Katariya knew that many carnivore tribes would uproar over a woman leading.

In moments like this, Katariya wished even more that her brother was still here. Without his support, his fishing lessons, or hours of archery and swordplay, she would have never seen her true potential. After years of lugging crates of mangoes and oranges, she was strong, working faster than most of the men. Through the years, she tried to prove herself worthy of her brother's love, keeping up with her fighting lessons even when her father hid her bow.

It was her mother's calm voice that broke her father's spout of anger. "Reevus, I'm sure the girls understand. Katariya has known the prophecy her entire life. She doesn't need another reminder. Let's finish this up. I need to get started on her hair anyways."

Katariya's mother was already moving around the kitchen, cleaning the dishes in the water basin. She gave her father a pointed look, in which he returned with a defeated sigh. As sweet as she was, her mother was not a woman worth arguing with.

"You're right. There's a big day ahead of us tomorrow. I'll be down at the barn before I'm off to bed. I'll see you girls in the morning."

He came around to each of them, placing an endearing kiss on their foreheads. With a loving kiss to her mother's cheek, he walked out the back door.

Sade cleaned up the kitchen while Katariya cleared the table to make room for her mother's combs, a large jar of beeswax, and tiny gold beads.

Making a nest on the floor with an old, quilted blanket, Katariya prepared herself for the sore neck and shoulders that would follow the hours she spent getting her hair braided. Sometimes, it felt as though she spent half of her life sitting on the floor, in between her mother's legs as the woman prodded, pulled and mangled her curly hair. It wouldn't be until the break of dawn that her mother would send her to bed with a tender scalp and long, beautiful braids.

Chapter 12

THE MORE WE TRY TO CONTROL NATURE,
THE MORE IMBALANCED OUR WORLD BECOMES.
- FENNEL HUDSON, A MEANINGFUL LIFE

The lush green state of Tulamund extended past the rocky mountain tops and touched every surface of the palace grounds. Despite wearing full-length gowns, Sade and Katariya could not escape the bite of the mountain's summer breeze. A deep emerald dress brought out the mossy flecks in Sade's green eyes and clung to every inch of her curvaceous figure. A braided tail hung over her shoulders, and gold face paintings patterned with rich ochre decorated her forehead.

Achieving a presentable look required more time and effort for Katariya. Clanging gold beads adorned her tightly knitted braids. A tight gold choker encircled her neck, and her oily skin required a second coating of ochre. The dress was a deep maroon, much darker than the bright red of the jaguar tribe's signature color but was slightly less harsh against her chestnut hair.

Upon reaching the sacred waterfall, they were transported in chariots pulled by oxen. They rose high into the heavenly mountains, where the clouds moved through and around them. The remnants of the goddesses' presence lingered in the vibrating energy of the sacred mountain.

As the ceremony drew closer, the energy surged through her veins, heightening her senses... clawing from within. It should have felt like a blessing, but for Katariya, it was a curse.

Once they reached the bronzed gates, they were directed through a courtyard. All around them were trees that seemed to have no end as their trunks disappeared into the clouds.

In the middle, a mosaic stone pathway was divided by vines and hedges, forming a floral dome of bright yellow, purple, and orange flowers above them. On either side, the king's warriors could be seen sparring. The sound of swords clashing, the grunts and groans of their efforts, and the swift movements of their bodies kept her mesmerized. Paired with the sounds of shifters in their human forms were the echoes of snarls, growls, and clashing teeth as a tiger and a jaguar battled to her left. On the right, a group of archers aimed at neatly assembled targets that were nothing like her tattered scarecrow.

Katariya desired to see more than just fleeting glimpses, but the chariot pressed on until they reached the palace doors.

Paintings of the palace paled in comparison to the grandeur of the real thing. Built from the soft cream color of limestone, each piece had been meticulously cut and lined with genuine gold. With the sun's rays gleaming off the stone, it created a unique pattern of sunspots that danced across the courtyard.

Uncontrollable vines webbed their way up the mountainside, trailing along the walls, merging the palace with the surrounding nature. Towers of different heights held trees growing in their crevices, and above her, a jaguar scaled the branches. Weaving between the towers, the wild cat moved swiftly, its fur rustling between the leaves of the yellowwood trees.

As Katariya exited the chariot, the entire courtyard flooded with guests. However, unlike her family, each tribe had a flag flying above them, signifying the ownership of their carriage. Panthers, cheetahs, leopards, tigers, maned wolves, and more were greeted by servants and promptly directed into the palace.

Before the sisters had a moment to compose themselves, Sade's future husband came barreling toward them. His face was framed by thick blond hair and set with the brightest blue eyes. The warrior's childish grin and soft baby cheeks contrasted with his massive stance and deadly muscles.

The sight of Sade left Bron speechless, his jaw hitting the floor. Katariya couldn't blame him. With her perfect sister dressed in a lavish gown fit for a princess, she wondered if King Cairo would finally offer her position to Sade instead.

The elephant shifter's feet, although not graceful, gravitated straight toward Sade, bypassing Katariya and her parents. Sade was long legged, but Bron's towering stance forced him to bend at the waist to meet her gaze.

He placed a soft kiss on her hand, and she let out a fit of girlish giggles.

"Sade Abara, you look absolutely breathtaking in that dress." His eyes were gleaming, moving appreciatively over the length of her emerald gown.

"Thank you. You look quite handsome in *and* out of your armor." She gestured toward his kaftan, lined with gold embellishments. It was extravagant but completely different from the gold-plated uniform of a Tulamund warrior.

"Ahh, well. The king insisted I dress up for the occasion, and I'm glad I did. We are matching, you know," Bron said, his eyes sparkling with delight.

Sade looked down at her dress and smiled.

"We are, aren't we?"

The dark green kaftan he wore was a shade darker than the vibrant emerald of her sister's gown. The coincidence made Sade giggle.

"I almost forgot. These are for you," he said, holding out the carefully wrapped package.

Made from the ivory of his own tusk, he presented a delicate pair of earrings. A pair to match the necklace that dangled around Sade's neck.

It was evident that Bron was infatuated with her older sister. The pain of chipping away at his own teeth to create a token of his love was agonizing, and the thought of forging a pair of earrings to match the necklace made Katariya shiver.

Sade always had a weak spot for boys. The compliments and grand gestures fueled her, but Katariya had never seen her sister so entranced by another shifter's presence.

He appeared to be a suitable man, but if his goal was to step into her brother's role, he had a lot to prove.

Oblivious to the other shifters around them, the couple stared at one another with soft smiles and gushing affection. It wasn't until her father let out three deep coughs that they finally snapped out of their trance.

"Goddess, forgive me, Mr. Abara. It is good to see you again," Bron said, his cheeks reddening.

"Do not fret, son. Please, call me Reevus," he insisted with a warm smile. Reaching upward, her father pulled the towering man into a deep bear hug.

One thing Katariya always admired about her father was his ability to make others feel welcome. His all-encompassing bear hugs weren't just reserved for his daughters. He had enough love to share with the entire kingdom. What she didn't like was how he called the man "son." Dead or alive, her father already had a son. Amos was irreplaceable, and hearing the endearment only deepened her concerns.

"Uhh yes, okay. *Reevus*. I am thrilled to show you around the palace. It took me a few years to remember my way, but I am confident that I can lead you to the grand hall." Bron laughed, and his entire body rumbled.

"Absolutely. I can only imagine how many rooms the palace holds." Her father cupped the small of her mother's back. "I believe you have already met my wife, Sabine."

"Bron, what a sweetheart you are. The flowers you sent were a treat."

Flowers. He sent her mother flowers. There was no going back now.

The soft song of her mother's voice welcomed the gigantic shifter. With little warning, he pulled her into a crushing hug that enveloped her small frame. A squeaky breath slipped from her lungs as he squeezed her.

"Oh, my! What do they feed you boys?" Her mother's eyes crinkled with amusement.

His cheeks flushed to a beet red, and he frantically pulled away. "Oh goddess. You would think after years of training, I would recognize just how strong I really am."

Amid the hug, he disheveled a few strands of her mother's hair and crinkled her dress.

Rushing to contain her composure, she said, "No, no worries at all. It makes me feel confident that King Cairo has a strong team of warriors to defend our kingdom. Your mass will surely help with the farm work as well."

The seven-foot shifter had thick muscles that stretched against the sides of his kaftan. Easily, he could attach three carts of mangoes, weigh it down with a ton of stone, and still be unfazed.

Nudging her, Katariya's father forced her to step forward.

"Don't be shy, Katariya. Say hello to Bron."

The elephant shifter paled as though he had completely forgotten not only Katariya's presence but her status as his future queen.

"Princess, I am so sorry. I should have welcomed you as soon as you arrived. Please forgive my manners."

His words fumbled out of his mouth as his hands flailed from side to side.

"Nonsense. You had your future bride to welcome and parents to impress. I'm sure you are nervous enough already. Please don't worry about me." Katariya craned her neck upward to smile at the enormous warrior.

"Still, you are our future queen. I should address you as such. Again, I apologize for my behavior."

His gaze shifted, and his words were hesitant, hinting at his shame.

She wanted to say something to ease the tension, anything to keep him from looking at her as though she had the power to punish him, but she found that when her mouth opened, no sound came out.

Despite being at a loss for words, her mind was loud, spiraling with the anticipation of seeing the king. Her dress seemed tighter as the panic rose. The unfamiliar sights and smells of the many species sent her into overdrive. If she couldn't find the calm within the rain, a thunderous storm would soon come crashing down.

Deep breaths. Her fingers picked at a loose strand on her dress. *Deep breaths.* She pulled the strand even tighter but somehow managed to send a quivering smile in his direction.

He gave her a wary look but made no comment as he turned toward her family.

"Shall we?"

Looping his arm with Sade, Bron led Katariya and her parents into the palace. Passing through the elephant sized golden doors revealed a grand entryway filled with bustling servants and carnivorous tribes dressed in luxurious gowns and robes.

The walls were bright white, decorated with carvings, pictures, and statues of jaguar shifters throughout history. This display was a grander version of the mementos and artifacts that decorated the halls of her family home. From its polished marble floors to its glittering chandeliers, the palace's ornate details left Katariya feeling out of place.

Warriors stood in formation around the room, their gold-plated uniforms casting a radiant glow on the walls behind them. The room itself was a choreographed dance, with servants gliding around her, preemptively fulfilling the wishes of guests. It was such a contrast from her normal life of making her own bed, catching and cooking her own meals, and cleaning up her own messes.

Was she expected to give up the simplest of freedoms? Did her future revolve around being waited on hand and foot like the other tribe leaders around her?

Katariya didn't know what she expected, but it wasn't this.

As though attempting to exceed her expectations, two small servants came rushing toward her. The girl with dusty brown hair held grapes over her mouth while a girl with beady eyes fanned her face with ostrich feathers.

"Oh, no! That's—" A grape was shoved into her open mouth.

She chewed and swallowed before muttering, "Oh gosh." She shook her head. "Thank you, but that won't be necessary."

The servant girl smiled back, her eyes darting around nervously as if she had committed a grave mistake.

A flurry of apologies tumbled out of her mouth. "I'm so sorry. We will soon know what it is you enjoy, princess. Perhaps you are cold? Can we offer you a warm towel and tea instead?"

Katariya stared wide-eyed as the servants waited for her command. *A warm towel and tea?* They seemed almost desperate to please her.

Unexpectedly, the servant holding the fan started to massage her hand. Surprised by the sudden touch, Katariya let out a squeal that caused both of the shifters to drop what they were holding.

When the bowl of grapes fell onto the floor, the grapes rolled right in front of a nobleman. He scoffed in disgust as the squishy fruit juices splattered against the bottom of his shoes.

"Oh dear! I am so sorry, sir. Let me clean that for you."

Quick on their feet, the two servants dropped everything they were doing. Grabbing a towel from a nearby table, they dropped to the floor to polish the man's shoes.

In the midst of all the chaos, Katariya was quickly led away, but not before hearing the servant girl's heartfelt string of apologies.

"Seriously, I'm fine. Thank you so much for your help, but I don't need anything right now. You all are far too kind." Katariya gave her a reassuring smile.

"Are you sure I can't get you *anything?* There must be something you long for. Anything, anything at all." The brown-haired girl begged, as though she needed to meet the needs of those she served.

"Well, ugh. Perhaps tea?" Katariya said, although her response came out as more of a question.

The girl nodded, her face content from receiving the order. "Yes, of course, my princess. I will bring tea to your table."

Once the servant was out of sight, Katariya turned to her waiting family. Their wide eyes mirrored her own, equally bewildered by the scene.

"Quite different, isn't it?" Her father shook his head with a soft chuckle.

"Bizarre is what it is." Katariya nodded in agreement.

It was Sade who finally voiced the question that had been on everyone's mind.

"Are all the servants herbivores?"

Bron looked around, as though he had never noticed the disparity.

"Ehh, yes. I believe so. We have lots of different species, though. Warthogs, aardvarks, wildebeest, ostriches, and capybaras. I know there are also a few hippos and a rhino who work in the kitchen. Why do you ask?"

"Oh, no reason. It was just an observation." Sade smiled politely at her future husband, yet the look in her eyes suggested his answer made her uneasy.

With a tender touch, he comforted Sade, guiding her through the tour until they finally arrived at the grand hall.

"If you follow me this way, I can take everyone to their seats."

CHAPTER 13

UNTIL THE LION LEARNS HOW TO WRITE,
EVERY STORY WILL GLORIFY THE HUNTER.
- J. NOZIPO MARAIRE, ZIMBABWEAN DOCTOR AND
WRITER

As they passed a ten-foot looming statue of a jaguar, the murmurs of awe and admiration from her mother and sister filled the grand hall.

The center of the room had a long, polished table filled with close to a hundred guests. The gawking crowd took sips from their bronze goblets and narrowed their eyes at the family of antelope shifters. Whispers circulated as they walked to the far end of the table. With her heightened senses, Katariya could make out faint mumbles, but every guest seemed to whisper at just the right octave to avoid eavesdropping.

"Katariya, you can take your place next to Prince Zahir."

Bron pointed toward the head of the table where the plates and cups were grander than the others. The royal family's seats were empty, but she knew that the king loved a grand entrance.

Each tribe already understood the customs, sauntering into the grand hall as though they had been there a dozen times for ceremonies and celebrations. They knew their places at the table and impatiently waited for servants to scurry around them, tending to their every need.

They gorged on the sliced meats, cheeses, and pastries and frantically waved their hands to request more wine. A woman stood in the corner singing a vibrant hymn, and conversation flowed between each carnivore tribe as they discussed their tribe's trade, land, and riches.

As Katariya went to take her seat, a young female servant dressed in tan smocks came rushing over.

"No, no, please let me get your seat for you."

With the chair already more than halfway out, Katariya insisted she could do it herself, but the servants arguably disagreed.

"Absolutely not. You are the princess. Let *us* serve you."

Letting go of the heavy wooden chair, she let the servant woman finish pulling out her seat. Without thinking, Katariya plopped down, only to discover her dress was now trapped beneath her. Slowly and carefully, she tried to free it. However, there was no real reason to be discreet when more than half of the guests studied her with wide-eyed fear and intense curiosity.

As soon as she had settled in, a brown-haired servant quickly appeared by her side, presenting her with a weighty teacup made of pure gold. On display were a dozen of her mother's teas. Sorting through the blends, Katariya settled on a sweet rose tea over a chamomile to keep herself awake and alert. A blend of black tea leaves, rose petals, basil, and lemon balm.

The smell of her mother's tea, which had been a source of comfort for her since she was a child, reassured Katariya that she might survive living in the palace. Even if she would no longer be a part of the antelope tribe, she would always have the knowledge her mother taught her, and she could carry on the practice of cultivating herbs to make teas and spices. It would be something she could pass down to her own children, even if they would never look like an antelope or share their nature. It was a part of her that would never change, despite whatever plans the goddesses had.

King Cairo hadn't arrived yet, but the festivities would not hold off for him. The room full of shifters talked among one another, their voices echoing off of the high ceilings. Eventually Katariya's parents were roped into a conversation on politics, none of which she could focus on, because the smells, the sights, and the overwhelming thought of living in the palace made her lightheaded.

Sade and Bron sat beside her, but they were too enthralled in one another to include her in their conversation. She took careful sips of her tea with one hand and pulled at the fabric of her dress with the other.

Glancing around the room, she took note that none of the other guests were herbivores. The elephants held a significant status, yet they had a strong disdain for the king and the restrictive rules that confined their time in their Animalia forms. Based on their opinions about Bron, Katariya didn't expect them to show up, but there were plenty of other herbivore tribes in charge of the kingdom's most profitable resources.

Panda bears, although living on the Isles of Beruk, were the lead producers of cloth and silk. Apes transported cacao from the Isles of Badania, and the other tribes living in the southern jungle harvested the oil from the oil-palm trees for cooking.

Out of all the tribes, Katariya expected the rhinos to attend because of their massive wealth from mining and trading gold. The entire palace was aligned with the element, yet not a single member of their tribe was sitting at the table.

To make matters worse, strutting across the room as though he too had owned the palace was the leader of the hyena tribe.

While the anointed leader was male, their species by nature was matriarchal. Certain species of apes, painted dogs, and elephants were also primarily led by females, but under King Cairo's reign, their leadership was disregarded, passing the title down to the female's chosen mate.

Dark, soulless eyes sat across from her parents, lining down the whole left side with eleven of their members. Each member of the hyena tribe wore black robes, lined with silver and etched with a picture of a small cackling hyena on the front breast pocket. They smelled of tobacco, must, and smoke, and their presence alone made Katariya uneasy.

"Reevus Abara. Funny seeing you here among the greats," the hyena leader barked.

He was speaking to her father but looking at her mother. His left eye was wonky, with a large protruding scar above the brow and his band of misfits had scars decorating their exposed hands and faces.

"Ahh Akuji, it's been a while, huh?" Katariya's father gave the hyena shifter a long, hardened stare before he gestured toward Katariya and Sade. "I'm sure you remember my beloved daughters. My dear Sade is to marry the army's captain..."

Akuji's gaze shifted toward Bron and Sade, who in return gave him a respectful smile.

"Yes. Well, I—" Akuji began, but was quickly interrupted by her father.

"—And of course, you should certainly know my other daughter, Katariya, the child of prophecy."

Katariya's father gave Akuji a smug smile—a smile that could have been confused with pride if not for the menacing look in his eyes. Reevus Abara wasn't one to gloat, but if the rumors about the hyena shifter's violent behavior were true, then he had a good reason to rub his successes in the man's face.

Hyenas were said to be responsible for a series of mysterious deaths, and from what she could gather, they were also responsible for the underground meat trade, offering a range of animals for sale including rabbits, chickens, rats, mice and pheasants.

Noticing her reaction, Akuji's focus turned toward her, looking up and down Katariya's frame before plastering his gaze on the cleavage peeking from her dress. Even with both of her parents present, the hyena leader's piercing black eyes held her captive, compelling her to lower her head in submission.

Attempting to steer Akuji's attention away from his daughters, Katariya's father raised his voice two octaves and said, "Aside from my daughters, is it not the antelopes who own most of the northern region? Our spice trade alone should be enough to earn me a seat at this table."

Her father took a long, slow sip of his wine as he waited for Akuji to make his rebuttal.

"Perhaps you are right. Sometimes I forget the antelopes hold so much power among the carnivores," Akuji said with laughter in his voice. His laughter started a chorus of cackling among the hyenas.

The rumbling laughter and scrutiny of the antelopes pushed Katariya from her subdued state. Through seething teeth, she said, "I'll have you know that my father *and my mother* make all of Tulamund's medicine with their herbs. I'm sure that gash on your forehead wouldn't have closed so nicely without my mother's calendula salve." She pointed to the jagged but fairly healed scar. "And as your *princess*, I expect you to treat me and my family with the respect we deserve."

Her words had been trapped as she stammered to the servants, but now they were clear and direct as she held Akuji's blazing, dark gaze.

The soulless man hadn't bothered with the pleasantries of greeting her properly. Normally, she would have been pleased with the lack of formality, but his arrogance ignited a burning desire to see him on his knees begging for forgiveness.

"I suppose you are right. My apologies, *princess*." Akuji's eyes turned inward as he seethed out her title. He gave her a menacing smile that flashed to a pair of wine-stained teeth. Katariya held his gaze, determined to wait until he was the one to look away, but their stare-down was interrupted by the sound of drums echoing off the walls.

Strutting into the room were two gorillas holding flaming torches. The thunderous beat was accompanied by a dramatic chant as a pair of monkeys came tumbling in, rolling into somersaults, spins, and back flips. The torches lit up the back walls, directing her attention to the ceiling where two chimpanzees twirled from golden aerial silks. Between them, two bonobos flew through the air and jumped through a set of flaming hoops.

The crowd was filled with gasps as a chimpanzee dangled by one leg and fell down the length of the silk. Effortlessly, he did a springing motion to propel him upwards, using his body strength to glide him across the grand hall. Circling above the seated guests, the crowd cheered over his daring performance.

Amid the chaos above them, the two gorillas holding the torches did a fire dance, swinging the flaming stick above them, below them, and between their legs. It was a breathtaking performance that had Katariya and the entire audience awestruck with every unexpected trick.

All at once, the aerialists stopped their show midair, their bodies suspended in the center of the room, and the dancers moved into two separate lines. From the far corner, King Cairo entered, his bright red robes billowing around him. The scent of lavender and rosewater clung to his beloved queen as they walked arm-in-arm. The pair were dressed to perfection and moved with a gentle elegance.

Queen Cherise had the most beautiful braided hairstyle, circled around the top of her head in a sculpted bun. Gold jewels decorated her thick black hair and accentuated not only the jewels that dazzled around her neck and wrists but also blended in with the large gold-crested crown nestled in between her braids.

Several shirtless warriors wearing gold plated skirts flooded in along the walls. Their skin was marred by scars, a testament to their years of training and defending their kingdom. Around their waists hung a belt, its weight heavy from the knives, machetes and steel swords it held. Their eyes scanned the room for potential threats, but they made no movements, not even the slight turn of a head. They were as rigid as stone, each one silently devoted to their task of protecting the king.

Trailing behind Queen Cherise was a pair of snow leopards, cousins who migrated with her from the icy lands of Tundre. Behind them stood Prince Zahir, surrounded by six other prominent members of the jaguar tribe. He was dressed in a bright red kaftan decorated with lavish gold beadwork. The fabric sparkled under the candlelit chandeliers, and against the backdrop of the impossibly white room, Zahir's skin glowed. He was feeling the effects of the shift just as much as she was, the aura of dominance held in his fiery orange-hued gaze.

"Welcome! Welcome!" King Cairo flung his arms. "It is a pleasure to see all my beautiful creatures. Thank you for joining us in this joyous celebration!"

The king's voice boomed, resonating from the high ceilings with its deep, velvety tone. Queen Cherise appeared flawless, playing the doting wife. With a proud smile, she gripped onto her husband's arm and soaked up his every word. Turning to her left, she flashed Zahir the same appreciative smile. The queen made the role look effortless, but Katariya knew her cheeks had to ache from smiling so much.

"My most trusted warrior, Bron, has decided to take a wife. Who better for my prized warrior than the beautiful sister of our future princess. Sade Abara will marry Bron Touré in just a few days' time." He gestured toward the blond giant. "When Reevus Abara steps down as leader, Bron will take over the antelope tribe."

There was a collective intake of breath, accompanied by soft gasps. The crowd was equally as shocked as Katariya had been when she had heard the news. The antelope tribe would experience an intense redistribution of power. Almost any child Bron and Sade had together would transform into an elephant shifter, moving the ancestral line in an entirely new direction. It wasn't impossible that their offspring would be an antelope, but the stronger the beast, the more powerful the spirit, and an elephant could crush an impala antelope with one mighty stomp.

It was unexpected and unfavorable for her father to accept the offer, but did he really have a choice when it was King Cairo who proposed the union?

The hyenas' leader nodded his head with a low, approving grunt.

"And because Reevus does not have a son, he will need an outstanding leader like Bron to take his place. Bron has shown incredible commitment to our forces and has climbed the ranks as a captain. I know he will do an excellent job leading the antelope tribe into the next generation."

Because Reevus does not have a son...

Katariya bit down on her tongue. The painful tip of her canine pushed so hard against the skin that she could taste blood. Everything about this felt wrong, not just out of place, or different, but morally wrong as though there was a hidden secret she didn't know about.

She could feel the heat of Zahir's eyes as he studied the distraught expression that surely slipped across her face. To distract herself, she took a sip of her tea, feeling the warm burn of the liquid moving down her chest. Taking a deep, ragged breath, she allowed the healing properties and the calming sentiment to center herself in the present rather than the haunting memories of the past.

Done with his speech, King Cairo glided toward the table. In a flurry, his servants quickly followed behind, ready to attend to his every need. They pulled out his chair, placed a napkin over his lap, and fanned him with ostrich feathers until he commanded them to stop with the slight wave of a hand.

Prince Zahir followed, sitting next to Katariya. The servants treated him with the same delicate care, and he happily accepted their doting behavior. As soon as Zahir was settled, he leaned over to whisper, his lips brushing against her ear.

"You look beautiful, Katariya, but I think you are in the wrong shade of red."

Being this close, she could smell the earthy pine of juniper berries. The aroma was bold and called to her beast's senses. Her mouth salivated in a way that she was unfamiliar with, drenched as if she were sucking on something sour. It had to be her shifter abilities that were making her drool over the prince. There was no way that this vibrating feeling was because of Zahir's flirtatious banter. There was no other explanation.

Leaning into him, only to avoid an eavesdropping Akuji, she whispered, "Ma tried her best to get the right fabric, but no one sells that color to anyone other than the jaguar tribe."

His eyes widened, taking a slow sip of his wine. "Your Ma could have requested the shipment. You are to be a jaguar shifter soon enough, and once you become my bride, you can have anything your heart desires."

The words rolled off his tongue and heat warmed up her spine. A rebuttal danced on the tip of her own tongue, but Zahir swiftly silenced it with a playful wink, refocusing his attention to the conversations being held at the head of the table.

Katariya sat in silence, watching as King Cairo gorged himself on wine, berries, meats, and cheeses, only slowing down to boast about his prized warriors. As he talked, she tried to let her mind wander, but throughout the dinner she couldn't help but notice the flickering switch in Zahir's eyes, shifting between a warm caramel and a vibrant orange glow. They never wavered as they pierced into her own, the beast inside making its presence known.

She couldn't bring herself to look away, even when he met her gaze with an unwavering intensity. His eyes lifted as she raised the teacup to her lips, and they flashed red when she took a slow sip. Mesmerized, his eyes locked on her throat, following the movement of the muscle as she swallowed.

There was a primal energy radiating from him, much like her own. It felt like static sparking between them, dancing across the hairs sticking up on her skin. Her Animalia senses were running high, and every action between them felt as though they were playing a new game with unspoken rules.

A crackling fire was roasting beneath them, and Katariya didn't know if she had the willpower to put it out. When his gaze bore down on her, her heart raced, and she struggled to keep the unsanctioned desire hidden behind her harden heart.

"Excuse me! Excuse me!" Akuji called out, snapping them out of a trance like the crackle of a broken tree.

Eagerly awaiting but vibrating with nerves, a small servant girl rushed to his side.

"More wine. I need something darker, *stronger,*" Akuji demanded.

He did *not* need anything darker or stronger. His teeth were already stained purple, and Katariya could only imagine that he was even more obnoxious when he had one too many.

"Yes, sir. Of course."

The small woman shuffled quickly through the kitchen. Akuji stared at the servants with a look of disdain, one that made Katariya wish she could trade seats with anyone else sitting at the table. King Cairo wafted an air of arrogance, while Akuji's smugness was reflected by a sinister glint in his eyes.

Beside her, Sade and Bron laughed alongside her mother and father at some unheard joke. Masking her uneasiness, Katariya put on a cheerful façade while the king continued discussing matters of the kingdom.

Just as quickly as she had left, the small servant girl rushed in with a full goblet of wine in tow. As she approached Akuji from behind, the shifter abruptly shoved his chair away. A loud clash of metal resounded as the goblet crashed against the floor, splattering wine all over the hyena leader.

"How dare you!" Akuji yelled.

Two servants ran to his side, wiping the wine from his robe. The fabric was so dark that Katariya could barely make out the color of the spill, but he fussed over the cloth as though it were completely ruined.

"Do you know what I had to trade for this silk? How careless are you, you foolish girl?"

The servant trembled, her eyes staring hauntingly at the mess. With no hesitation, Katariya attempted to help, but a firm hand against her thigh pushed her back into her seat.

Servants rushed around, and within moments, the wine was gone. The floor was buffed to a glossy shine, as though it had never happened, but the girl continued to kneel, waiting for the king's punishment.

"I'm so sorry, my king. It was my fault. I'll give up my rations for his robes—work extra hours if you command it. Whatever it is you think I deserve." Tears brimmed her light blue eyes.

"Nonsense, nonsense. How about you spend some time serving the hyenas? My dear friend, Akuji, is an honorable man." "Honorable" rolled off the king's tongue but was laced with a venom that had both Katariya and the servant girl shuddering. "You will return when *he* believes you have paid your debt."

King Cairo took a slow sip of his wine as though he was used to making a show of how he dealt his punishments. Turning his gaze toward the hyena, he asked, "Does that seem fair to you, Akuji?"

"Yes, my king, that shall be grand. There is plenty of work to do in my private quarters." His eyes were menacing, and his voice was just as deadly.

Katariya stared wide eyed at the king, who paid her no attention. The focus of the entire room was on King Cairo,

Akuji, and the crying servant girl. From how violently her tears fell, Katariya guessed that the king had just suggested the worst scenario for the servant.

Just being around the hyena made Katariya's skin crawl. She couldn't imagine what it would be like to act as a servant to the wretched man for an entire week. Akuji's suggestive tone and the way he licked his lips as he gazed down at the girl made her stomach lurch. She found herself involuntarily leaning into Sade to distance herself from him.

"Up now, girl. Back to the kitchens until I fetch for you later," Akuji said with a sinister grin on his face. As the young girl scurried past him, he patted her on the bottom, causing the girl to squeal and retreat to the kitchen.

All the men in the room let out a simultaneous laughter at the girl's reaction. Even some of the women found Akuji's behavior amusing, stifling their giggles behind their perfectly smooth hands. Out of everyone, the king's laugh roared and echoed off the walls, causing a sickening shrill to move through Katariya. Zahir was frozen, refusing to take sides until the king's strong hand slapped against the prince's back, causing a choked laugh to escape from deep within his chest.

Never had she seen anyone treated so harshly, nor had she seen a crowd of royals shamelessly mock a servant before. It was a wakeup call, a slap in the face that had her wondering why the goddesses thought she could fit in with a group of heinous carnivores.

CHAPTER 14

THERE ISN'T MUCH A LION CAN DO AMID FLIES.
- LIRZOD BASHA, SHAMBALA SECT

When the laughter died down, plates of perfectly plated dishes were set in front of them and, as shocking as the commotion was, Katariya felt slightly better after a few bites of the unique dishes. The chefs working in the kitchen made great use of her tribe's spices, and the comfort of their flavors eased away the tension she felt when Akuji's eyes landed on hers.

The thunderous pounding from the drums grew louder, and the dimmed lighting set the stage for the next performance. Instead of monkeys diving through the air, two chimpanzees walked out with a blank white sheet. Walking on two feet, the apes wasted no time, draping the sheet over two long metal poles, creating a curtain. They placed a flickering candle behind the sheet, and its flame created a warm, gentle glow that illuminated the space.

The chimpanzees exited the stage, and the music changed to a low, soft beat that glided through Katariya's eardrums. Out of nowhere, a zebra shifter galloped to the center, her black and white animal form creating a shimmering silhouette on the walls. Her thumping hooves pounded in rhythm with the music, and the crowd roared with excitement.

With a graceful sweep, the zebra girl shifted behind the curtain. The angled light revealed the promiscuous shadow of a curvaceous woman. The dancer moved her hands down her body in a very sultry motion. Sliding to the right, the woman peered out to reveal a black-haired velvet beauty, her long locks flowing down to the small of her back.

With the sway of her hips, she teased the crowd by keeping her seductive frame hidden in the shadows. Her provocative dance incited hollers filled with oohs and ahhs and piercing whistles.

The hyenas made the most noise, but King Cairo was not far behind as he blared degrading comments.

"I wished all herbivores moved with her same quickness. If they did, I think we'd all be a little more inclined to share a bed with the plant-eaters."

Katariya's parents didn't care to watch the provocative display, choosing to focus on their food instead. Sade and Bron were quiet, stealing quick glances at one another while playing a silent game of footsie under the table. Katariya discovered it by the accidental brush of Sade's foot against her calf.

The unexpected touch caused her to squeal, which in turn made Zahir look in their direction where he could see the slight rustle of the tablecloth between the warrior and her sister.

Zahir's attention was partially focused on the performance, but Katariya imagined that most men would shamelessly want to watch a naked woman dance. He only offered a faint grin when his father made a joke, then swiftly shifted his attention back to her, giving her leg a tight, reassuring squeeze.

The moment his hand gripped around the fabric of her dress, she became increasingly aware of the heat that penetrated through the thin material. Squirming under his touch only urged his beast to continue as he kneaded his fingers into the tense flesh of her upper thigh.

Moments ago, she had a strong desire to destroy something, preferably something of importance to the king. An expensive item that would cause him pain, a fraction of the suffering he had caused her and her family. Now, under the prince's firm touch, she found the incessant need to pick, to destroy, to chip and bleed, melt away.

As the drum's tempo changed, the woman transformed back into her zebra form. Hidden behind a curtain, all Katariya could see was the flash of light as the dancer's spirit flooded down from the heavens. Shifting at impossible speeds, the dancer made no sounds of discomfort as her body contorted through the shift.

Without hesitating, she transformed again, tumbling into a different pose as her animal body turned human. With one leg wrapped around her head, the flexible shifter transformed back into a zebra. Leaving the curtain, the black and white beauty galloped and leapt through the air, her hooves clacking on the marble floor.

Katariya winced as the dancer transformed for a third time. Balancing on one hand with her legs split wide open caused a string of flirtatious whistles to echo off the walls.

Reaching for her tea, Katariya took small sips of the sweet rose, but even the comfort of her mother's herbal blends could not ease her discomfort. Carnivores were salivating, watching the herbivore shifter put on an elaborate display that would pain even the king's strongest warriors.

Feeling trapped, Katariya tried to create space between her and the prince by moving his hand away from her leg and pushing it toward his lap. He looked down at her with great concern and did his best to apologize.

In a surprisingly sweet and bashful tone, Zahir stammered, "I'm sorry—I, I won't watch anymore if it causes you discomfort. I may be caught up in my head most days, but I'm not that foolish. As your future husband, I understand you may not like me—ahh, admiring other women."

Without waiting for her response, he immediately redirected his gaze away from the performance, choosing to stare deep into her eyes. He offered her a nervous smile and she found herself blinking at him in surprise.

Looking back to the performance and then back to Zahir, she whispered, "Honestly, it's not that. I can't deny that she's absolutely breathtaking. It's just—shifting is supposed to be raw, a true testament to her inner strength, and yet the entire room seems to make a mockery of it. Shifting gets easier over time, but there's always some discomfort and she has already transformed what— three—four times now."

The zebra was black and white again, moving through the air, the candlelight flickering off her melancholy stripes.

"Ahh—well. It's just a show, and she gained great wealth for her talents," the prince said with a casual shrug.

"That's beside the point. Everything about this evening has been uncomfortable," Katariya said a little too loudly.

Zahir's eyes widened at her unexpected tone, and both her father and Akuji snapped their attention toward her outburst.

"Not enjoying the show, princess?" Akuji asked. His tongue rolled every time he mentioned her title, and it felt like ants crawling against her skin with each syllable.

"Absolutely not. You can't see her face, but you can't tell me she's not in pain. No one can shift that many times without suffering," Katariya sneered, her voice carrying across the table, drawing the attention of the king and queen.

Shaking his head in disapproval, King Cairo said, "Now, now. Why don't we all calm down? Katariya, dear, can you not attest that the herbivores are some of the strongest shifters?"

Surprised by the peculiar question, she stammered, "Yes—yes, they are, they—"

"So, you would agree that the zebra girl should be strong enough to manage a simple dance."

King Cairo swirled the wine around his goblet, his expression remaining unimpressed.

"But she's not just dancing, she's—"

"Zahir, control her." The king barked out the command, and Zahir's hand swiftly returned to the burning spot on her upper thigh. The command had enough bite in it to undo any sweet moment or mutual understanding she and the prince had developed. His fingers pressed down, and the display of dominance only served to ignite her fury.

Blood bubbled beneath her aching skin and bones and, without thinking of the consequences, she said, "I don't see any of *you* transforming into your Animalia six times in a row."

It may have been just a coincidence, but the music slowed down, and the zebra shifter's performance suddenly came to a halt. The unexpected outburst caused a wave of silence to wash over the room as everyone turned toward her.

In seconds, King Cairo was rising from his seat. The stillness was so profound that even the sound of his chair scraping against the marble floors made a reverberation throughout the hall. Katariya tried to hold her breath, but she was still huffing in anger. Her inner beast, her past, and her looming future were demanding she put an end to the dehumanizing behavior.

King Cairo's words were laced with venom as he growled, "I'll have you know, during the Red War, I transformed over a hundred times moving through the battlefield. I promise you I can shift a few times for a silly little dance."

Interrupting the chaos, Akuji played his role as the king's minion as he barked, "The jaguar tribe feels threatened by no one, little girl."

Had the hyena not poked his nose where it didn't belong, Katariya could have been coaxed by the king's low growl to calm down. The mocking tone of his voice made the beast rumble beneath her skin, so close to the surface that she felt like she could have shifted without the help of the ceremonial cleansing.

Rising from her seat with teeth seething and sweat pooling above her brow, she said, "Is that so? Then why does King Cairo still have warriors searching for my brother? Do you feel threatened that his lion is going to take your throne?"

The accusations were vomiting out of her mouth before her mind caught up to the meaning of her words.

The king's power was absolute, and nobody dared to challenge him. Evidence of his strength and fury was in his orange eyes, burning into a bright, fiery red. Visible steam puffed from his flared nostrils as a rage burned from inside him. On the surface, he was a man, but there was a thin line between his physical body and his jaguar spirit.

Without waiting for his father's response, Zahir grabbed her by the arm and dragged Katariya across the silent room. King Cairo's eyes continued to burn into her back, but no matter how heated his gaze was, her anger rose above it all.

Everything she had seen this evening had been too much: too flashy, too degrading, sickening—a disgrace to the goddesses. King Cairo lived with little respect for their culture and traditions, and Katariya found that she now had very little respect for him.

Animalia were supposed to be a part of a unified culture. Their goddesses blessed them with the spiritual gift to stop the violence between man and animal, but no matter how hard Atlaua tried to keep her creations from killing one another, they remained separated. Disparities that had nothing to do with their food selection seemed to divide them. The greed behind land, gold, and diamonds, and the violence that came with it.

To Atlaua and to animals, they were just earth, metal, and sparkling stone. Humans take too much. They were too violent, deadly, and hungry for power. Animals gave unto the earth just as much as they took. There was a balance with the Animalia, but under King Cairo's reign, the kingdom had tilted in one direction.

She fought Zahir's grip until she saw the sorrowful expression on her father's face as he profusely apologized to the king. Fear was frozen in her mother's eyes, and Sade's tears were muffled into Bron's shoulder.

There was an apology stuck in her throat, but it wasn't one she was willing to give the king. It was an apology to her sister and parents for endangering the future of the tribe and destroying her sister's engagement celebration.

Katariya had one purpose—one mysterious threat that forged a promise. Her future as a princess was her only shot at finding Amos, but she couldn't keep her mouth shut.

Tugging forcefully, Zahir spun her down the white corridor as tears brimmed in her eyes. With a mutual tremor of fury, the pair tumbled out the bronze plated doors with a loud clang.

CHAPTER 15

RESERVE YOUR LOVE, NOT FOR THE SLOW AND
TAMED, BUT FOR THE WILD AND ADVENTUROUS.
- MICHAEL BASSEY JOHNSON, SONG OF A NATURE
LOVER

As soon as they rounded the corner, Zahir pinned Katariya against the cement wall. One of his hands clenched around the fabric of her dress, tightly cinching her waist. His other hand was placed next to her face, caging her in between him and his beast.

"What are you doing, Katariya?"

His teeth pulled back in a threatening snarl. Orange-hued eyes shot daggers that pierced through her skin, and into her bones. She gazed at him, speechless, listening intently for his next words.

"I know how much you miss him, but this is not the way to go about it."

"And what do you know?"

Her eyes flashed with anger as she attempted to shuffle from his tight grip. Moving away caused him to squeeze her hip, and his fingers dig further into her sensitive flesh. As he leaned closer, the sound of his heavy breathing filled the small gap between them. A shadow from his large, wide stance towered over her, darkening her view of anything else around them.

With his face inches from her own, his velvet voice whispered, "I have watched you over the years, sat next to you every day in our lessons and prayers. Did you really think I didn't notice how the life drained from you the second my father sent your brother away?"

His inquisitive gaze seemed to take in every detail of her face, but she had never noticed this practice before. During lessons, she would catch him glancing her way, but she'd chastise him for copying her work. Had he been admiring her? Studying her like he seemed to be doing now. No, no, this was new. There was a primal energy in his intense gaze. Beneath the orange irises, his beast was on the surface, flooding him with desire.

"What does it matter? It's not like you care. We aren't friends, and we are certainly *not* true lovers." She tried to brush off the feeling his intensity gave her, but it was impossible to drag herself away from the magnetizing pull her beast felt as she stared at his own spirit.

Zahir's chest heaved, his breathing deep and rhythmic. "We fight and we banter, but it is within our spirit. That is who we are. We may not be friends, but there is no reason for us to be enemies, Katariya."

Zahir leaned closer until the heat from his body could be felt by her own.

"For my entire life, both my father and the kingdom have claimed that you were meant for me. Regardless of the prophecy's truth, I have always thought of you as *mine*."

A shiver rippled down her spine. Against his strong hold, Katariya's dress molded to her body, amplifying her silhouette. The fabric was suddenly too tight, too itchy, and too hot. *He* made her feel too hot.

"Yours?" She stammered with a bone-dry tongue. "How can I be yours when your father sentenced my brother to death? Amos didn't leave, Zahir. He was banished to a deserted wasteland."

As much as blood boiled, she had to fight her animalistic urges. Using her inner beast's strength, she yanked herself from his hold and sprinted across the stone pathway.

Without his body hovering over her, she could now see that Zahir had pulled her away to the palace gardens. Around the courtyard, lightning bugs danced around the bushes of blossoming flowers, twinkling like the night sky mirrored above.

A lush jungle nestled between the clouds with stone pathways pulled apart by vines. Large hedges were sculpted in the appearance of a roaring jaguar shifter. In the middle stood a massive statue of Atlaua splashing a steady stream of water into a pond filled with croaking toads and tri-colored koi fish.

Losing her shoes, Katariya took off in a sprint. No longer caring about the dress nor her tightly braided hair, she moved through the greenery as though she were an animal running in the jungle.

Her escape was short-lived. Zahir's heavy footsteps closed in on her just seconds after she passed the statue. The koi fish swam closer as though they were expecting a special treat.

"Can you slow down? Can you please just wait a—"

The scent of juniper berries followed as he propelled himself toward her. Before he could lay a hand on her, Katariya turned around and shot Zahir with a deadly look that left him speechless.

"Do you know how hard it is to pretend to be this child of prophecy? Pretending to care about a city, about a kingdom who sentenced my brother to death."

Her voice was laced with venom. The beast inside her raged, and through deep breaths, Katariya's anger never lessened. They would have this discussion now or never.

"He may not be dead, my father said—"

"You say that your father fears the Sandstone king, but yet you offer me no proof of his existence. No proof that the man you speak of is Amos. You won't even let me question the king. Why should I believe you?" She pushed a jabbing finger into his chest, and he took her closeness as another opportunity to wrap his arms around her.

Surprised by his sudden proximity, she stumbled forward, squealing as they both took a tumble onto the cold, hard ground. Landing on top of him, she felt the smooth fabric of his shirt under her palms. His hands cupped just below her waist as he tried to steady himself from the fall.

Neither of them made any movements. Zahir swallowed, and Katariya's eyes focused on the lump moving up and down his throat. His breathing was shallow, and his arms trembled. The faint thump of his racing heart echoed in his chest. She could hear and feel his nerves—see his lustful gaze.

The dizzy spell was broken as he ran his fingers up and down her side. She attempted to pull herself away from him, but he quickly flipped her over, causing her to land on the ground with a loud thump.

He used one hand to hold both of her hands above her head. Teeth scraped against her throat, and a low growl slipped from deep within his chest.

Time was impossibly still, moving in slow motion as her inner beast seemed both flustered by his dominance and annoyed by her willing submission.

Brushing his lips against her ear, Zahir let out another breathless growl and inhaled deeply. "I wouldn't lie. I swear everything I told you is true, but I worry about you. Sandstone is no place for a woman, no matter how skilled you are with a sword. If I bring you hope, you'll recklessly head to the city gates in pursuit of him, and then the prophecy will be determined as the truth."

Zahir wasn't wrong. Almost every day, Katariya thought about leaving the city to search for Amos. Her heart yearned for his comfort, and as she neared her Animalia ceremony, the need to be united grew stronger. It was as if her beast had been with her all this time and felt the same sufferings she had.

"You say it's no place for a man, so how do you expect me to forget about him? His beast may have some control over him, but he's still my brother." She searched his eyes, hoping to see some sort of understanding.

When she found none, she pleaded, "You said he was alive, so if he is, he must have been able to conquer the lion's spirit. If anyone could do it, it would be Amos. You knew him enough; you knew his ambitions. He was going to be a warrior, Zahir! A herbivore ready and willing to fight for our kingdom."

He took a deep breath, and although she was upset, the rise and fall of his chest pushing against her caused her breath to grow shallow.

"He was a good man, a great fighter, a good brother to you and your sister. I will admit he would have made a great leader for the antelope tribe, but the lions were said to kill species by the hundreds. My father, who has fought bears, tigers, and gorillas, fears no one but the lion's spirit. As much as you think you have a choice in leaving the city, you don't. I refuse to let you go."

"Refuse? You don't own me, Zahir. It's not even the true will of the goddesses; it's your father who has demanded our union!"

"The goddesses chose you to be someone great. How can you refuse Tulamund the next line of noble Animalia shifters? Your parents' status, *ruined*. The antelope tribe, *ruined*. And your sister? Do you think she'd be able to marry a warrior if you weren't the chosen one? Do you not wish to see her happy?"

She hated the way he was speaking to her, so plainly as though she were the only one blind to the truth. It was written clearly, signed and sealed by the goddesses, king, and the priests and priestesses.

How could she *not* see it?

Hesitant to state her own truths, her voice wavered. "I do, Zahir. I know how much Sade has suffered, but how do you expect me to live in the same palace as your father? Cowering around every corner, trying to avoid him. Fearful that every warrior he sends out of the city is planning an attack on my brother. It will always be that way. An all-encompassing misery."

He pulled one of his hands away from her, tightening his grip on her jaw.

"One day I will be king. It won't be but a few years after we marry and produce an heir that my father will pass the throne down to me. We can rule the city together. Send warriors out to search for your brother. We can bring him back to you."

Katariya shook her head.

"You expect me to believe that you would allow my brother to remain free when you say his beast is violent and unstable?"

"I don't know about freedom, but we can make a safe space for him, somewhere to control his beast. Maybe there is an herb or tea your mother can make to sedate him."

"You want to make him a prisoner?" she nearly shouted.

Tulamund rarely kept prisoners. The options were to obey the laws of the king or face exile. There weren't long-term prisoners in their city because confining an animal to a cage was enough to make them go mad. If they locked her brother away, the gains he had made in taming his beast would vanish in a matter of days.

"I don't know, Katariya. I don't know what you want me to say. Taking care of the kingdom is my responsibility, and, as my father has reminded me many times before, we can't let history repeat itself. You don't seem to grasp the consequences of allowing the lion to roam free."

Zahir leaned back a few inches to gauge her reaction, and she chose to send him a scowling glare. The extra space between them allowed her to take a deep breath, but on release, it came out sputtering.

"I understand more than anyone. I'm the one who lost a brother. I'm the one who has to leave everyone behind. What's so great about that?"

"We are working hard to build a better kingdom. Sometimes, things don't work out how we want them to, but maintaining safety and controlling the beast is my father's number one priority." His voice was steady and sure, and he spoke with the assurance that his father's plans would succeed.

"Better? You know there's not a single herbivore at your father's table. Just a herd full of herbivore servants tending to his every need. And then there are the ape shifters swinging from the ceiling for his entertainment. How long has he been treating the herbivores as second-class citizens?" She took her free hand and pushed against his chest. "And when did your father become companions with the hyenas? They have never been trusted, and yet he has their leader sitting two seats down from him, discussing politics and sharing a glass of wine."

Unable to break from his hold, she dug her nails into the fabric of his kaftan and snarled just inches from his face. Her beast made her confident, powerful, and sure of herself.

Grabbing his chin, she spoke quickly, her voice unwavering. "The shifters of Tulamund may not know it yet, but I can see the shift in power. I know your father only plans to marry Bron to my sister to gain access to our lands."

His mouth was set in a hard line, and his expression was impenetrable despite her attempts to rattle him. "Tulamund is a city for all species: carnivores, herbivores, omnivores. It's why our blessed land has the resources to keep our species satisfied. We may be humans, but we are also animals. There will always be a system of hierarchy in place."

"But we aren't animals, Zahir. Your father has a firm system that ensures that we don't succumb to the animal's nature. Humans do not have the same system. They are already at the top of the food chain. I don't understand your father's intentions. If you say it's to not upset the goddesses, I hate to tell you this, but if the lion has returned, then they must already be furious."

Her chest thumped as the wild creature in her fought against him for control. No matter how hard she tried to break away from his embrace, his grip only seemed to tighten.

"I became your intended years ago, and yet my tribe has never been invited to ceremonies and celebrations. My father was refused a spot on the king's council way before my brother's ceremony. I've watched hundreds of shifters climb up these mountains, riding on the backs of herbivores, tossing them aside as though they were rotting carcasses."

"Carnivores have always ruled Tulamund. It's just the way it's always been. Do you know why my father sends his warriors to the Outlands? It's because he's trying to make the land safe for herbivores to roam. All they ever do is run the length of the river. Don't you think they would be much happier running through the plains?"

"It sounds to me like your father wants to run herbivores out of the city. Is this your idea too? Is this how you plan to run your kingdom? With the herbivores outside of Tulamund's walls."

The fact that the king thought he could boot the herbivores out of their land was preposterous. Katariya was a generational child of the impala antelopes. The land had been in her family's tribe for nearly a thousand years, and they would continue to cultivate the soil for herbs and spices for a thousand more.

If the antelopes were forced outside of the city's walls, would they also be forced to give up their trade? She could never imagine a team of carnivores working together on the farm. Their species were no longer used to manual labor, and they had become accustomed to filling their bellies rather than harvesting the crops.

"Is this not what the antelope tribe wants? Shifters are always pushing for more space. This would be a solution. It could change everything for the better."

"You're telling me you want to change things for the better? I always knew you were a fool, but I never knew that you were a liar. What happens when the goddesses are wrong? What will you do when I transform into an antelope tomorrow?"

Zahir rolled his eyes, as though he believed her suggestion to be impossible. "There's no way. We have all heard the prophecy. Priestess Osha has never been wrong."

"The priestess receives messages from the goddesses almost daily, and somehow, she didn't know my brother was going to transform into a lion. I think there is a strong possibility that she was wrong about me."

With a dismissive snort, the prince shook his head in disagreement.

"I can see the fire. There's a spark in you. It ignites the same way as when my eyes flicker with the beast. You have a hunger inside of you, one that is far more powerful than an antelope."

She hated to admit it, but he was right. She had a fire in her heart, a spark of passion, and right now, her beast was focused on the heat radiating between the tension.

With great effort, Katariya shook off the ripple of desire and continued, "I have spent my entire life trying to figure out what the goddesses have seen in me. After tomorrow, we will have the answer, and I pray to the goddesses that you are wrong. I pray to Atlaua that you fell for an antelope shifter. That you dreamt and fantasized about an impala girl."

"The goddesses would not torture me with these beastly urges, if I wasn't right. You are mine, Katariya. My beast longs for you."

For a second, her heart fluttered, but she was reminded of the increased urges of the new shifter abilities, and she shrugged off the feeling.

Looking him straight in the eyes, she said, "Your beast craves me because it sees me as prey."

He shook his head, and his pupil dilated. "That's not true. Since day one, I have always known that you were going to be a carnivore. You are the girl who wrestles painted dog boys and causes scenes in the city markets. You have never fit in, but that's never been a bad thing. I make mistakes, I may be slightly foolish, but the beast of a jaguar is much more cunning than an antelope. You don't think you are great, but maybe it's because you grew up in the wrong tribe."

"You think I will have it better here? The carnivore women hang on the arms of their men like trophies. I don't carry the same beauty they do."

His words never faltered, but her heart nearly stopped when he said, "Your wit and strength are what make you so beautiful, Katariya. I have never met anyone quite like you. Once you shift, you may find that antelopes are more narrow-minded than you previously thought. The world is a little different when you can scale the treetops and reach the heavens."

Maybe his words had some truth to them, but she didn't see things the same way he did.

Pulled into a moment of clarity, she said, "I am different. I wasn't made for this city, but if I am destined to be a jaguar, then the goddess gave me these skills to defend and search for my brother."

Zahir's face drew into a hard line, frustrated by her inability to see reason. "Katariya, I swear that once I'm king, I will send a whole team to search for him, but I cannot allow you to leave the city. There are too many dangers, and we have a kingdom to run."

"You mean *you* have a kingdom to run? When have the women of Tulamund ever had a say in its ruling? You say that I am yours, that you have always known, but I'm not anyone's. The only person who truly understood me was my brother, and you and your father are keeping us apart!"

Her muscles strained against his hold, and tears pooled in the corners of her eyes. His arms caged her in as he took in her desperate state.

The pair sat in silence for a few moments. He couldn't deny the truth. That was what this moment was: a sharing of truths, no matter how ugly and hurtful they were.

"I'm sorry," he whispered.

Giving into the weight of her troubles, she fell apart in his arms, letting out tears she had been holding onto for years. A whirlwind swirled inside her. A combination of the stress from her new shifter abilities and the horrendously draining events of the evening.

Deep down, she knew a breakdown was bound to happen, but Katariya hadn't imagined she would cry every time she privately spoke with Zahir. The jaguar shifter was pushing past her defenses, and she found that she was tired of the fight.

Despite the tears soaking into his kaftan and wetting his neck, Zahir held on to her tightly, whispering words of comfort in her ear. They sat in each other's arms for a few minutes, and eventually, the soft whirring of the wind and the low rumble of her sobs slowly turned into soft sighs.

When she was calm, his irises danced around her bloodshot eyes before he pulled her into a deep, thunderous kiss.

Her fingers ran through his hair, tugging on the end of his braids, and she let out a throaty moan when his tongue grazed hers. As soon as she welcomed the kiss, he moved his lips against hers with an intensity that made her tremble.

Satisfied with his conquest, Zahir leaned back and murmured against her bruised lips. "I missed this."

"Missed what? Unless you are confusing me with someone else, that was our first kiss."

He rolled his eyes, and a low laugh vibrated through him.

"I missed the banter. I missed your fire, that thunderous spark. I can feel it rumbling against you when you are this close to me."

He bit down on her bottom lip, and she let out a squeal that was quickly silenced by his tongue circling through her open mouth.

The beast inside her was fired up, angry at the world, but somehow complacent in his arms. She kissed him with the same urgency and melted against him.

Neither of them made any movement to pull away from one another. Their hands were grabby, their lips were swollen, and a purr vibrated from Zahir's chest that captured Katariya in the spell. To seal the kiss with perfection, the captivating scent of citrus and juniper berries wafted from his pheromones and called to her senses.

"Prince Zahir, Princess Katariya! Where are you? Sade wanted me to check on—"

With a jump, Katariya and Zahir shoved themselves apart. Quickly, they turned to stare at the elephant shifter with glossy eyes, red cheeks, and disheveled hair.

Looking up and down their forms, no doubt noticing their state of being, Bron shamelessly laughed, "Perhaps, it's a good thing I showed up. You wild cats can't be making babies in the palace gardens."

Shaking her head, Katariya ran a hand down the length of her body, attempting to smooth her dress. "Oh, no. Ugh, please don't tell Sade what happened."

She was thankful her sister had not been the one to stumble upon her and the prince in a compromising position and felt a wave of relief wash over. Bron was sworn to keep the prince's secrets. Her sister was not.

"Your secret is safe with me, but trust me, if I can wait, you both can too. The way Sade bites her lips is enough to drive any man crazy."

Bron's gaze became distant, as though he were envisioning her sister in the same position he had caught Zahir and her in just moments before.

"And when she—"

"Oh no, don't. I do not want to hear about you lusting after my sister," Katariya interrupted.

His wide, droopy eyes gave the impression of innocence, but his lack of filter was obvious as he tried to start up his rambling again. "It's hard not to when she—"

She interrupted him once more. "Please Bron, don't tell her about what you saw. She already thinks ill of me."

"Ill of you? Your sister doesn't think ill of you. Jealous perhaps, but who wouldn't be? You are Tulamund's princess. Sade admires you, Katariya. She's always going on and on about her fearless sister. She told me she wishes she had just a small amount of your courage."

"She admires me?"

Throughout their childhood, Sade and Amos were constantly bickering, trying to put an end to Katariya's wild behavior. Both of her siblings had different ideas on how a princess should behave. Amos wanted to ensure that Katariya knew how to defend herself, while Sade discouraged the swordplay, grumbling about the prophecy and the importance of her safety.

"*You are putting her at risk,*" she would say.

Never in her life had she imagined her sister to be jealous of more than just her status as a princess. Fearless? Courageous? Katariya felt she was just the opposite. Every day since her brother's exile, she felt her world crashing down like a mudslide.

She was barely holding onto the strength and confidence that Amos instilled in her. Evidence of her lack of strength was the weak-kneed kiss she had given the prince just moments before. She melted like soft clay in his hands, and for a few moments, she almost welcomed the idea of becoming a jaguar shifter. To her, that was not fearless or courageous.

"I know she doesn't express it, but losing your brother was hard on Sade, too. It changed the outlook of her future, but things happen for a reason. If her proposals hadn't been delayed, then we wouldn't have met, and I can't tell you how excited I am about our union."

Bron's eyes held a special warmth whenever he spoke about Sade, and his words conveyed the strength of his feelings. Marching up to Bron with a pointed finger, Katariya threatened, "If you ever hurt my sister, I swear to the goddesses, I will personally make sure you regret it."

Bron was so tall that her finger barely reached the middle of his chest. His eyes widened and blinked rapidly before he let out a bellied laugh.

"I may not be afraid of the other Abara sister, but you, Katariya—you're scarier than a gorilla on a rampage."

Zahir let out a huff and retorted, "You're telling me. She's going to be ruthless when she accepts her jaguar."

They all walked across the courtyard with tension in the air and the gray haze of clouds lingering in the night sky. Katariya attempted to straighten her dress while the prince adjusted his robe.

Eventually, they found her shoes in the middle of the grass, and Bron could not contain his teasing banter.

"Oh goddess, you both have so much to look forward to. With both of you shifting at the same time, it will surely fire up your senses, and you two can cozy yourselves away for winter and—"

Zahir let out a low, hearty laugh as he stated, "Okay, that's enough, Bron. Not in front of the lady. You can come to my quarters, and we can discuss—"

Katariya took a pointed elbow and jabbed it into the prince's side to silence him.

"Ow! And you still think you are going to be an antelope? Not with that strength." He rubbed his aching side.

She stepped in front of them, blocking their path from the grand hall's entrance. Wagging her finger between them, she narrowed her eyes and mouth into a threatening scowl.

"You two will not be continuing this conversation whether it is about me *or* my sister. Better yet, just pretend this never happened!"

Both men gave each other knowing smiles, and Katariya huffed the entire way back to the palace. Storming back into the grand hall with her head held high, she was determined to bite her tongue through the rest of the dinner.

PART III | CHAPTER 16

KNOWLEDGE IS LIKE A LION;
IT CANNOT BE GENTLY EMBRACED.
- A SOUTH AFRICAN PROVERB

Katariya went through the rest of the dinner unscathed and unnoticed. King Cairo pretended as though she didn't exist, and she found solace in the tender touch of Zahir's hand under the table.

When they arrived home, the two sisters talked for hours. Sade overflowed with enthusiasm over her newfound love for Bron while she pulled out different fabrics and patterns for the wedding. Eventually, Sade fell asleep, laid out between tulle and lace, and Katariya retired to her room, finding it increasingly harder to suppress the dizzying sensations of the Animalia spirit as the day reached its end.

Existential dread crept in as Katariya listened to the rain patter against her bedroom window. As the mind drifted, she was reminded of her wrongdoings and all the reasons she didn't deserve this supposed greatness. If Amos had been the bearer of the prophecy, then maybe he would have been more fortunate in the species his soul attached itself to.

No matter what Katariya did, she couldn't stop tallying how many times she had mouthed off to her parents. How many times had she lied to her sister about going to prayer lessons when she was really down by the river practicing her fighting skills? All the times she failed to say a thankful prayer when she caught a fish. Oh, how Katariya wished she hadn't teased a painted dog boy for having a set of crooked teeth.

Analyzing the mistakes she made as a child and the normal acts of teenage defiance would have no real sway in the goddesses' decision tomorrow. Katariya knew their selection was not only based on birth and blood, but also from the contents of the soul. However, she had spent her entire life trying to mold herself into this role and prepare for the transition into a jaguar. No matter how hard she tried, it never settled in her bones.

She wanted to detest the notion, to test the boundaries of her parents and the high standards that the women of Tulamund were supposed to hold themselves to. If she accepted her fate, then maybe she wouldn't feel like her skin was crawling, blood pumping through her veins like a beating snare drum.

To distract herself, she tried to think about her brother, but eventually her thoughts drifted back to the kiss with Prince

Zahir. Surprisingly, the thought of the kiss filled her with a bubbly warmth that differed from the fiery boil of her beast raging from within. It was a pleasant distraction from the panic in her chest.

Zahir had not only been nice to her but had also tried to comfort her in a time of need. The ceremony was happening to the both of them, and if he was not scared, why should she be?

Everyone in her tribe knew how badly the loss of her brother had broken her. For months, she would wake up drenched in a layer of sweat, and when she woke, her cheeks were sticky from the tears that came with the night terrors.

The image of the king's jaws tightly wrapped around her brother's neck would play on repeat. Haunting her so badly that it took weeks before she could eat. The simple utterance of her brother's name created a wave of nausea, and she had vomited almost every time.

Time heals all wounds, and while it was true that with time things had gotten easier, there was still a gaping hole in her heart, and she had given up trying to make it scab and scar.

From outside her bedroom door, a loud thump paired with the sound of barreling footsteps pulled Katariya from her thoughts. The silence of the night was broken only by the occasional chirp of a cricket, hinting at how late it was. Everyone in her house should have been sleeping.

The footsteps moved closer, and the door rattled.

Throwing off her covers, she jumped from the bed and searched for a weapon. The only defense was a rotting wooden sword. Her knife and steel sword were hidden in the barn, and she hadn't been lucky enough to find the bow her father hid months ago.

As the knob rattled and the door quietly crept open, it revealed the intruder to be her father dressed in a heavy raincoat. Behind him was the shadow of another shifter looming in the darkness. As they fully stepped into the room, their lanterns sent a soft, orange glow that illuminated their faces.

Her father sputtered in disbelief. "Katariya, what are you doing awake?"

Katariya had a similar look on her face, her jaw dropping. Standing in her room was Priestess Osha, flashing her a sympathetic smile. The hood of the priestess's cloak covered her long black hair and most of her face, but there was no doubt it was the okapi shifter.

Throwing the stick to the ground, Katariya straightened her back and attempted to smooth down her braids.

"Blessed priestess, what—what are you doing here?" she stammered.

The priestess opened her mouth then slammed it shut. Taking a visible deep breath, Priestess Osha said, "You need to get dressed, pack a bag, and please hurry."

Scrambling around the room, her father shoved a green leather satchel in her hands and dragged her the rest of the way out of the bed.

"What do you mean, 'pack a bag'?" Katariya's eyebrows raised.

"We'll explain soon, but not now. Please Katariya, my sweet girl. Do not ask questions; grab your things and hurry. We need to leave." Her father continued to shove clothes into her bag.

Looking toward Priestess Osha, Katariya hoped she would offer some clarity, but her face was drawn in a hard line.

Staring at the satchel with uncertainty, she packed for several occasions. A kaftan, long sleeve and short sleeve blouses, and two pairs of trousers. It took her a minute to make up her mind, but she decided it was best if she brought her ceremony dress. A part of her wondered if they were making the move to the palace now, but it was such a peculiar time for travel.

Tossing Katariya another thick pair of trousers and a long-sleeved shirt, her father instructed her to change. They spun around to give her privacy, and the eerie silence filled with unanswered questions.

When she was dressed, they ushered her through the halls, quietly passing the rooms that held her sleeping mother and sister. When Katariya tried to open her mouth to ask if they were coming, her father's hand silenced her. They tiptoed down the stairs, put on their hooded jackets, and exited through the kitchen's back door.

When the door slammed shut, Katariya spun around with a multitude of questions. She had barely opened her mouth when her father barked, "Not now. Not here. Let's go."

Extending his arm, her father adjusted the hood of her coat before clasping her hand. He pulled her through the orchards, weaving through the rows of fruit-bearing trees.

Priestess Osha trailed behind them but suddenly stopped to ask. "Do you have a weapon she can use? A sword or a knife. It may be best to bring it."

Stopping in her tracks, Katariya tried to feign innocence by stammering her words. "No—I would never—I..."

Her father rested a hand on her shoulder. "It's okay, sweet girl. I need you to go get your knife *and* your sword."

Never in her life did Katariya expect to be allowed to use a weapon, but she did not take more than a moment to hesitate. Spinning around, she sprinted toward the old barn.

Moving the broken wheel and sorting through a pile of hay, she threw the knife into her satchel and attached the sword to the belt around her waist. While she grabbed her gear, her father climbed the ladder to the second story barn. After rummaging around for a few minutes, he came down holding the bow he had confiscated from her many times before.

Fixing the bow over her shoulder, he shoved two dozen arrows into her bag until it overflowed. Without a word, they guided Katariya out of the barn and into the eerie darkness.

The three of them flew through the expanse of her family's property as though they were propelled by a purpose. Her jacket's hood protected her from the harsh rains, but she could still feel the crisp air of the howling winds against her face. The storm that came on the evening of the ceremony arrived like clockwork, falling from the heavens at the same time of day each year. It rained so heavily that the valley filled, and the entire southern region was converted into a huge marshy pool by the end of the week.

With every step she took, sludge and mud seeped through her shoes. The soft glow of their lanterns lit up a small circle around them, but the looming darkness was ominous, and with every other step Katariya took, she stumbled blindly.

There was not a soul on the road, not even a straggler coming out of the tavern. The kingdom was fast asleep, waiting for the events of tomorrow to unfold.

The merchants' goods and stalls were covered by tarps that created an even louder drumming as the rain pounded against them. It wasn't until they reached the end of the carts and stalls that she realized that the direction they were facing was not that of the king's palace. The night sky hid the mountain, but she was familiar with the land.

If they were headed north, then they would have been standing in an open clearing, facing the grand staircase that directed them to the waterfall. Instead, they traveled south until the stone road transformed into a dirt path and vanished into the trees.

Coming to a full stop, Katariya tugged on her father's arm. "Papa, where are we going?"

Her father brushed her off, his voice strained as he said, "We need to keep walking. We cannot slow down. Please, just be brave for me."

"But Pa, none of this is making any sense. Just tell me where we are going," she begged, stumbling after him.

Priestess Osha gently placed her hand on Katariya's arm. "It is for your safety that you follow us. I do not know why the lion has returned. I no longer hear the goddesses' whispers; no one has in quite some time. His na—your name. I heard the goddess call for your protection, and I must do what I can to ensure your safety."

Katariya could only stare. The panic in her chest did not allow room for her to mull over the priestess's words.

With a tug, her father pulled her along. Fear quivered in his shaky voice. "Let's go. I can explain more soon. Things I should have told you, things about you and your brother."

If Katariya could have seen his face, she would have known he was crying. She crashed into her father's side, his weight sagging into her.

It was not the pressure of his body that weighed her down, rather it was the whirlwind of the confusion and the exhaustion of the impossibly long evening that felt heavy. In the late night, when she should have been preparing her body for the Animalia ceremony, Katariya was scrambling in the mud, blindly following her father and priestess into the darkness.

"Reevus, I know this is hard, but if you want to do what's best for her, we need to keep moving," Priestess Osha said.

"You're right." He nodded. "Come along, Katariya."

Pulling her from the desperate hug, her father led them down the dirt path into the thick brush and foggy mist. The darkness of the forest enveloped them as thunder crackled in the distance.

CHAPTER 17

THE TRUTH IS LIKE A LION. YOU DON'T HAVE TO
DEFEND IT. LET IT LOOSE; IT WILL DEFEND ITSELF.
- ST. AUGUSTINE OF HIPPO

For thirty minutes, they trekked through the forest until they unexpectedly entered a lengthy, wide tunnel. Katariya settled in and took a moment to observe her surroundings, realizing they were standing inside a large, hollowed-out tree. It was enormous in width and length, and even with the low light of the lanterns illuminating the bark, she was unable to see where it ended.

"You can come out now."

Priestess Osha set a lantern on the ground and walked down the tunnel.

From the shadows, a dark mass emerged. Once it was revealed by the light, Katariya propelled herself forward, jumping into the arms of someone she hadn't seen in years.

"Uncle Ram!"

The massive warrior pulled her into one of his tight, over-bearing hugs. He smelled of mulled wine, spices, and rolled tobacco. A unique scent she associated with the legend.

As a former mercenary, Ramar had seen it all. He wasn't related by blood, but with the hardships of war, many of the men who fought together bonded on the battlefield. In every good war story, it was her Uncle Ram who saved the day.

"It's good to see ya kid." His deep grumbling voice vibrated against her.

Priestess Osha remained in the darkness, but Katariya stared at the two men, expecting someone to finally give her answers.

The silence between them was ominous and, just like at dinner the night before, it seemed like she was the only one left in the dark. Stuck reading expressions and searching for clues in between their hesitant responses.

As her father went to sit down, the fibers of the wood scraped against his back. A grumble of annoyance escaped him as his jacket tore down a jagged seam. Brushing off an act that would normally pull her father into a hot-headed temper, he patted the ground beside her and directed her to take a seat.

"Come and rest for a little while. I have much to explain."

Uncle Ram took that as his excuse to look like he was busy inspecting the cave, slowly turning to join the priestess in the darkness.

Moving her sword to the side, she took a spot next to her father, careful not to touch the rough wood. A need for comfort had her instinctively leaning into his body for support, and upon contact, he pulled her into a close hug.

His voice started off low, accompanied with a few ragged coughs. "You and your brother are more alike than you think."

Katariya's brother was her kindred spirit. In her youngest memories, even from the age of a small, waddling toddler, Amos had always been the one to look out for her. Everyone in her family treated her differently, but with Amos, it was in a good way. He was attentive, joking, and tried his best to be lighthearted. For years of her life, she aspired to be exactly like him.

"There's no easy way to say this, but you and your brother do not share my blood."

The rumble of thunder crashed down just as his words rattled across her brain. Her mouth hung low to the ground, filling with the musty, humid air of the ceremonial rains. Incoherent ramblings stuttered alongside sputtering gasps.

Did he just say that he wasn't her father? Did she say that out loud? She honestly couldn't tell. The announcement was dizzying.

He cleared his throat, and she could see the hurt and shame flash across his light brown eyes.

"A few nights after the war—" he started, then stopped as though he knew there was no good way to explain the unexpected news. "Priestess Osha came knocking at our door, and standing behind her was a child holding a newborn baby."

"*Pa.*" The endearment suddenly sounded peculiar as soon as it came out of her mouth, but she tried not to let her voice waver. "I understand the war was violent. You have walked with a limp my entire life, but what does this have to do with Amos? What does it have to do with me?"

Priestess Osha's voice made her shiver. "The current. The river's current moved backwards, guiding you and your brother through the Outlands and into the city. *Backwards*, through the rain that was pushing all of the magic into the plains, you and Amos safely made it upstream. There was no greater sign of the goddesses' existence than hearing her voice and witnessing the both of you safely floating from the ashes of war."

"But the lion—the prophecy." Katariya shook her head.

"When the priestess came to me. When I saw your face. A brave little boy holding the smallest little creature. I couldn't turn you away. Not when the goddess so strongly believed you were in danger. I would have done anything to protect you—will do anything." Her father held her gaze. "Your mother and I kept this secret from the king to ensure you and your brother's safety. If I had known, if we had known what you truly were, we would have never let your brother attend the ceremony. We had no idea what the prophecy was truly asking."

Ram emerged from the darkness, startling them with a jump.

"Reevus, ya gotta wrap this up. The rain is settlin' and soon we'll be visible from the treetops. We need to get a move on if we're goin' to get out of the city before night falls."

Her father softly nodded, his face contorting in concern as his eyes dashed across Katariya's face.

Priestess Osha's voice raised to gain their attention. "I cannot answer everything, but I need you to know there is a strong chance that if you go through with the ceremony, you will transform into a lion, just as your brother had."

Secret after secret. Lie after lie. Katariya could only blink at her rapidly before a sobbed croaked.

Shaking her head, she pleaded, "This cannot be. Pa, please tell me this is a lie. A cruel joke. A test, if you will."

"I'm so sorry. It killed me when they took Amos. Breaks me to think it could happen to you. I can't let you suffer the same fate."

Her heart throbbed in her ears, and panic thundered through her quaking body. The veil over the secrets and lies was suddenly peeled away, exposing her to an unsettling truth. The weight of her spirit felt heavy—oh so heavy that she jerked away from her father to shoot a spray of vomit on the wooden walls behind her.

"You have options Katariya, if you don't have the ceremo-ny—if we can keep you out of the river until the rain passes, the gift will pass too. You'll remain human. The king may be furious. He may no longer let you marry the prince, but he wouldn't banish you. You can come back. You'd have a home with me, your Ma, and Sade."

Priestess Osha nodded in agreement, Ram refused to meet her gaze, and her father choked on a sob.

Katariya's body convulsed, and tears damped her cheeks. Attempting to clear her vision, she swiped her shaky hands against the wet hair plastered to her face. Overcome with hurt and the sodden state of her clothes, she felt her spirits sinking further.

Once, the shifters of Tulamund believed the lion spirit had left them forever, yet her father now argued that Katariya shared the same bloodthirsty spirit as her brother. Since Amos's exile, she spent years learning about the history of the lion. There was insanity and madness behind the beast, and the terror they had caused Tulamund during their reign would never be forgotten.

The kingdom had thought that her brother's shift had been unusual, even more rare than lightning striking the same place twice. They had been raised to be passive gatherers rather than aggressive hunters. It was out of character for Amos to transform into a wild beast, but if he shared a lion's blood, there wasn't much that he could have done to change his fate. With the beast's powerful bloodline, the lion's gift was almost guaranteed to manifest itself.

Her father grabbed her shoulders and shook them in an attempt to pull her out of the panicked daze.

"I never thought Amos would have transformed into a—a monster. Not even the Priestess suspected that the lion had made its return. Your brother had always been a sweet child. He had a knack for finding trouble, but he had good intentions."

His eyes strayed to Ram, who was impatiently waiting by the tunnel's entrance. His head was stuck outside the door, looking around for potential witnesses.

"So what? You just found us and kept us? How does one hide two children from the prying eyes of the kingdom?" she asked.

The hoarseness of her voice trembled in a pitch that was just above a whisper. She had a million questions, but Ram's lingering presence and tapping foot signaled that they were running out of time.

"Priestess Osha." Katariya's father took a quivering breath. "She's done her part in keeping the king and the kingdom clueless. She bent the truth. The entire antelope tribe has been sworn under a sacred oath."

A detail Katariya had skipped over suddenly rose to her mind. Turning to Priestess Osha, she asked, "*The Outlands*? You said I came from the Outlands."

Nodding slowly, Priestess Osha answered, "A few nights after the war, I heard you crying and, in your tears, I heard the prophecy. I came to your mother and father, begging them to keep you both safe. Your father showed his nature throughout the war, and the antelope tribe does not quarrel with the need for status. I trusted him to protect you. The kingdom made their speculations, but the prophecy was enough to keep them from making threats or accusations. It also helped that Amos looked exactly like you, a near twin."

Katariya's father grabbed her arm and gave it a gentle squeeze. "You may have come from the Outlands, but the prophecy was as clear as day. The goddesses demand your protection from our very own king."

Her mind flashed to the image of her brother shivering, mumbling, fearful of the king's wrath. The prophecy was true after all. King Cairo and his lethal carnivores posed a dangerous threat to her and her brother's life.

In the faint light of the lantern, she could see her father's bloodshot eyes. As he recounted the story, she sensed his desperation. The sadness and guilt were clear as tears poured down his cheeks into his long, graying beard. It hurt to watch the man who raised her, the man she thought to be her father, breaking down in her arms.

She hugged him tightly, trying to replicate the warmth of his bear hugs that she had come to cherish. Her stomach was further settled, and her breathing was even, but Katariya couldn't find the right words to say. She wanted to tell him she understood why he kept the secret. Her heart longed to tell him that everything was going to be okay, but she didn't want to add another lie to the fire.

Until today, her future had been predetermined, but now she faced the unknown that was covered in a web of lies and concealed uncertainty.

"So, what now? Uncle Ram takes me out of the city, he keeps me away from the river, and... I deny my gift. Live the rest of my life as a human," she said, trying to make sense of the situation.

"We can't have you here. The king will demand to witness your transformation. He'll force you in the water, and he'll come knocking at our door if we don't attend the ceremony. We'll say you ran away in the middle of the night. We'll tell them that the pressure of the prophecy has become too much for you." He rose from the ground, careful not to step in the mess of her empty stomach. "If you leave now, you can get far enough south that you should have a decent head start. Ram can easily navigate these lands. He'll lead you far away from the kingdom."

Her father reached down to offer a hand, and Katariya took it and rose to stand beside him. Holding onto her shoulders, he said, "We will come for you as soon as the rain has passed. It may be a few days or even a week, but once it has settled, we can bring you home."

He tightened her jacket and tucked her braided hair inside her hood. His eyes studied her as though he was trying to memorize her face.

"Come on, kid, we gotta get a move on." Ram's tapping foot stilled, but his arms were still folded across his chest as though he were losing patience.

Panic crept its way back in as Katariya's mind spiraled with so many questions. Quickly, she blurted, "But what happens if I don't marry the prince?"

"We'll deal with the repercussions this will have on the farm and the tribe later. All I care about is that you will be alive." Her father's eyes narrowed. "They will never know the true nature of your spirit if we never activate it."

It wasn't a great plan, yet her father seemed so sure that it would work. In his eyes, there was worry, guilt, and shame mirrored back at her, but his voice was wrapped in love. He squeezed her hands tightly.

"It will be okay, I promise. Be good for your uncle, and if you really need it, do not hesitate to use your bow."

Everything was falling apart. The prophecy haunted her every single day of her life. For years, she prayed to the goddesses to understand their reason for choosing her. There was a longing to be like her parents and Sade. A dream of living with the swift agility of an antelope shifter. Although there had always been a disconnect between her and her family, nothing could have prepared her for the truths that had been revealed.

There were two options, one that was not much greater than the other. Katariya would have to choose between losing her mind to the madness of the lion's spirit or give up her birthright as an Animalia shifter.

It was odd for her to admit it, but some part of her wished that the king's interpretation of the prophecy had been true. Right now, she would have given anything to be a jaguar shifter, just like Prince Zahir.

Ram's low, gruff voice bellowed out a deep, growling command. "Alright kid, we gotta get out of here. Reevus, ya need to hurry back before anyone notices ya walkin' through the city." He turned to the Priestess and bowed. "Osha, good to see ya as always."

"Until next time, Ram." Priestess Osha gave a slight nod.

"Come on, kid. We're gonna have to move quickly. If we aren't down by the marsh when the sun comes up, the entire southern region is goin' to spot us. We gotta go now," Uncle Ram grumbled, then mumbled under his breath about no one taking this as seriously as they should.

Pulled into another hug, Katariya was wrapped within her father's warm embrace. As her father held onto her shoulders, his face searched her own.

"Please remember that I love you. Always remember that Ma and Sade love you, oh, so very much."

Despite the honesty in his eyes, Katariya knew she wouldn't be able to get all of her questions answered until she returned. She would have to put her faith in the goddess and pray that she would make it back unharmed.

Staring into his light brown eyes, she found herself studying his features. Before now, she had always assumed her nose was the same shape as his. His eyes and face now appeared narrow, and his eyes weren't hazel at all. They were light in color, but they were clearly brown. Katariya could no longer see any similarities between the two.

Ram guided her to the edge of the tunnel, and his low breath could be heard from the depths of the hollowed-out tree. The men shared a wordless understanding, like warriors passing secret codes and messages. There was nothing for Katariya to do or say that would make the situation any better.

Without warning, her father disrobed, transforming into his impala antelope form. The thick trees of the jungle seemed to part as he galloped away. Priestess Osha slipped from her cloak, and the majestic gallop of the okapi left Katariya breathless, the moonlight shining brightly against the white lines of the Animalia's dark coat.

Flashing her a solemn look, Ram waved his hand, directing Katariya to follow. Plunging into the darkness, she trailed behind him, uncertain of what was to come.

CHAPTER 18

STUDY THE NATURE AROUND
YOU, BUT ALSO WITHIN YOU.
- FENNEL HUDSON, A MEANINGFUL LIFE

Katariya blindly followed her uncle through the jungle until they reached a small dock with six or seven boats tied to the edge of the water. The heavy rains caused the river to overflow, and the rapids crashed, rocking each boat from side to side. In disbelief, Katariya raised her eyebrows and spoke for the first time since they had begun their journey.

"Are you *trying* to make me shift?"

Ram gave her a half shrug.

"Might not seem like it, but we'll be safer if ya risk it."

Katariya could see the fiery red that clouded the king's vision when faced with the threat of the lion, and she knew he would not hesitate to do the same to her. Shivering at the thought, she carefully followed her uncle onto the platform.

The pair boarded the smallest vessel out of the entire fleet. Despite the boat missing a plank, it carried them swiftly down the river.

She had never traveled much farther than the market, and hours passed in silence with no clues as to how far they had gotten. Katariya's head began to spiral, and her uncle tried to find the right words, but as someone who was never great with emotions, Ram chose to avoid making eye contact.

Over the next few hours, they listened to the buzzing of cicadas mixed with the sounds of her hiccups and sniffling, snotty nose. To distract herself, she made mental notes of the many types of plants and trees: rattan palm, acai palms, lowland nepenthes, and bucket orchids. The tall yellowwood trees were a maze, and the thick foliage of the dense forest was not contained to the trails.

As they coasted down the river, the low protruding branches and trees brushed against her. The emotional weight of the day pulled her down with every wet leaf that smacked her in the face.

"You've grown up a lot, kid. Have to say that I kinda missed ya." Ram's boisterous voice shattered through the unnerving silence.

The customs of the Tulamund were different from the freedoms of living on the Isles of Beruk, an island completely filled with bear shifters, where Ram was born and raised. Ram's job as a mercenary had him moving around all the time, but even if it didn't, he never stuck around the city for too long.

"Too many rules" as he would say.

In keeping up with his restless nature, his visits with her family were brief. Each stay, he would give her and her sister beautiful gems and necklaces, while Amos was gifted with an assortment of tools and weapons. Despite the fact that the bow was gifted to Amos, Ram encouraged Amos to teach Katariya how to wield it.

To put it simply, Ram was a loud-mouthed, grumbling bear who didn't care what anyone had to say or what they thought. He was someone she looked up to.

"Thanks Ram," Katariya replied, wiping her nose on the end of her sleeve.

"What's it been? Two years now?" he asked, using the oars to guide them around a rocky bend.

"Three," she answered quietly.

He nodded but made no further comment. Their eyes drifted away from one another as they thought about how long it had really been since her brother's ceremony.

Quickly changing the subject, she asked, "Where are you living now?"

Lifting a large tree branch to allow her to duck under, Ram grumbled with disinterest, "Here, there, the marsh, the Outlands. Been makin' the transition from merc to bounty hunter. Lots more money in a good bounty."

Ram was a no-nonsense kind of man who had been wearing the same jacket for over twenty years. His coarse black hair was an unkept mop sitting on the top of his head. He had dark brown doe-eyes and a shaggy beard that was dirty and lopsided in a way that Katariya guessed he last chopped it on a drinking binge.

If he wasn't grumbling his words, he could be seen with a stick of rolled tobacco hanging from his mouth. If they had met under different circumstances, she doubted that her father and Ram would have become friends. While her father was noble and reserved, her uncle was loud, had a lack of morals, and was a master of all weapons. They couldn't have been more different.

To prove her point, Ram let out a hearty chuckle and said, "I don't know. Just been tryin' to avoid the city lately. Everyone there has a banana up their behind, and the work I do involves breaking a few laws here and there."

Katariya couldn't bring herself to join in on the laughter. There was a question burning on the tip of her tongue. She was biting it hard, reminding herself that he was here to help her.

As carefree as the bear shifter was, Ram was also observant. There had been a shift in her demeanor that had him saying, "I know. I know I shoulda been there. It was stupid, I took a job and ended up back on Beruk. When the news carried across the coast, it was too late. He was already gone."

In a burst, Katariya let out the bubbling question. "Did you look for him? Do you know where he is?"

Her uncle took a deep breath, and visible steam mingled with the mist of fog. A single lantern provided a soft glow, casting a warm light on his face as he crafted a thoughtful response.

"My contacts only go so far once we're outta the king's barriers. I'm sure your Pa told ya I was once a captain. Spent years breaking from shackles tryin' to leave that horrid palace. I got the trainin' but travelin' to Sandstone without a team—" He shook his head. "I'm sorry kid, but even that's too risky for me."

Katariya gave a dispirited nod, and they fell back into silence until the wind began to howl, spitting drops of water all over their faces. Tugging her hood closer she asked, "Where exactly are we going?"

She wasn't familiar with the layout of the southern land, but she had prior knowledge of the branch of water that flowed into the Outlands. It contained the essence of their creator, but as a branch from the main river, it only held a fraction of the heavens' magic and was heavily guarded by the king's army.

It was the same river that carried Amos and Katariya into Tulamund. The disbelief behind their heritage had slithered to the back of her mind. She was burdened with thoughts of her brother, who had never been given the opportunity to suppress the lion. Exiled and punished by a spirit that may also be coursing through her veins.

"We're in the heart of the leopards' den. They're all asleep in the treetops." He pointed up as though she could see their treehouses in the forest brush.

She tried to look inside herself to access her new senses, but without an Animalia gift, her eyes wouldn't focus in the dark.

"We've got about a day or so down the river, maybe more if the rain slows down. We'll get to the marsh and head into a tavern. Hang around for a bit while we wait on an old buddy of mine to give us a ride out of Tulamund."

"Is it safer than this boat?" Katariya asked.

"Ya, probably. This one here,"—he gestured to the barely floating vessel— "is for fishin' and travelin'. Malau's boat is for shipments. My hope is that the king's guards will be pre-occupied with the ceremony, but ya know, in case we run into anyone, they'll just assume that anything the boats holdin' is cargo."

The plan sounded too easy, too well thought out. Curiously, she asked, "How long have you and my father been planning this escape?"

"Nearly three years now, I guess. We mighta lost your brother, but we couldn't lose ya too."

Despite her inability to accept her new reality, Ram's gaze was filled with compassion, and his hardened face briefly softened.

"Malau will guide us through the delta and drop us off on the other side. *If* we are lucky, we'll travel back up north and reenter the city through the mountains. We can waste some time hidin' out in the plains and wait for the rain to stop before ya make your grand appearance." He spoke in a laid-back, offhand manner that was accompanied by a casual shrug.

When he gritted out the word *"If"*, Katariya felt sick, knowing the reality was that the odds weren't in their favor.

"And if we are *not* lucky?"

"If we are not lucky, someone recognizes ya. We get caught, they send a few guards, and ya get taken back to that dreaded palace and meet whatever fate the king decides."

Ram wouldn't sugarcoat it for her. If she didn't get out of the city safely, she would be met with the wrath of King Cairo and face the same fate as her brother.

Instantly, she began to tremble, shaken by the weight of her cursed reality. The lies were sinking into her pores and burning at a hole that grew even larger as the spirit of the beast called out to her.

Before today, her entire life had been mapped out. From whom she would marry, to her role and the species that lurked within her heart and soul.

Now, she was faced with the loose strings of fabrication and the falsehood of her entire life. Her family. *A lie.* The prophecy. *A lie.* The contents of her soul were questionable, and not knowing who or what she was made her feel *empty.*

"Do you truly believe the prophecies?" Katariya asked timidly.

She had seen what the Animalia spirit had done to her brother. How he thrashed with uncontrollable rage and muttered nonsense under his breath, fighting off the beast inside. Her brother's downfall was a stark reminder that the spirit of the lion was far from gifted or great.

For her entire life, she had been told that the soul never rests until it receives the Animalia gift. If she became a lion, the beast inside would drive her to madness, blind her with rage, and fill her with bloodlust. If she didn't accept the gift and kept herself out of the river, then she would live as a human with half a soul. Without the spirit, an even bigger void would form in her heart.

Inside, there was a longing for the flutter of magic against her skin. Katariya had dreams about what it would feel like for the spirit to not only envelop the body but to seep through the flesh and bones into the soul.

Most days, she woke up remembering dreams where she galloped through the open plains as an antelope. Her mind never once imagined her spirit as a jaguar, but she did recall the haunting of a lioness lingering in her dreams the weeks following her brother's ceremony. She thought the appearance of the beast was a part of her night terrors, but now she wondered if the goddesses were trying to tell her something more.

Ram let out a deep sigh, and his fingers tapped against his leg. Laced with a tinge of sadness, he said, "I don't know, kid. After your brother's ceremony—I just don't know. This world will take a chunk out of ya, chew ya up, and spit ya out into tiny bones and broken pieces. Sometimes I pray for somebody to talk to, but honestly, I don't know if anybody's really listenin' anymore."

The silence descended once more, and the heavy weight of his words mulling over her heart and through her mind. The rain stopped, and a thick fog surrounded them. The river was swollen, pushing the boat down the stream.

It was the end of summer, and the days were still hot, yet under the dense forest shade, in the middle of the night, the air was cold and left a chill in her bones. The end of the evening was marked by the gradual decrease in the chirping of the crickets, replaced by the gentle, melodic voices of the birds singing in the treetops.

No longer needing to use the oars, Ram reached into his satchel and pulled out two jars and two tiny, intricately designed spoons. Dipping into the jar, he handed her a spoon covered with a light sticky substance.

Dumbfoundedly, she stared at the spoon in her hand. Under the faint light of the lantern, she couldn't completely see the details, but she could feel patterned lines under her fingertips, the point a jagged chunk of clear quartz melded onto the end.

"It's honey. Eat it. Lots of sugar. Fuels and fattens ya. We got a couple hours until we reach the swamps. We'll catch a fish once we're deeper in the south," he said as he dipped an identical spoon into his own honey jar.

Slurping down the honey, he pushed the other jar into her hands. She licked the spoon and silently stared as he shoved a spoonful into his eager mouth.

Katariya had just days to decide her fate. As she tried to sort through all the options, her head began to swim.

Her spirit was strong. Rumbling through her skin and itching its way into her veins, her blood, and her heart. She couldn't envision a life without the Animalia spirit. The world would view her as a plague, no better than the soulless poachers set on destroying the kingdom. If she did accept the spirit, the king would either hunt her down or she'd lose her mind to a violent rampage. There was no great option, but one was better than the other.

Despite her thoughts, she paused to indulge in the delicious honey and took the time to admire the intricate and dainty spoons. Her eyes flickered to the massive bear, and she wondered why such a gruff man would own such delicate trinkets.

CHAPTER 19

A GAZELLE RUNS FASTER THAN US; COCKROACHES
ARE REMARKABLY TOLERANT OF RADIATION;
EVERY BEING HAS SOME SUPERIORITY; IN
REMEMBERING THIS, BE VERY HUMBLE!
- MEHMET MURAT ILDAN, CONTEMPORARY TURKISH
PLAYWRIGHT, NOVELIST

After two full days of travel, Katariya and Ram reached the tavern. Traversing the swampy jungle had left her famished and exhausted. Somehow, she was able to catch a few hours of sleep, but at this point, she would have followed anyone who could provide her with a hot meal and warm shelter.

The so-called tavern was a small wooden shack at the edge of the jungle, patched together with mismatched slabs of wood, each piece slapped over weathered holes and water damage. Heavily leaning on one side, the shack was far from safe or inviting for a young woman, let alone the future princess. Yet outside the tavern stood a small brown-haired woman with a broom in her hand, unlocking the front door.

"Mornin' Ram. Haven't seen ya around here lately. Especially not this early," the barkeep said with a wide, teasing grin.

The woman had an enormous set of top teeth and a smile that took over every inch of her tiny, narrow face. Although she was on the shorter side, Katariya could see that the barkeep's clothes were tight around thick muscles. Her curly hair was in a sloppy bun sitting on the top of her head and she had a knife strapped to her waist.

Another woman with a weapon... Katariya's brow arched as she eyed the tiny blade. This day was filled with so many surprises.

"Ahh, ya, I've been tryin' to lie low. Been on a few jobs that have kept me away," Uncle Ram said.

The inside of the shack looked just as rough as the outside. There were six tables and benches made from rough cuts of wood that were thrown on top of tree stumps to keep them steady. The tavern had a stale odor of ale, vomit, and the faint smell of urine.

At the end of the shack, there was a long bar, empty with only three stools. Behind the counter was a wall filled with a plethora of amber bottles and canteens filled with wine and pale ale. To the left, there was a small kitchen where she could see an older man standing at a clay oven stirring a pot.

When Katariya searched through her senses and worked past the stench, she could smell the faint aroma of a stew, beautifully spiced with coriander, turmeric, and a hint of cumin. With a deep inhale, her mouth watered, and her stomach rumbled, clearly not satisfied by the teeny scoops of honey.

"And your friend here? Is she a part of those jobs you're talking about?" The woman's eyes shifted, scrutinizing Katariya's appearance.

Few shifters in the north were fond of the southerners, and likewise. They had different standards on how they lived their lives, and there was great judgment between the different regions.

Many of the southern tribes were free-spirited and spent as much time in their shifter forms as the king allowed. While the northern tribes still shifted, it was primarily to meet their spirits' demands. There were quick spars and horn butting, sprints, and gallops, but no one in the north spent more than an hour or two in their gifted forms.

In the southern jungles of Tolego, there were monkeys freely swinging in the treetops, tigers casually lounging in the sun, and crocodiles swimming up and down the length of the river. There was nothing but trees, thick foliage, and Animalia shifters.

If the barkeep saw the elaborate braids that were hidden under Katariya's hood, the woman would instantly know that she was from the north. While most shifters with similar hair textures wore braids, carnivores never failed to impress, challenging themselves with unique patterns, new techniques, and often decorated each lock with gold hoops and crystals.

Under the woman's harsh gaze, it took everything for Katariya to not reach up and check that her hood was still placed tightly over her vibrant chestnut hair. She doubted this woman had ever been in the northern region, but if she had, she would recognize Katariya as Tulamund's future princess.

"Oh no, Scout. This is my partner, *Karina*, one of the king's mercenaries. A killer with her bow and arrow." He gestured to the bow slung over Katariya's shoulder.

Ram spoke the lie with a steady, unwavering voice, and Katariya struggled to keep her expression neutral. Of course, he would need a good cover story, but she hadn't known that King Cairo used mercenaries. Why would the king need to hire someone to do his bidding? He had an entire army of skilled shifters to use at will.

The woman, Scout, eyed her with a furrowed brow, expressing her disbelief. If what he said didn't throw her off, her appearance definitely would. Scout was probably questioning Katariya's choice of clothes and judging her clean face, hands, and fingernails. She looked rough from days of treading through rain and mud, but she still looked neat and tidy compared to Ram, Scout, and the older gentleman in the kitchen.

"Oh, you don't look too much like a mercenary. Much too... pretty." Scout met Katariya's eyes with a scowl.

Instead of cowering under the woman's intense gaze, she pushed her shoulders back and committed to the lie.

"I work both sides. The pretty face is how I reel in the targets."

Scout stared at her with a blank face before keeling over in laughter.

"Mighty fine work, girl! Usin' what the goddesses gave you, am I right?"

Katariya couldn't bring herself to laugh but gave Scout a soft smile.

"Can we set these back here?" Ram asked, pulling the bow off of Katariya's shoulder.

She then passed him her satchel and sword but left the knife strapped to her belt.

"Yeah, of course Ram. You don't have to ask." Scout grabbed the satchel from his hands. She tucked their belongings behind the bar, then grabbed a canteen off the counter.

"Well, what can I get ya? We got a nice catfish soup going. Should be done in ten minutes. I can get ya a drink while ya wait."

Scout filled two drinking glasses with an amber gold pale ale. The suds bubbled at the top as she slid them across the counter.

Ram immediately grabbed the glass, downed the ale in one big gulp, and let out a loud belch.

Katariya stared back with a mixture of amazement and disgust. She was shocked by how quickly he downed the drink but was unnerved by his lack of manners.

It didn't seem to bother Scout, though. She let out an exasperated laugh and slapped her hand against the counter. Within seconds, his glass was filled up again and halfway down his throat.

"Long trip?" Scout snickered.

"You have no idea," Ram mumbled, taking the last gulp of his second drink.

When Scout went to fill up his glass again, he raised a single finger as though to signal that he needed a minute.

"Ya hungry kid?" He turned to Katariya, and her stomach rumbled.

"I'm gonna go ahead and take that as a yes. I'll let Tatu know, and I'll have him bring it out to you when it's ready," Scout said, already walking back to the kitchen with her broom in hand.

Katariya sat sipping her pale ale, intrigued by the almost nutty flavor it had. She couldn't imagine ever getting used to all the new senses, but she found that when the smell was pleasant, she quite enjoyed the shrivel of happiness that ran through her body at the aroma.

The senses never dulled, but in time, they became less noticeable to the shifter. She was sad to think that after this week, her new gifts would be gone forever. Nothing seemed to settle in her spirit, but then again, how fast was she supposed to get over eighteen years of lies?

The minute long drinking break was really only a minute. Reaching around the counter, Ram grabbed the canteen of ale and filled his glass with his third drink.

"Woah, I don't think you can just take that. Don't you have to trade for it?" Katariya asked, completely stunned.

With a dismissive wave, he said, "I've known Tatu and Scout for a long time. Been coming here since I was sixteen. Scout will say she'll put it on my tab, but we both do a few unconventional services for each other."

His eyes arched up as he wiggled his brows suggestively, and it took Katariya a few seconds to figure out exactly what he had meant. She grimaced and he let out a full-bellied laugh.

Katariya hadn't gotten that kind of vibe from the two of them. Scout was muscular, and Katariya could tell that the barkeep could pack a mean punch, but she was also very short. She had to be at least two feet shorter than Ram because the top of her head only reached the center of his torso.

"Scout and Tatu are good, honest shifters. This little shack might not look like much, but I keep an eye on this place. Lots of trouble around these parts. I provide a little muscle. I get free meals, drinks and a little bit of comfort," he continued.

"But she said you hadn't been around for a while? So where have you really been?" Katariya asked.

"I didn't lie to her. I've been on a few jobs that have been keeping me away. Tracked down a fox shifter just last week. Shifty fella thought he could scam a couple tigers out of a large hunk of diamond. Caught him just last week up your way, trying to pawn it off in the market."

"So, what happened to him?" she asked hesitantly.

"I didn't kill him, if that's what you're asking. I got out of the business of killing years ago. Bounty hunter work is all about the delivery, but I don't ask questions of what they do with the shifters after I track them down," he admitted.

"So who protects this place when you're gone?"

"Lots of guys within my circle would happily slap around a couple of birdbrains, but I worry about 'em when I'm not around. Scout and Tatu would give ya the clothes off their backs if ya needed them. Being too nice can oftentimes get ya in a heap of trouble," Ram said as he finished his drink.

While he was on the third glass of ale, Katariya was still working on her first. He didn't appear to be reacting to the drinks, but she guessed that with his size, he had to drink a lot to feel its effects. As he reached to fill his fourth glass, Scout came rounding the corner and pulled the canteen out of his hands.

"No more for you, big fella. I need ya to help me with something in the back," Scout giggled, pulling Ram up from his stool.

"We'll be right back—ugh, make it fifteen to twenty minutes. My friend should be here soon to take us to his boat. He's a real big fella, ya won't miss him." Ram said, stretching out his arms to indicate that his friend was even larger than his own towering height.

"I'll have Tatu bring out your food if we're too long. I know this one's just gonna wolf it down when he gets his, but I hope ya enjoy yours when it comes out. My uncle takes great pride cookin' his stews." Scout gleamed with pride.

Ram ran his fingers up and down the tiny barkeep's side, and she squealed as he ushered her into the back room. Katariya hoped there was more than just the kitchen back there because poor Tatu was going to get a show if there wasn't. From this angle, she could see the elderly man, and he paid little attention to Ram and Scout as they sauntered past him.

Staring down at her drink, Katariya slowly swirled her finger around the rim of the glass. Just days before, she spent the evening with the jaguar prince. They had seemed to come to an understanding, but their argument in the courtyard had brought up so much more.

Fueled by the heated mix of frustration and desire, she has little time to process what his kiss had really meant. There had been a fiery warmth flickering in his cat eyes and a glow in her cheeks as they pulled away from one another. In that moment, they had not been a prince and a princess but rather two lost souls trying to make sense of a star-crossed union.

Taking a sip, Katariya wondered how the goddesses could lead her to such an impossible decision. Lose herself from the lack of spirit or lose herself to the spirit of the beast. That thought had her finishing the glass and pouring another.

CHAPTER 20

A LION DOES NOT FLINCH AT
THE LAUGHTER COMING FROM A HYENA.
- SUZY KASSEM, RISE UP AND SALUTE THE SUN

With a deep inhale, Katariya attempted to use her new abilities to smell the delicious stew. Her sensitive nose betrayed her and an onslaught of ale, urine and vomit left her gasping. The stench wafted through the air and seeped under the crack in the tavern's door.

As she turned around to investigate, the door busted open and in sauntered three grimy men completely covered in the ghastly scent. The strangers nearly kicked down the door as they barged in, throwing their coats on the table closest to them. They surveyed the room until the man in the middle caught Katariya staring. He gave her a toothless grin, accompanied by an unsettling wink. With a nod, the stranger ushered his companions closer.

From their smell alone, Katariya knew she did not want their attention. She turned to face forward and stared blankly at the bottles on the shelves. Taking slow sips of the ale, she willed her unnecessary panic away and tried her best to ignore their intense gazes.

There was no way that any of these men were Malau. She couldn't imagine her uncle being friends with men who wafted an aura of darkness and had eyes as dark as an endless pit. The smell of the men made her nose crinkle and she stiffen as their eyes seared into her back.

"Oh, look at you. Aren't you a pretty young thing?"

One of the men moved in closer, his presence looming over her shoulder. Katariya held her breath and shivered as he deeply sniffed the base of her neck. In the southern regions and the Isles, it was common to sniff out someone's Animalia species, but his unsettling wink gave her the notion that he wasn't just smelling her to figure out what kind of species she was.

Katariya ignored him and instead took another drink. She silently murmured her prayers and wished that Ram, or his friend, would barge through the door. It wasn't exactly what she had prayed for, but suddenly, Tatu rounded the corner holding a big bowl of stew and a fresh slice of bread.

"Catfish stew for the young lady," Tatu said, positioning the food in front of her, passing her a dented silver spoon.

His eyes widened and flashed with a look of fear as he took in the men that were surrounding her. Even though his eyes showed fear, he forced a smile, flashing her a set of wide bucked teeth that were identical to Scouts.

Tatu was an elder with coarse white hair and a full beard that hung down to the middle of his chest. It was braided into three knots and tied together with a small gold bead at the end. He was tiny, somehow even shorter than Scout, and he lacked muscles, frail from old age.

Tatu wore a tan smock with a tattered black apron wrapped around his waist. The apron was dusted orange from turmeric and covered with splashes of the brownish-red soup. He was clearly not a clean cook, but the soup smelled delicious, and the familiar smell of spices made her mouth water.

"What can I get ya, fellas? The usual?" Tatu turned to the man behind her, already grabbing drinking glasses from the bar.

"Ahh yeah, bring it around, Tatu. Fill another one up for the lady while you're at it." The man who sniffed her sat down on the stool beside her.

Tatu walked around the bar and placed the canteen on the table. There was familiarity between Tatu and the strangers, but she couldn't imagine they were his favorite patrons.

As he came back to fill up her half empty glass, a loud crash crackled from behind her.

One of the men sneered. "What is this? We didn't ask for the cheap stuff, old man. Is this how you treat us hyenas? Do we need to send word to the boss man that his little rats are being stingy?"

She turned around to see the canteen knocked over and the ale spilled all over the floor.

"So-sorry sir, let me fix it," Tatu stammered.

He sprang into action, grabbing an even bigger bottle that had been hidden below the counter. He filled their cups, then used his own apron to soak up the sticky mess.

"Much better, Tatu, much better," one of the strangers snickered, sickeningly amused by the old man scrambling about on the floor.

Katariya's body shook with anger at their cruel treatment. She was already on edge from her expected shifter abilities, and she could feel her temperature rising and her blood boiling. In all tribes, it was shameful to disrespect elders, but it was even more offensive that they acted so heinously during the most sacred time of the year.

She quickly rose from her seat. Reaching out a hand, Katariya helped the frail man up from the dirty hardwood floor. Tatu gave her a slight smile before scurrying behind the bar, distancing himself from the men.

Turning to go to her seat, she was stopped by a firm hand on her shoulder.

"Hey, where do you think you're going? Don't you want to sit with us? We'd be happy to keep you company."

Katariya tried to shrug off their hold but was whirled around to meet their gazes trailing up and down her body.

"No, thank you, I'm fine. I have food to eat, and I prefer to keep better company. Plus, I am waiting for my friend to come back; he went to grab something from the kitchen," she retorted, persistently tugging out of his grip.

His gaze drifted to the back. With an unsettling squeeze, he let Katariya go, and she let out a tremendous sigh of relief.

There was no commotion coming from the back room, and while she was thankful that she did not have to smell the two lovers, she was silently cursing Ram under her breath. Soon, they would find out that she was a liar. Their shifter noses would tell them that no one else was in the building, and once they realized she lied, they would go back to sizing her up as though she was their next meal.

They stared at her with hooded brown eyes so dark they appeared black. The surrounding skin around their eyes was darkened as though they hadn't had a good night's rest in weeks. She could feel their intentions as they looked her up and down, slowly licking their lips.

Every single one of them was filthy, gruff, and had menacing looks in their eyes, but none of them looked as bad as the man who sniffed her. His black attire was tattered, torn, and covered in dirt. Evidence of burn marks from smoking several illegal products was not only on his pants but also on different spots trailing up and down the skin of his scarred arm.

There was no way a man like him could ever live in the north, but he was exactly the type of man she imagined a scummy leader like Akuji would have working under him.

"I don't see your *friend*. Why don't I sit down and join you instead," he argued, taking the seat next to Katariya.

She sat down and tried her best to ignore him but was overwhelmed by the pungent scent he emitted. With all her might, she used her senses and searched through the grunge to smell the flavorful spices and the tenderness of the catfish in her stew.

At first, she stuck with small, ladylike bites, but they quickly turned wild and ravenous. The aroma alone had been enough to make her mouth water, and the taste of the fish stew had her involuntarily moaning around her spoon.

Every shred of the men's focus was on Katariya as soon as the moan slipped from her lips. From the corner of her eyes, she could see the sniffer casually sipping his drink with a smirk on his face. He looked over every inch of her form before he leaned in for a second time and tried to smell her once again.

Leaning backward, Katariya tried to put as much distance between them as she possibly could. When she leaned back, her balance was thrown off and her spoon flew out of her hand, clattering onto the sticky floor.

He took the startling moment to move even closer.

"You have no scent. You're shivering, shaking, and have a forehead damp with sweat. I'd say we got a new shifter on our hands here, boys. What do you guys say we throw her in the river and see what's hiding underneath?"

His friends' eyes widened as they nodded eagerly in agreement. His voice was gruff and raspy, but she had no problem hearing his words or understanding his intentions.

"I bet she's a wild little beast," another one of the men snickered. The twisted grin on his face gave away his sinister desires, sending a chill down her spine.

The anger, the nerves, and the weird vibrations in Katariya's body had her wishing she could throw herself in the river and transform into the bloodthirsty beast to kill the lot of them.

She looked at Tatu for support, but he kept his back to her and appeared to be wiping an invisible mess on the counter.

"Are you going to say something to them?" she barked, desperate for some back up.

Tatu ignored her and instead handed her a replacement spoon before walking off into the kitchen. Her heart stopped at the realization that he was leaving her there to fend for herself.

"Oh, she's gotta get a man to defend her. This will be an easy one, boys. She's so soft and pretty. I'd say we have a northern doll on our hands," the sniffer said, leaning closer.

Katariya could feel his hot, sour breath on her face, breathing over the top of her stew. She tried her best to keep her eyes straight and was startled when his hands grazed the side of her cheek.

"Hey, don't touch me!" she yelled, pushing his hands away.

She grabbed the knife around her belt and pointed it out in front of her, trying to use it to create distance between them.

"Oh, she has claws, fellas. You know my buddy Kubar here. He likes them when they're feisty," the sniffer snarled, completely unaffected by the weapon pointed in his face.

Instead, he reached to grab the knife, allowing his hand to tightly wrap around the sharp end. Forcefully, he pushed the weapon down, letting the blade bite into his skin. There was pressure as she resisted his hold and tiny drops of blood fell from his hand. Her eyes widened as the knife cut deeper and blood dripped down his arm.

His eyes remained unchanged. There was no fear or pain present. When Katariya finally removed her eyes from the blood-stained knife, she was swept with a dizzying quake that had the knife slipping from her grasp.

With a flick of a wrist, the sniffer snatched the knife away from her shaking hands. Slowly, he took the bloody end and wiped it along the length of his shirt.

"It's much better when they bleed, but I'll take the first cut for you." He lifted the knife to his face and used his long, dangling tongue to lick the weapon clean.

Her brain kicked into defensive mode, and she tried to take the knife back, but she wasn't quick enough.

Immediately, Katariya was pulled backward by two large hands wrapping themselves around her shoulders. Shaking her upper body, she thrashed back and forth, begging for release, but their nails extended into a tight grip around the tender flesh of her arms.

"Oh-Wee! Would you look at that?" The man who held her hollered, "She really is a beaut. Look at that gorgeous hair."

Somehow, when he grabbed her, the hood of her jacket had fallen, exposing her thick, braided hair.

"Get off of me! Help! Somebody help!"

Where was Ram? Wasn't he supposed to be protecting her? Her father entrusted the man with her life, and he was off somewhere else, receiving attention from some woman. Where was the friend they were supposed to be meeting? Clearly Tatu would not help her, but was no one else around to put an end to their wicked game?

"Oh, it'd be so easy just to cut it all off. Snip, snip, snip," the sniffer sneered.

He held the knife in one of his hands and grasped a handful of her hair in the other. She felt a slight tug and looked down to see one single braid sitting in her lap.

Her eyes puddled with tears. Hair, fur, and feathers were sacred. Each strand was a representation of her power and spirit. The single braid left her with a chilling realization; these men were just as evil as the savages in Sandstone.

"A little keepsake for after we are through with you." He took the chestnut-colored braid, gave it a long sniff, and dangled it in the air.

The third man, who was at least ten years younger than the other two, invited himself to join in on the attack. He came stalking toward her with the same predatory look in his eyes as his two friends.

"No, no, no, no, NO!" Katariya screamed as someone pulled her backward.

"Wait, wait a minute," the younger man called out.

The hands stopped being as aggressive, but she could still feel the tight grasp of someone clawing their fingers into her shoulders.

The younger man grabbed the braided strand of hair from his brooding friend. He rolled it around in his fingers for a few seconds before switching his threatening look to that of inquisition. His eyes darted over the features of her face and back to the strand of hair.

"Come on, Attor! Let's get her down to the water," the sniffer barked.

The younger man came down to look her straight in the eyes and frowned.

"You better quit touching her. Boss is gonna wanna know we've got the runaway princess on our hands."

"Princess? How can you tell?" The man holding her knife leaned closer to inspect Katariya's face.

"I remember her. She was at the palace a few nights ago. Not only do I remember her outburst, but I'd never forget a woman in a tight red dress." He licked his lips and winked at her.

Katariya steeled her face, her eyes stinging as she fought to keep her expression neutral. Even if her face didn't give away her identity, she was positive that hyenas were more than capable of hearing the thump in her heartbeat.

She didn't recognize him. The entire dinner she had been more focused on avoiding their gazes than meeting their eyes. Their leader's crude comments had been enough for Katariya to know she never wanted to be caught in the same room as a hyena, but fate had a funny way of playing sickening jokes. Now, the goddesses were working in overdrive doing everything they could to break her spirit.

"Ah man, Attor. Come on, just a little fun. The prince will never even know," the sniffer said as he took the tip of the knife and ran it down the length of her leg. He didn't so much as nick her, but nonetheless, Katariya held her breath.

"No. If Akuji doesn't smell her, mother will. She'll have your head because that's not just any girl, she's the princess. If we deliver her to mother unharmed, we might be sitting pretty for a little while," Attor argued.

"Ahh, pretty girl. Do you know how much fun we'd have had if we'd gotten to play?" Kubar whispered in her ear, his breath chilling her bones in the most unpleasant way.

Exhaling, she let go of the tension that had been building in her chest. Katariya was thankful that she would not be ravaged, but her relief only lasted a few seconds.

Fear stirred once again as Kubar said, "Don't relax too much. Our mother is the *mistress* of all wicked games."

His slimy tongue licked her cheek, and tears violently fell from her eyes. A hoarse, strained cry escaped her lips as a result of being ignored for so long. The hammering in her chest worsened as she came to the conclusion that no one, not even old Tatu, was coming to her rescue. If Katariya considered Akuji cruel, then she was frightened to think how much worse his wife could be.

Kubar and Attor grabbed her by the arms and pulled her across the bar, heading toward the exit. The sniffer grabbed their belongings and a canteen of ale before following.

Katariya thrashed and kicked the entire way, forcing all of her weight to the ground until she fell over. Her attempt to flee was futile as they used their superior strength to drag her across the rough wooden floor.

CHAPTER 21

THE MORE YOU LEARN ABOUT THE DIGNITY OF THE
GORILLA, THE MORE YOU WANT TO AVOID PEOPLE.
- DIAN FOSSEY, AMERICAN PRIMATOLOGIST AND
CONSERVATIONIST

The kidnappers didn't get very far. As soon as the men reached the door, Attor was knocked over, tumbling into Katariya. They crashed into a wobbly table, falling into the pile of wood and wreckage.

This was her chance to escape. A combination of adrenaline, fear, and instinct had her scrambling across the floor. Focused on gaining freedom, she failed to hear the threatening growl of an even bigger menace.

Standing in the doorway was an enormous gorilla. The shifter had thick black fur with a dust of silver on his back, and while his broad-chested build was animalistic, his eyes were human. Eyes that flashed with rage as he scanned the room, letting out a bellowing scream that echoed and rattled off the walls.

Tables shook as the gorilla beat his chest. With a thunderous grunt, the beast descended on Attor, brutally throwing the hyena's body against the wall. Falling victim to the gorilla's wrath, the shifter's body lay limp, passed out on the floor. One of the four threats was now eliminated.

While the gorilla was preoccupied with the hyenas, Katariya rushed to hide behind the bar. Peering around the side, she made note of their positions in the room. If she moved fast enough, she could run through the kitchen and out the back door.

The gorilla relentlessly pounded into one of the hyena's chests, his sharp teeth ripping at the man's arm. The sniffer stood in his hyena form: tan fur, dusted in soft black spots, with a hunched back and dark eyes.

Katariya retreated completely behind the bar and stared longingly at the exit. The sounds of snarls, rumblings, and roars reverberated against the tavern's walls as the two species attacked one another.

The cackle of a hyena quickly turned into chilling shrieks as the gorilla ripped off his victim's leg, tossing the limb over the top of the bar.

By the grace of the goddesses, Katariya's shifter abilities kicked in, pumping blood and adrenaline through her, forcing her up from the floor. Throwing the satchel over her shoulder, she clenched her bow and readied herself to make a dash across the room.

With a deep, ragged breath, she bolted and ran into the empty kitchen. The first door on the right was hanging wide open, but no one was inside. Rattling the knob to the second door, she silently screamed when she found that it was locked.

Suddenly, the sound of thrashing body parts clashed with the snarl of teeth and claws stopped. Instead, large footsteps barreled toward the kitchen.

Fear-stricken, she refused to face the brutal fists of her attacker. There were two options: she could either run like the antelope, or she could face her enemy head on like the ferocious lioness.

With poor judgment, Katariya spun around to face the raging gorilla, but was surprised to meet the sunken eyes of a brown bear with a jagged scar running down the length of his chest.

With no time to pull out her arrows, she sprung like an antelope and made a run for the exit. Her stomach churned as she realized how much worse her situation had become. Along with the gorilla, who could split his enemies in two, there was now a brown bear stalking toward her.

Katariya tried to barge through the back door, but found it was jammed from the other side. No matter how hard she pushed, the door would not budge.

The shadow of the bear loomed over her, making Katariya appear even smaller in the shadowed cast of his powerful frame. She closed her eyes and prayed for a quick and easy death. A slash through the heart. A bite in the neck. Quick and easy.

As she waited for his jaws to descend, she heard Ram's voice rumbling in place of the bear's huffing.

"Hey kid, hey kid. It's okay. It's me, Ramar."

Ever so slightly, Katariya opened her eyes. The tall shadow of the brown bear was no longer hovering over her. In its place was Uncle Ram, with a matching scar running down his chest.

In the panicked moment and the near kiss of death, she failed to recognize her uncle. A deep sigh turned into a manic laughter as the stress of the day came crashing down on her and all of her senses. She tried to clear her mind, but her vision grew fuzzy, and her head swirled with a pounding headache. The adrenaline slowly ebbed away, and the weight of the trauma settled in.

"Oh god, kid. I am so sorry." Ram reached around to grab the apron hanging on the wall, using it to cover the lower half of his body.

Reaching out to her, he pulled her into a hug that was so tight she felt like she couldn't breathe.

"Shh, shh. It's over now," he murmured into her hair. Wisps of her thick, chestnut-colored curls, which had once been braided, now hung in frayed, loose strands.

Katariya understood the attack was over, but the stress was pouring out of her with violent, panicked sobs. Her arms thrashed, trying to distance herself.

Her mind still viewed him as the enemy, but he held onto her tightly and stated, "That's okay, ya can hurt me. Lash out. Cry it out. Scream if ya need to. Whatever ya need to release the pain."

"Where were you?" she wailed a blood-curdling scream. Snot dripped violently down her nose, covering his bare chest.

"I—I'm sorry. I know I shouldn't have left. Scout lives down the road. I didn't think anythin' of it. We were only gone for twenty, maybe thirty minutes. Seriously, Katariya, I'm so sorry," he pleaded.

"I called out for you—and Tatu, he ran away. I was so scared. I thought they were going to—or worse, kill me."

Katariya shuddered, thinking about all the things they had done to her and all the things they could have done if the gorilla hadn't shown up.

"I know—I should have been listenin' or lent an extra ear. It had just been so long, I was caught up in the moment. I didn't know until Tatu came to get us."

"I can't—I can't Ram. They knew who I was, and even then, that wouldn't have stopped them," she wailed, her breath catching in her throat, turning her violent cries into pathetic hiccups.

"I know. This is all my fault, and your father is going to kill me. They didn't harm you, did they?" he asked, looking over every inch of her, searching for any cuts or scrapes.

Katariya shook her head, thankful to avoid any actual injury. However, it was the what ifs that threw her into a panic. The whole time, she wished she had her animal spirit to protect her. She was no match against her attackers. While she was more confident with her bow and arrow in her hands, when faced with real danger, Katariya couldn't bring herself to use the weapon.

If she didn't go through with the ceremony before the end of the week, she would be giving away her Animalia gift forever. She wouldn't have a fraction of the strength and skills that her attackers had, even if she got better at fighting with a sword or hand-to-hand combat. Without her Animalia spirit, Katariya could never truly defend herself in a fight against a shifter.

It felt like a lifetime before her heart slowed down and her breathing returned to normal. Ram picked her up with ease and used his shoulder to forcefully push the jammed door open. They walked around the building and headed to the front. Neither of them said anything as she silently wept.

As they rounded the corner, they were met by Scout, who came running at full speed with words of apology.

"I'm so, so sorry. I shouldn't have pulled him away. Please forgive me. Oh god, ya must have been so scared." Scout was crying almost as violently as Katariya had been just moments before.

Beside her was a small capybara. The large brown rodent stared up at them with wide eyes. It took her a second to recognize him through the beady eyes, but there was no doubt that the bucked-toothed Animalia was Tatu.

Capybaras were excellent swimmers but terrible fighters. At his age, he could have been pushed over too harshly and, unfortunately, would meet his maker. It only made sense that he ran for help instead of trying to defend her.

Katariya pulled away from Ram's arms. With a deep breath, she attempted to compose herself or what was left of her tattered state. Pushing her hair away from her eyes, she pressed her jumbled shirt down and straightened her shoulders. With her bow clenched in a tight fist, the weapon seemed to calm her spirit.

She closed her eyes and took in the smell of dewy grasses, the faint scent of a hibiscus flower, and the deep, musty aroma of rain and sludgy mud. It poured through her, washing away the scents of blood, sweat, and tears.

"Come on. I'm gonna need your help moving the bodies before ya leave," Scout said with a hint of apathy, grasping Ram's arm and guiding him forward.

He paused, measuring Katariya's reaction as he said, "You don't have to go in there. You can stay out here if you need to. I'm sure it's not a pretty sight."

Katariya aggressively shook her head at the idea. "No—no way. I don't want to be left alone."

"I know. I'm sorry. We are just gonna... clean up and then we can head out right away." Ram placed a hand on the small of her back as he ushered her inside the tavern.

The room was a wreck. The place was already thrown together by scraps of wood, but now every table had been turned around, flipped upside down, or knocked on its side. Chairs were scattered across every surface, with blood splattered on the walls.

Scout and Tatu moved quickly through the room, jumping straight into repairs, not even taking a second to access the damage.

The gorilla was nowhere in sight, but it was impossible to not notice the three dead bodies. Each of their deaths was more violent as the beast's rampage had progressed. Taking in the sight of her enemies, Katariya suddenly felt a surge of unexpected triumph. The hyenas would cackle at her misery no more.

CHAPTER 22

SOMETIMES, I AM THE BEAST IN THE
DARKNESS. SOMETIMES, I AM THE GHOST.
- HEATHER DURHAM, GOING FERAL: FIELD NOTES ON
WONDER AND WANDERLUST

Tatu's rodent form scurried to and from the kitchen much faster than his human body. Katariya, on the other hand, struggled to make her legs work. Her eyes locked into the pit of the hyena's dark soulless eyes. The threat of his words echoing like a knife piercing her eardrums.

In a chant, she repeated: *No longer a threat. No longer capable of harming me. Dead, no longer alive.*

Kicking his lifeless head to the side, she watched as it slowly rolled under the table, the face turned toward the wall. She was unaware that Scout and Ram were watching her, but when she met their gazes, their eyes weren't judgmental. Instead, they were brimmed with worry, hesitant that she would finally snap and start destroying the entire room in a fit of rage.

Katariya didn't throw any chairs or break any glass. There were no more tears left for her to cry either. Instead, she walked over the bar, grabbed one of the many bottles, and took one, two, three big gulps.

She didn't quiver as it burned down her throat. Her face didn't twitch like the last time she drank. Instead, it went down rather easily, feeling like a reboot to her broken down nervous system. Picking up one of the wobbly bar stools, she sat down and nursed the bottle.

Scout gave Ram a silent, pointed look before she ran off to the kitchen. There was a lingering moment that fluttered between Katariya and Ram as he thought about what to say.

Reaching around her, Ram pried the bottle from her clenching hands and took a big swig.

"Gotta be careful of this stuff. Strong enough to burn ya wounds, strong enough to burn a hole through your stomach," Ram grunted, pushing the bottle far enough away that she couldn't reach it.

"I know. I just—I don't want to feel anymore," she whined, putting her head in her hands.

The drinks were settling in. Her skin no longer crawled, and her fear slowly dissipated. She now understood why Zahir was inclined to overindulge in the burning brown liquid.

"I get that. I do, and I'm sorry. None of this should have ever happened, but I need ya to get it through your head that things might get worse," Ram stated, staring deep into her slightly glossy eyes.

"I don't know how anything could be as bad as this." She swung her arm around, gesturing to the wreckage. "If the gorilla hadn't been there—if you hadn't been there, who knows where I'd be and what would have happened?"

Katariya couldn't reach the amber bottle, so instead, she reached around the counter and grabbed the canteen that was still half full of pale ale. Her uncle didn't stop her from filling a glass but quietly observed her.

"I'm gonna be honest here, kid. I know the plan is to leave the city, hole up somewhere for a few days, and take ya back, but—" He hesitated. "I'm not sure it's goin' to work out that way."

"What do you mean?" Katariya asked.

"You're gonna be seen as a traitor to your kingdom. That's never been taken lightly and has always been a cause for exile. If ya don't go through with the shift, you'll be a human."

He took another sip of his drink and said plainly, "Without the gift, you'll be a poacher in their eyes. Even if ya somehow are accepted back into the antelope tribe, I've heard rumors that denying your gift can make a person real crazy. Depressed, crying, said to die of heartbreak. Then there's the crazy idea ya transform, ya turn into a lion, and lose your mind either way."

Even though Ram looked remorseful, he had not taken the liberty to cover any of the cold, hard truths. No one knew what her fate would be. She'd say that maybe a priest or priestess would have an idea, but even Priestess Osha couldn't predict her brother's spirit. Everything about this day, everything about her life, was a big mix-up, a mistake, and the farthest thing from greatness.

Katariya had dreams of being a fighter ever since she was a little girl, but when faced with real danger, she cowered in fear. Shivering like a leaf, frail, weak. The opposite of the lioness.

The bodies around the room were a reminder that she was not capable of the goddess-given greatness, and without her shifter gift, she could never defend herself from men with ill intentions.

"I'm sorry, kid, but I'm telling ya now. Ya need to toughen up. Blockade that heart, be alert, and trust no one. It's a gamble on how the next few weeks of your life are gonna go. Your Pa and I will fight for ya against the king, but if ya can't fight your mind, can't fight the needs of your soul. We might lose ya no matter how hard we try."

It seemed like a lose-lose situation. She'd either be longing for the beast or destroyed by the beast itself, but either way, the odds were not in her favor.

"Well, that was a lot of fun!" A booming voice exploded from around the corner.

Strolling out of the kitchen was a broad-shouldered man with veins bulging on thick biceps, calves, and thighs. He was about seven feet tall in his human form and incredibly stocky with dozens of scattered scars covering his dark skin. Cuts, scrapes, and burn marks. Reminders of mistakes, accidents, victories, and losses.

It became very obvious that the man strutting into the room was Malau. He grinned ear to ear despite the circumstances, and Katariya questioned the type of company she suddenly kept. The men who were leading her to safety were dangerous, and the likelihood that she was going to survive the journey was becoming worrisome.

Malau was covered in splattered blood that gruesomely decorated his entire body, including the edges of his lips. It was evidence of the terrifying jaws he used to snap the neck off of the hyena. He had a wide smile on his face that seemed to suggest that the violent deaths he committed did not faze him.

In fact, no one was fazed, acting as though today was just like any ordinary day, and that made Katariya wonder what truths she really knew about the kingdom.

"Malau. Hey man, I'm so sorry. Ya shouldn't have had to deal with this, especially not by yourself," Ram apologized.

Malau nodded his head in understanding as he walked to the bar, filling his drinking glass with wine from one of the canteens.

Katariya barely noticed Scout standing behind them, pushing a wheelbarrow for what Katariya could only assume was for bodies and the various body parts.

"No problem at all. It was good to let my beast rage for a minute. Those suckers have been causin' problems throughout the marsh for months now. Lost a full case of rubies from an ambush just last week."

Malau slurped down his drink like it was water instead of wine. Slamming his glass on the counter, he said, "Not sure if they were the same fellas, but their leaders are fearless. Feels good to help dwindle down that threat."

Ram's eyebrows raised as he let out a large huff. "I didn't realize how bad it was getting. I mean, I've only been gone a few months."

"Life changes quickly in the jungle. Including me. I mean me, of all shifters, has to smuggle *the princess* out of the city? I can't believe you'd get me involved in—" Malau scoffed, his arms flailing in disbelief.

Scout's wails interrupted the gorilla, tears streaming down her face.

"Oh, my gosh. Ya mean to tell me that I endangered the princess's life? Oh, my goddess. I'm so sorry, princess. I don't know how I could ever make this right."

Katariya rose from her seat despite dealing with a pair of wobbly legs. Moving to the other side of the counter, she pulled Scout into a comforting hug.

"You must have been so scared," Scout pulled her tighter.

"I'm surprisingly okay. It might be the ale, but I promise you Scout, I'm alright. I know you don't know what's going on, but this barely compares to what I'm dealing with right now."

The small woman's sparkling bright green eyes were now red and watery. A harsh contrast from the rough and tough woman that kept a wheelbarrow around to pick up bodies.

Her voice did not falter as Scout replied, "I don't know what you're going through, but my Pa always told me that life happens the way it's supposed to. Whatever it is, it will work itself out."

Katariya desperately wanted to believe that. It was just that the words of a prophecy, words that came from the goddess of life herself, had deemed Katariya as great, yet the hardships of today proved otherwise.

"So, no one is going to tell me what the hell we are doing smuggling the princess out of the city?" Malau scowled, impatiently waiting for an answer.

"It's a long story but trust me. It's for her own good. Her life is in danger," Ram replied with a shrug.

A short, sweet answer, one that would not satisfy a curious soul, but his dismissive tone was threatening enough that most shifters would not ask any further questions.

"I know that. I just saved her life moments ago," Malau said with a smug look in his eyes as he appreciated his handy work. With one large gulp, he drank the rest of his wine and quickly got to work.

Picking up two bodies thrown over each arm, Katariya watched as a trail of fresh blood poured down the leg of the dismembered hyena.

"No, there are bigger, more complicated threats at stake. We can't say, but just know if we can safely get her out of the city, the antelope tribe will be in your debt forever," Ram pleaded.

"This isn't just gems, drugs, and dumping dead bodies. This is smuggling the princess, and if I get caught, I'm at risk of exile—at risk of death!" Malau argued.

Katariya strutted across the room to stand in front of Malau. He had all three bodies stacked on top of one another, but he paused to listen to what she had to say.

Malau was so tall that she had to look straight up in order to look at his face, and Katariya found it was hard to maintain eye contact when he had so much blood on his lips.

Boldly, she said, "I can't say why I need to flee. It's safer if no one knows the truth, but I promise you, if we don't get out of the marsh by the time the ceremony starts, my life will be in danger." Her eyes softened. "I don't want you putting your own life at risk, so if we need to, we will take the boat ourselves. You can add stealing to the many crimes they are going to accuse me of."

Scanning her face, Malau searched for the truth in her eyes and in her words. It only took a few moments before his shoulders slumped, and his reservations dissipated.

"Alright, princess, I believe ya, but once ya are back in the city, ya gotta send down some tea. I've only been lucky enough to try the orange cinnamon, but I swear to the heavens, it was the best thing I've ever tasted."

Katariya forced a smile and nodded back.

"Of course, for saving my life, you can have all the teas and spices your heart desires."

There was a strong possibility that her promise was a lie. If Katariya was able to return home, she wasn't completely sure that her family would have the same wealth and status as before. Even if she didn't have the means to send him a crate full of tea and spices, she was determined to deliver any gifts she could.

Not only did Malau save her from the hyenas, but if he got them out of the city, he would help her escape the wrath of the jaguar king.

CHAPTER 23

EVERY CREATURE WAS DESIGNED TO SERVE A
PURPOSE. LEARN FROM ANIMALS FOR THEY ARE
THERE TO TEACH YOU THE WAY OF LIFE.
- SUZY KASSEM, RISE UP AND SALUTE THE SUN

C rowded onto the large fishing boat, Ram and Malau
took turns rowing from the jungles of Tolego into the
Outlands. The trio traveled through the dense swamp, into
the thick brush and parting deltas, until they found a spot to
dump the bodies. Ram tied heavy rocks to the scattered limbs,
and they sat in silence as the corpses slowly sank and bubbles
rose to the surface.

The silence lingered for a while until Malau couldn't control himself. Like a waterfall, questions poured out of him,
rushing out in a stream.

"So, how long do you have to dry the herbs?"

"How does your Ma make the orange flavors pop?"

"Is it true ya gotta banana-flavored tea?"

Katariya answered all of his questions —

"Five to seven days."

"Orange zest soaked in orange juice."

"No, but I'll be sure to tell my Ma about the request."

After a few hours of rowing through the tangled streams, Katariya lost all sense of direction. They didn't see any other boats, but at one point they passed a small cluster of crocodiles floating on the water's surface. Their scaled bodies slithered through the tall grasses, and their beady eyes gleamed with curiosity.

Malau waved at the crocodiles, and they acknowledged his presence with a slight swish of their tails. The group went back to swimming, and in moments, they disappeared into the never-ending web of streams.

Katariya suspected that most of the kingdom was on patrol, searching for their lost princess. She was their future, the first prophecy in years to call out a child by name and a call for the kingdom's protection.

What would happen if they failed to protect her? What wrath would the goddess bestow upon those who failed their one request?

Running away was Katariya's only option. Revealing her lioness's identity would be cause for immediate execution. Her father would be seen as a traitor, the priestess' lies would unfold, and the antelope tribe would face consequences for their role in her father's deceit.

Would they send them to Sandstone? No, they couldn't send an entire tribe, but her father, her mother, Sade...

It was better if they didn't know what beast lay beneath Katariya's skin. There was madness at each end of the stick, but only one resulted in her family getting hurt.

Inside, the beast was buzzing, agitated for release, susceptible to the lulls in the rain as the ceremonial storms began to drift away. There was also lingering fear. Her mind was haunted by dreadful thoughts of the tavern and the hyenas, the what ifs of their horrid plans.

Amos raised Katariya to be fearless despite the unknown threats of the prophecy, and she took the necessary risks to fulfill her promise. She kept up with her training, but that wasn't the only promise she made. She just wasn't sure which way her heart was leaning.

Along with her troubled thoughts, Katariya was sweaty, nauseous, and lightheaded. A combination of a lack of food and the mixture of wine and ale had her slurring, "Uncle Ram, do you think we'll see my brother? Maybe he *is* alive. Maybe he can save me from the lion spirit. Maybe we can—"

"Okay kid, that's enough," Ram interrupted, slapping a hand over Katariya's mouth.

For such an enormous man, Malau let out a surprisingly high-pitched squeal.

"Wait, did she say *lion* spirit?"

"Yeah, well, apparently I do not have antelope ancestry—" Katariya began the tale with so much enthusiasm, one would think it was an epic and grand story rather than a tragedy.

"Alright. No more. We gotta get ya sobered up."

Ram jumped up from his seat, grabbed a side of the boat, and rocked it from side to side. The smallest little wave had the wine and stew coming up, spewing out along with her pain and fear.

"What, what are you doing, are you crazy? What if I fell in? What if I shifted and killed you!" Katariya yelled.

"You're fine. I wouldn't let ya fall in, and even if ya did, we'd deal with it."

"What do you mean 'deal with it'? Would you kill me? Send me to Sandstone? Tie rocks to my limbs and throw me in the river?"

As tears threatened to spill from her eyes, Ram firmly clasped her chin, demanding Katariya's attention.

"I won't let anything bad happen to ya. Whatever choice ya make, just know me and your Pa will fight for ya, and I got enough friends across the water to make the king think twice about wagin' a war. You'll be okay, kid, and I'm sure your brother's okay too."

Katariya nodded but wasn't sure she really believed it. The herbivores couldn't stand a chance against the carnivores, and when it came down to it, was her life really worth starting a war?

Malau loudly clasped his hands together, drawing their attention to his wide-eyed gaze.

He pleaded, "No way, ya can't just leave me hangin' man. Please, can ya finish? The princess started off with, *I do not have antelope ancestry.* That sounds like the start of a great story. I mean come on, don't ya trust me, Ram?"

"No, I trust ya. I really do, but the less ya know, the better. Ya just gotta trust that what we are doin' is the best thing for the princess."

Malau's eyes shuffled between the two of them. Ram had a stern look, indicating he would not budge. Katariya was sick to her stomach, no longer paying attention to the conversation. Her story long forgotten.

"Fine, I do. I trust ya with my life, Ram, but I'm telling ya, y'all are gonna get me some of that banana tea." Malau shook a wagging finger between the two of them.

Ram gave him a smirk and agreed, while Katariya could only muster a soft groan.

They traveled the rest of the day with very little conversation. Katariya was saved from Malau's endless questions, but only because every time she tried to speak, she found herself leaning back over the side of the boat. After two or three questions, accompanied by her sickness, Malau took it upon himself to be quiet.

She slept most of the day and into the evening. The night croaks of the marsh were similar to the caws of the jungle.

It was a full night of sweats and groans until she woke up at dawn to find they were near the shore.

Snapping his finger, Ram attempted to pull her out of her dazed slumber. His eyes were intense as they scanned the shoreline for any immediate threats.

"Hey kid, when we dock, I'm gonna need to shift. Ya gotta be cautious, far more than ya would behind the wall. It's different out here. Stay alert, move quickly, and follow my lead." He roughed her hair and strapped her bow to her shoulder. "Keep an arrow in your hand. Walk into this like we are expectin' trouble, and I promise ya, if you're prepared, we'll be alright."

His grumbling voice came out as a clear command. Snapped upright, clinging to every word, Katariya nodded as his power rumbled through her. He wasn't the king, nor did he have the controlling spirit of the lion, but Ram was once a captain, and his spirit oozed with the strength of a bear.

As soon as they reached the shoreline, Ram immediately transformed into the large brown ball of fur. He gave a slight nod with his snout in Malau's direction before he trotted away.

Turning toward the gorilla, Katariya gave a soft smile and said, "I promise, as soon as I can, I will get you that banana tea. I'll make it myself if I have to, but seriously, thank you for saving my life. I don't think that tea is enough to repay you."

His cheeks glowed, and she giggled at the sight of the bashful beast.

"Awe no, don't laugh. It's an honor, but there's no need to thank me. It was my pleasure."

Once Katariya was on dry land, she said a silent prayer before gathering her weapons. She then took the time to ready a feather tipped arrow. It took a few minutes before her uncle came trotting back, and with a final wave, Malau pushed the boat away from the shore and began his journey back to Tolego.

Using his snout, the bear nudged her forward, and Katariya took it as a sign to pick up the pace. Remaining vigilant, she kept a low stance on the ground and disappeared into the fog and the tall grasses.

Ram thankfully kept a human pace to his trot. With his nose moving high and low, he and Katariya were on alert, scanning the plains for potential threats. Tapping into her animal senses was much easier in the Outlands. For miles on end, she could detect the crisp clean air, lush grass, and the dew of the misty fog.

In the distance, the mountain's jagged slopes were covered in dense, lush trees, paired with beautiful purple and yellow flowers, but ahead was nothing but rolling plains as far as the eye could see.

It had been four days since the ceremony, and her skin felt as though the beast was clawing from within. Yesterday, it rained off and on for a few hours, but Katariya knew she was running out of time. Not only did she only have days, or even hours, before her gift would be lost forever, but how long would it take for the prince to find her?

It wouldn't take long for them to track her scent. She was sure her father had a plan to throw them off, but no one truly ever went missing in Tulamund.

Katariya could keep running, but without the gift, how soon would the four-legged beast catch up to her? Another day or so at best. They were foolish to think that they could escape the king and his army, but still she pushed forward, thinking of her family's safety.

After a while, Ram slowed down and transformed back into his human form. Katariya dropped the bag and turned around to give him privacy as he rummaged for his trousers. Once he was dressed, he grabbed the canteen and took a sip before passing it back for Katariya to have her fill.

Thirstier than expected, she found herself drinking down the bottle in three large gulps.

Patting the bottom to get a few more drops, she asked, "How long until we reach the main river?"

"Takes a little while. Half a day or so. Maybe more." He rummaged through her satchel. "Ya know, it would be a lot easier if ya could run with me. With a shifter gift, we'd be there in no time."

He said it as though that was a plausible and safe option. Nonchalantly, as if she wouldn't turn into a bloodthirsty savage the moment she fully submerged herself in the sacred river.

Glaring at him, Katariya snapped, "It's not like I have a choice in the matter."

Ram gave her a casual shrug. "Ya have a choice, but choosin' the right answer isn't up to me."

Everything he said sounded like a trick. The impossible choice, a decision that would change her life forever.

Not thrilled with either option, she shook her head and whispered, "*A choice.*"

Katariya didn't really believe that, and the exhaustion was finally creeping up on her. There was a strong desire to throw it all away. Give up her swordplay and archery and her Animalia gift to live a quiet and shut-in life on her family farm.

It was the safe option, but there was an itch that she would never be able to scratch away, and that was a longing to be reunited with her brother. To break the promise would be one thing, but to give up her search for Amos wasn't something Katariya was sure she could live with.

Ram nodded and pulled the honey jar from the satchel. "Yeah kid, it's your choice. The way I see it, ya gotta pick which consequences you're willing to deal with."

With his dainty spoon, the giant bear shoveled spoonful after spoonful of the sticky substance into his mouth before he reached inside her bag to hand her a small piece of bread.

"Eat it. Ya gotta try to get some of your energy back."

Katariya did not hesitate to take the hardened bread from his hands, but she stared skeptically at her bag, knowing there was little room for her arrows, her clothes, the canteen, and their supply of food. When did he put them in there and how did she not notice?

"Give me that."

She snatched her satchel and rummaged through its contents.

All of her clothes were missing. The arrows were still there, but the only garment was the dress her mother had sewn for the ceremony. It was the least functional piece of clothing, but as she stared at its detailed pattern, decorated with hand-sewn leaping antelopes, she was thankful that her uncle hadn't tossed it out.

Her mother had known she was not a true antelope, but she still spent hours crafting the unique indigo dress. The sentiment tugged at an ache in her tender heart.

"Seriously, all my stuff is gone," Katariya groaned.

Ram made room for important things to help them along their journey, but seriously, did he have to throw out all of her clothes?

He shrugged his shoulders, and with a mouthful of honey, he mumbled, "What? I kept the pretty little dress. It's a waste of space, but it's still your ceremony gift."

His doe-eyes glazed with the reminder of a bittersweet memory. "I remember when my Mama made me a robe. Wasn't nearly as fancy as yours, but it was made from fine leather and had a tiny bear stitched into the right pocket." He pointed to his chest. "Even in the dead of summer, I wore that damn thing almost every day. I loved it. I really did."

"What happened to it?" she questioned.

"Lots of years of travelin' and lots of movin' around. I don't know for sure. It's hard to keep track of your stuff when you're in my line of work. Today and tomorrow, I'm here with ya. Next month, I'll move onto the next job," he stated, tightening the lid to the honey jar, packing it up for the next part of their journey.

"Is it lonely not having a tribe to call your own?" she asked, questioning her future.

In both scenarios, she would either be a lonely human or a forsaken lioness. Belonging to a tribe was something she would never experience again, not really. Without a shifter spirit, she would be an outcast, seen as nothing better than a giftless and wretched poacher.

Katariya always felt like she didn't belong, but could she handle being an outsider in a world where she already felt so disconnected?

"I wouldn't say I'm lonely. Shifters come and go from your life all the time. In and out of your circle, they pop by for a few to say hi. They make ya smile, make ya laugh, angry, sad, all of it. Ya just gotta learn to appreciate the moments ya have with 'em and know that the time they were there served you well," he answered earnestly.

From looking at him, Katariya would have never guessed that her uncle was so wise, but his words resonated deep within her spirit.

The family that loved her and raised her had served her well. They taught her kindness and raised her in a home with unconditional love. She cherished the relationship she had with her brother and, although she and Sade could never meet eye to eye, Katariya would have gotten into a lot of trouble if her sister hadn't kept her in line.

She hated to think that her brother had already served his purpose. How could a bond that close be gone forever? Even after all these years, none of it seemed real.

Her own parents risked their lives and their tribe's future to harbor two children born from the Outlands. They spent their entire lives loving these children as their own, just to be torn apart from one another.

Then there were her birth parents, who were unknown, but they too had served their purpose. Her time in their care had been fleeting, and perhaps her brother shared some distant memory of their life from before, but they had given them life, connecting their spirits in a blood-bond that would tie them together forever.

Her life was filled with a sea of sadness, regret, and despair, but she couldn't deny that the moments of joy, laughter, and love were worth the crash of a few waves.

CHAPTER 24

WATER WAS HOW THE DESERT WOULD BRING
EVERYONE TOGETHER. THE ANTELOPE'S DAILY
PRAYER, WEIGHING THE MORTAL NEED OF WATER
WITH THE MORTAL DANGER OF OBTAINING IT.
- MIKE BOND, THE LAST SAVANNA

Katariya could no longer feel her feet. It was no longer raining, but the clouds remained, hovering above them, sending her signs of an impending doom. Ram didn't seem tired at all as he casually walked on all fours beside her.

Without the mountains to shield her, the wind roared and pelted against them. While she had previously thought they would head straight into the vast grassland, there were miles of thick, sludgy marshes trailing into the plains.

As her shoes grew soppy, her motivation dwindled, and the burning desire to accept her Animalia spirit crept in. Even the surrounding air seemed to be laced with the essence of the spirit, calling to her in ways that she never thought possible. It was a cold rush and a searing burn all at the same time.

When they reached the end of the marshy beaches, Ram's bear walked straight into the thick, sludgy water. Taking a moment to herself, Katariya threw her satchel on the ground and took a seat, leaning her back against a smooth rock.

The bear swam while Katariya watched from the shore. Sweeping his slashing paws through the murky water, Ram pulled out a gasping fish. She drooled at the sight of their next meal.

Reaching his snout into her satchel, Ram grabbed his trousers, quickly shifted, and then got dressed. He drove his knife into the fish before it had floundered into a suffocating death, and with precision, he removed the outer scales, leaving behind its tender flesh.

"What can I do to help?" Katariya asked, licking her lips.

She was eager to get the process started. There was a ravenous hunger taking root deep within the pit of her stomach. Seeing the raw flesh wouldn't normally ignite such an insatiable appetite, but her Animalia was in overdrive, vibrating her spirit with a gluttonous need.

Ram dug a shallow pit to start a fire, and without looking up, he replied, "Can you try to find some twigs or grasses? The dryer the better."

Nodding, Katariya rose and began to walk along the marshy coast. It didn't take her long to find enough sticks and brush to make the fire, but the sight of plump blueberries distracted her from the main task.

Creating a pocket in the front of her shirt, she used the pouch to carry the berries, and for a few seconds, she was transported back to the farm amid a busy harvest day. With a basket filled to the brim and sticky red fingers from mushy raspberries. In between stains of red were deep blues from blueberries melted together to create shades of purple from the two fruit juices. It was easy to pretend that she wasn't really here when she was doing mindless work.

Her father had been quite adamant that if she gave up her gift, she could return home. He was confident that the antelope tribe would be secure as long as he was leading, but if Sade married the elephant shifter, wouldn't that power eventually go to him?

"Hey, that's far enough!" Ram called out, shaking her from her thoughts.

He was still in her line of sight, but her feet had carried her farther than she had intended. With her shirt overflowing with berries, she carefully walked back to the spot, juggling the pouch and an arm full of sticks.

"Hey, it's fine as long as ya stay along the coast. It's safe here." He grabbed a handful of berries from her shirt and tossed them into his mouth with a loud, squishy bite.

"Why is that? Where are all the shifters, anyway?" Katariya passed him the wood so he could start the fire.

Taking a small rock, he used the flint to create a spark. In moments, little embers steadily grew into a roaring fire, cooking their fish and wafting the air with its delicious aroma.

"Rivers and lakes are sacred. It remains a safe space for all tribes and clans. No fighting is allowed here. No crime and no death." Ram's eyes focused on the fish, carefully rotating it over the flames to avoid charring it. Their stomachs growled simultaneously.

"The tavern was right next to the marsh, and the hyenas still attacked. And what about Malau? He killed them."

His explanation of a safe space meant nothing to her when she had almost been kidnapped. As thankful as she was that Malau had saved her, he still killed three shifters along the river during the most sacred time of the year. Was the gorilla worried about his soul, or was he a nonbeliever like her uncle?

"Yes, but that was in the city. We're in the Outlands now, and as savage and cutthroat as the clans are here, there's one thing that they respect, and that is the sanctity of this river. Malau, goddess bless his soul, did what anyone would have done. Those hyenas shouldn't have been on our turf, and when he realized who ya were, there was no stopping him," Ram said.

Pulling the fish out of the open flame, he set it on the log beside them to allow it to cool. They were too hungry to worry about a burnt mouth and barely waited a full minute before they were digging in. As they took a bite, the sound of their moans could be heard through the howling wind.

"And you trust me to believe that?" Katariya asked.

It was hard to believe that if the shifters of Tulamund couldn't stick to the rules, the shifters in the Outlands could resist creating mayhem up and down the river's length.

"You've only seen a small portion of this land. They don't have homes sittin' on the river like we do. They travel daily, sometimes hundreds of miles, to drink and bathe. It means so much more to them than it does to us. Especially this week."

"So, if it's so important, why is nobody here?" To the west, she could make out the silhouette of the mountains, and in every other direction, there was nothing and no one as far as the eye could see.

"Well, we're barely out of Tulamund's land. They don't usually travel this close to the border. Another half a day's walk, and you'll reach the split between the mountains. That's where they're all gonna be." Ram pointed to the northeast.

Looking at the ominous, darkening clouds, he said, "Rain's gonna start comin' down. I say we camp here for a few hours, stay the night if we have to." He wiped his hands clean of the fish flakes. "In the mornin', I'll take a quick dip, fill up on water, and go. We're gonna wanna leave before the buffalo herd gets here. Trust me, ya do not want to bathe after a thousand buffalo have been swimmin' through it."

Here, right now, Katariya was the closest she would ever get to Sandstone. There had never been a clearer path to her brother's destination.

If she could safely get to the next river, the sacred body of water would keep her safe. Tulamund's river funneled from the mountains and into the Outlands, stretching far and wide until it reached the outskirts of the desert. In a few days, Katariya could be in Sandstone—she could be with her brother.

It was possible. Risky, yes. Probably foolish, but perhaps a path that led her straight to her brother was her true destiny. She wasn't entirely sure she could make the journey as a human, but it had her thinking—if Amos was alive, then perhaps he had overcome the maddening bloodthirst of his beast.

The lion was the only spirit with enough total control and dominance to keep the Sandstone shifters from killing one another. If he could create and lead an army, then he had to be sound of mind, right? And if Amos had mastered his beast, then perhaps he could keep her from losing her mind too.

There was a small voice inside her head that was egging her on. It was the natural instinct to become one with the animal spirit and transform into an Animalia. Katariya tried to shut down the idea, but it was so tempting. The power of the beast was coursing through her veins, and the water was just a few feet away. With a spirit as strong as a lioness, no one could stop her. No one could stop her from being reunited with Amos.

The memories of her brother had never dimmed or faded. Shifters in Tulamund tried to erase him from their tribe's history, but Katariya could never forget the softness of his soul. She could picture it clearly: a crinkle in the corner of his eyes as he flashed her a wide, toothy grin.

Sometimes, when she closed her eyes, she would see the lion staring back at her. A shaggy golden mane that matched his bright, glistening eyes. If she put aside the bloodlust, she could see how confident and brave her brother could be with such a powerful gift.

Breaking her from her wandering mind, Ram hopped out of the water and in a flash was in his human form. With the waterline covering his lower body, he shook his hair out as though he were shaking out his thick brown fur.

"I'm gonna do a quick scout before we set up camp for the night. There's a tarp folded up real tight in the front pocket of your bag. It won't cover much, but it should help with the rain a little."

The second half of their trip was lucky. They hadn't received more than a sprinkle for the past few hours, but looking up, she could see that the lingering cloud was transitioning into a threatening storm.

"Go ahead and put out the fire, kid. It's not likely we'll receive any visitors, but just to be safe, it'll keep our visibility low."

In a flash, he was back into his shifter form, climbing out of the water and disappearing into the tall grasses. Besides the doom of the darkening clouds, the sky itself was turning into a hazy gray as the sun waned on the horizon.

After the fire was out, Katariya found a dry patch of grass near the river. Unbraiding her hair, she let the stress of the day unfold as her curls bounced around her shoulders. The soft moonlight against the water was the only light she needed. Her night vision was slightly increased from her shifter gift but nothing compared to the glow of the moon. Knowing that a lion's night vision was four times stronger than her own made her curious about the different night dwellers lurking in the distance.

The brash mix of ocean and river water created a film over the surface. It was impossible to see the bottom, but Katariya could still see her reflection in the murky haze. There was a slight difference in her appearance. Her cheeks were thinner, with eyes that told a story. Her face lacked color, and her jaw was tight.

The magic called to her, willing her to connect the human body with that of an animal's power and spirit. Conflicted, she couldn't think of anything else to do but to pray to the goddesses for mercy. Staring at the dazzling night sky, she thought if she looked hard enough, she could see a glimpse of the heavens.

Within the stars, she could see none of the world's truths. It was a gut feeling, one that she would have to trust. Maybe, just maybe, the prophecy was right all along. That somehow, by a miracle from their gracious goddesses, Katariya would transform into a jaguar. The perilous journey would have been for nothing, and the rest of her life would remain unchanged. She would run back to the palace in her newly accepted form and be met with the welcoming arms of her family and Prince Zahir.

Without spending another second thinking about the consequences, Katariya walked into the cloudy water with her eyes focused on the heavens. Her body moved involuntarily, guiding her through the swirls of algae and sludge. A sprinkle from the heavens fluttered on her cheek bones, and with a smile, Katariya began her prayers.

"Atlaua. Mother creator. I give myself to you."

Closing her eyes, she walked until she was waist deep into the water. She took a deep breath, and, on its release, Katariya let go crashing into the sacred river.

PART IIII | CHAPTER 25

OH YES, THE PAST CAN HURT. BUT FROM THE WAY I SEE IT, YOU CAN EITHER RUN FROM IT, OR LEARN FROM IT.
- RAFIKI, DISNEY'S THE LION KING

No lesson, prayers, or words from the wise could have prepared Katariya for the rush that flowed through her. Every fiber of her being burned underneath her skin as though she had been set aflame. She floundered under the cold water, but her blood boiled.

Unable to keep herself afloat, she sank to the bottom. The haze of the water grew to a darkness where her mind slipped in and out of consciousness. A darkness that grew still until, suddenly, a bright light blinded her vision.

When she had blinked away the flashes, the white spots focused into a vast field of wide-open grasses. Katariya felt weightless, as though she were floating, free from her flesh and bones.

Blinking rapidly, she was torn between multiple versions of the here and now. Memories, lifetimes, fragments of the universe.

Blinking again, Katariya was instantly transported from the open plains into a dense tropical jungle. Everything that surrounded her was untouched, alive, and overgrown. Monkeys howled in the distance, and the echoed caws of a toucan shattered with the sound of a roar.

Upon the third blink, her vision shifted to sandy beaches, where a pack of wolves ran along the water's edge. The whirlwind shift in reality made her dizzy, causing Katariya to blink over and over again into new locations. Here, the sun, the moon, the stars, and the clouds all existed as one entity.

In a dizzy spell, she tumbled backward, crashing through the heavens and into an open field.

This time, she was not alone. Animals swarmed her, trotting through the grass, jumping over rocky boulders and swimming along the river's edge.

As far as the eye could see, there were herds of antelope: bongos, gemsbok, eland, and sables galloping as a giant herd. They walked forward, their beady eyes watching her with apprehension, as though she weren't supposed to be there.

Katariya slowly crept through the grasses to avoid spooking the beasts. When she reached out to touch a gazelle, hoping to connect with the spirit, it dissipated, like pollen in the wind, barely visible to the eye. On the second attempt, she reached for an impala with coarse, dark fur, and the creature dissolved, evaporating into thin air.

What if she didn't have to choose the lioness? What if she could connect with another spirit? The impalas did not accept her, but perhaps the jaguar would.

She blinked again, transported to the desert, where camels sauntered through the sand dunes. She didn't linger long. Over and over again, she traveled through the light of the heavens until she was back in the jungle.

Through the trees and dense fog, she could see a jaguar. Its tawny-colored fur with black rosettes decorated the beast from head to toe. From the tree branch, the creature stared curiously, swishing its tail back and forth.

Muscle memory had Katariya ducking under branches, even though they disappeared with the smallest touch. She crept closer, stomping through a layer of mud that did not stick to her shoes.

Unmoving and unblinking, the jaguar kept its gaze fixed on Katariya as she scaled the tree. Every move she made was stalked by the deadly predator. The wild cat licked its lips and let out a low, growling rumble.

This was Katariya's one shot.

Straddling the trunk of the tree, she shuffled closer. In its eyes, Katariya could see her own reflection. Moving to touch the beast's head, just like the antelopes, the animal spirit disappeared.

A harsh wind knocked her down as though the goddesses were upset with her antics. Tumbling backward, she fell from the tree and spiraled through the air.

A booming feminine voice rattled through each flicker in time.

"Stop running, child. You cannot run from destiny."

Transported back into the plains, Katariya was surrounded by herds of antelope, zebras, rhinos, buffalo, giraffes, and more. Her body ached as it slipped between two realities, but she pushed forward, running into the thunderous herd. Frantically, Katariya grabbed onto any animal spirits she could reach. She grew desperate for the beasts to connect with her soul, but the more animals she touched, the faster they disappeared.

After swiping her hands through a dozen spirits, the remaining beasts took off in a full sprint before disappearing into the bright light of the horizon. The herd of antelope was gone. There was no wildebeest, no zebras braying, or even a long neck of a giraffe in sight.

The only creature who remained was a lioness with deep golden eyes staring back at her.

Katariya firmly planted her feet in the loose soil and prepared for the worst. The lioness studied her, slowly flicking her tufted tail as she made her observations.

Katariya trembled in fear, suddenly coming to the realization that the only way she could exit the heavens was if she connected with the spirit of the lioness.

The golden-brown beast gracefully descended from the boulder, her fur glowing in the sun's rays. A trail of dust and glittering magic trailed behind the lioness as the animal walked toward her.

With wobbly legs, Katariya took slow, apprehensive strides to meet the beast in the middle. For a few moments, they were locked in a mutual gaze, fear reflected in their eyes. Without showing her sharp claws or teeth, the lioness almost appeared to be a peaceful cat, patiently waiting for Katariya to make a decision.

With a shaky hand, she reached out to graze the side of the lioness's snout, much like she had done when Amos's lion had reached for her many moons ago. This time, the beast felt solid as she placed her hand in the center of its head.

Grasping her fingers around the thick golden fur, Katariya felt her spirit melting and mixing with the lioness. Tiny bits and fragments of the universe absorbed into her body, and the bright light enveloped her.

As the two beasts connected as one, every tendon, joint, and bone cracked and stretched. She struggled to take on an entirely new shape and size.

No sound escaped her lips as she let out a painful cry.

With a jolt, the bright light vanished, and she found herself standing in the middle of the tall grass. There was a second heartbeat combined with her own. It was larger and louder but created a harmonic melody.

Her movements felt the same as she stretched her neck from side to side and slowly rose from her crouched position. The grasses that were once up to her knees, now clouded her line of vision.

Sweeping her tongue against the roof of her mouth, she could feel ferociously large, pointed teeth. There was a slight scratch of fur against her lips as she licked what would normally be her bottom lip. In its place was a snout, covered in thick, shaggy fur and filled with a set of dangerously sharp canines.

With unfamiliar legs, she wobbled to the river. In place of her curly chestnut hair and freckled, spotted golden skin was a magnificent lioness staring back at her with curious golden eyes.

Thick golden-brown fur covered her, with a dark brown tuft hung on the end of a long, swishing tail. The beast in front of her was so familiar. To Katariya, the unity between the two species made her feel as though lioness had been watching over her from the moment she was birthed into existence. The spirit was a warm sensation that wrapped around her heart, merging the two as one.

The lioness had enormous paws, each one twice the size of Katariya's hands. Two circular ears sat on the top of her head, much different from the human ears that cupped the sides of her face. The whirling of the wind sounded stronger, and the vibrations carried differently from their new placement.

Katariya and her beast were in sync, the energy that connected them electric and alive. There was no fear, no confusion, and no intense bloodlust. There was a lonely lioness and a lost girl, but together, their heart beat with a renewed purpose.

The stress and trauma of the day and the fear of what was yet to come was behind her. In front of her was a magnificent lioness who longed to run through the plains, bask in the sun's warmth, and together, they would accomplish greatness.

Katariya walked forward, stumbling with every other step as she attempted to gain speed. With no end to the horizon, they ran together across the plains, feeling the wind in their fur and the sun on their faces. A sense of peace and gratitude.

The moment of freedom couldn't last forever. As Katariya ran faster, the world around her began to crumble. Her vision dimmed, and the white clouds slipped into a hazy gray.

Reality crashed down, and the lioness pulled her from the heavens. *Pain.* The dreadful pain of the shift caused Katariya to roll and tumble into darkness.

CHAPTER 26

THE WILD HEART CAN TAME ANYTHING, EVEN A LION.
- MICHAEL BASSEY JOHNSON, SONG OF A NATURE
LOVER

Katariya heard the faint mumble of voices before she could see. There was a heavy weight of pressure on her chest, as though someone was pounding against it.

Her mind longed to flutter back into the darkness, but suddenly, water spewed from her, and a breath of air filled her aching lungs.

Jolting forward, more water rushed from her mouth and nose with violent coughs. It took a few seconds before Katariya's cold, pale body warmed with life. The shock of nearly dying was not as surprising as seeing a strange, brooding man gazing into her eyes, his lips seemingly pulling away from hers. Her eyes danced, unable to focus, but she was almost positive he had gifted life back into her lungs.

She was alive. *Oh, thank goddess, she was alive.*

Katariya was staring. Not just staring: she was getting lost in the dark green eyes of her hero. He was staring too, studying her with a crinkled brow. The sides of his hair were shaved, but his coarse black hair trailed into a long-braided tail, swept over his shoulder.

There was a familiarity in his mossy green irises, but Katariya was positive she had never met this shifter before. His slightly crooked nose showed that he had been in a fight at least once in his life. It was pierced with a gold hoop dangling in the middle of his septum. Scars covered the length of his arms and torso, and anywhere that wasn't already marked by violence had been covered in intricate tattoos.

Her brain was too frazzled to remember which type of tribes were adorned with that type of piercing, and although it was not popular in the north, she didn't hate the way it looked. It did, however, raise an alarm. Katariya was in the Outlands, and this man, shirtless, covered in the thinnest fabric, and decorated with inked, foreign symbols, was an Outland shifter.

Deadly. Ruthless. To be feared.

There was another problem. No matter how much she willed her body to move, the beast inside her pulled in the opposite direction. A split between two halves that had her adrenaline pumping. However, it was not stronger than the rush of nearly dying. Katariya was in shock, and it kept her complacent in his arms.

Her clothes were torn, destroyed by the shift. A thoughtless mistake she made as the water and spirit called to her. Even though she couldn't find the drive to break free from his grip, Katariya refused to be bashful. Her lioness had no qualms about their current state, and her captor didn't seem to care because he was barely covered himself.

Her vision shifted with every other blink. Everything was too loud. There was the sound of the river's rushing current, still heavy from the rain. The soft chirp of crickets and the deep croaks of frogs echoed along the riverside. There were heartbeats and heavy breathing. Rustling leaves and tiny creatures lurking between them. It was more than she could have ever imagined.

It was too much.

Until now, she hadn't even realized that it was dark outside. The moon and many stars above them gave her guidance, but it was her Animalia gift that allowed her to see clearly in the darkness. The near-death experience had her so overwhelmed that she barely noticed that the stranger was running a soft, comforting hand up and down the length of her arm.

His caress was soothing, yet Katariya's agitation was too strong to be calmed. Her blood boiled, and her skin itched, longing to be back in its lioness form. No matter how comforting his touch was, this man was a threat to her lioness, and the beast tried to push itself to the forefront of her mind.

A low growl came from deep within her chest, one that was far more animal than human. One that wasn't of her own accord. As though suddenly realizing that a wild beast was lurking in his arms, the jade green speckles of her hero's eyes flitted from distress to deep concern.

"We're gonna need to tie her up. She's gonna try to shift again."

Katariya's attention was pulled from the handsome stranger to see another man and a woman staring back at her.

Both of them had tall, muscular frames, light brown hair, and a pair of piercing gray eyes that seemed to cut through her. Their mouths were expressionless, like chiseled stone, but their eyes were expressive, showing every thought that fluttered across their minds.

They were not foolish to question Katariya's abilities. Her beast was powerful, and even though she couldn't distinguish the scents of the other species, her lioness had already measured up the competition and was sure of its dominance.

Satchels, including hers, were slung over their shoulders, and they both held ropes and cloth ties in their hands. Katariya couldn't believe that her luck was so bad that she would be kidnapped twice in one day.

"Absolutely not, Tongo. Put the rope down." Her hero abruptly turned to the other male captor, shaking his head in disapproval.

His gaze filled with warmth as he reassured her. "We don't want to hurt you, Wild Kat. No rope, no ties. We just want to talk."

The deep, vibrating rhythm of his voice matched his broad chest and wide stature. He was absurdly muscular, like she was hugging an elephant's leg, and his neck was so thick she could see the veins pulsing beneath the skin.

Her stomach rumbled when she realized that not only did he captivate her attention, but she was staring at him with a savage hunger. Alarmed at how badly she wanted to sink her teeth into the bulging veins.

Katariya and the beast had similar, but different thoughts on how they wanted to devour him. His size would appear to be a challenge, but her lioness reveled in the idea of taking down the shifter. In fact, she had been so focused on wanting to feel his pulse that she barely noticed that he called her Wild Kat.

"Hey, now, snap out of it. I'm not the kill you need." He gave her a stern look and tightened his hold on her arms.

It took a few seconds for his words to resonate. There was a twinge of fire in her line of sight, and all she could see was red. Red rage, thick, pulsing, deep blood, red.

Her ability to calm the beast only worsened when the woman tossed a freshly caught fish onto the ground. Katariya and her lioness stared longingly at its tail flapping, making a desperate attempt to slither back to the river.

In seconds, she was lunging for the fish but was held back by the stranger's tight grip on her forearms. There had been a rush of power surging through her, but her inexperience as a new shifter had Katariya questioning how to release her Animalia form.

Unable to shift, she growled inwardly at her beast and outwardly at her captors.

"Now, wait a second. We need to talk first," the hero proposed as a demand.

Katariya tried to tear her eyes away from the fish but couldn't. She needed it. Desperately, she longed for a taste.

Grabbing her by the chin, her hero used a death grip to capture her attention.

Forced to look into his eyes, Katariya growled, "What do you want from me? Let me go!"

Her temperature rose when she heard him snicker. "It's kind of cute when the little lioness growls."

Cute. Katariya was not cute. She was furious, vicious, and uncomfortably starved.

"Look, Kat, I know it might be hard for you to believe it, but we aren't here to hurt you. We were the ones who saved you." His voice was calm, and his eyes softened. "I need you to calm your spirit. Picture your family, remember the taste of your favorite food, or listen for the faint sound of a favored lullaby. Anything to calm the beast. You are safe, you will be fed, and together, we will help you find your brother."

Katariya's eyes attempted to focus. There was haziness that pulled her to and from the animal's spirit world. However, the mention of her brother had piqued the cat's interest.

What did he know about her brother? Who was this mossy eyed stranger?

When she opened her mouth to ask, the only sound that emerged was a deep, throaty growl. Panicked that the beast was ready to unleash, she reminded herself of his words.

Calm your spirit. Picture your family. Open up the bottle cap and listen to the sound of their laughter; feel the sun on her face.

Letting out a deep, exasperated breath, Katariya pictured the bright sparkling grin of her brother accompanied by the sweet song of her sister's laughter caressing her inner ear. The memory resonated with the beast.

For the first time since her shift, Katariya was the one at the forefront of her mind. Her lioness settled into a soft purr, wrapping around the favored memory.

If she traveled west, she'd be back with Sade and her parents. Despite her lineage, memories of her mother and father filled her with a sense of peace. Back to the warm comfort of her father's all-encompassing hugs. The coziness of her mother lulling her to sleep with the soft melody of a lullaby.

Despite their disagreements, Katariya missed the jaguar prince. His firm touch, the leathery, smooth caress of his voice, and the desire she saw mirrored in his eyes as she returned his insatiable kiss. Would his jaguar look the same as his father's, or did he have a distinct pattern to his black rosettes?

In the other direction was her brother. Deep down she knew Amos was still out there; her beast was sure of it. She felt the pull, pushing her to become one with her pride. Her heart, however, was torn in two.

Deep down, the decision to shift wasn't about her lioness or the need to be powerful. Katariya would always choose Amos above everyone. Being like him, with the power to defend herself above all creatures, ensured her ability to search through the savage desert land.

"Brother? What do you know about my brother?"

"I know you are the *oh so great* princess of Tulamund—"

"*Was*. I *was* the *oh so great* princess of Tulamund." Katariya rolled her eyes.

His laughter mimicked that of a purr, and in return, her lioness lay belly up, reveling in his calm aura.

"Okay, *was* a princess," he said, his eyes crinkled with amusement. "Your father commands the largest tribe in Tulamund. You and your brother both possess the ability to shift into lions, and you are a proud lioness. Running away has made you an enemy of the kingdom, and you need *my* help," he announced in a heavy tone.

Who did this man think he was?

"I know my life story. I may have almost died, but I have not lost my memory. There's no need to remind me of my fate," she snarled. "Is there a point you are trying to make? Just tell me what you want and what this has to do with my brother."

The stranger huffed, and the sound of his annoyance made Katariya's skin prickle with anger. She was bored with the mind games, and her beast was growing restless.

"What I'm trying to say is that we can take you to safety," the hero said with sincerity in his speckled green eyes.

"I swear you are talking in riddles. Can you move along so I can enjoy my meal? I have a friend nearby, and if I scream, he'll end each and every one of your lives," Katariya shouted, glaring at all three of her captors.

Where was her uncle? Had Ram witnessed her shift and abandoned the mission? Was he already heading back to Tulamund to tell her father she had succumbed to the bloodthirsty beast?

"No need to get feisty," the hero snapped, sending her a death glare.

"What do you know about feisty? Let me go, and I'm sure my lioness will be glad to show you," Katariya barked, thrashing her arms in an attempt to break free.

"She's not gonna listen. She's too far gone. If we hurry and get her to him, we might avoid getting our heads ripped off."

It was the woman who spoke this time, her voice hard and firm like a captain. For a split second, her aura caught Katariya's focus, but the trance only lasted a few seconds. Her rage returned, and her lioness resumed her thrashing struggle.

The other man, known as Tongo, stared down at her with apprehension. He grabbed the fish by the tail and dangled it in front of her face. She licked her lips in anticipation, her ears twitched, and her eyes rolled into the back of her head.

The barrage of sights, sounds, and smells was almost too much for her to handle. The gnawing hunger in her stomach outweighed any power that her captors held over her.

First, she would nourish the beast, and then she would remind her enemies of the lioness's dominance.

"It feels wrong to take her if she doesn't know all of the details," the handsome stranger replied.

The words went in one ear and out the other. Katariya vaguely understood, but nothing they said was more important than the fish just a few feet away from her. She didn't care for whomever was going to make her feel better or what was in store for her. Food would make her feel better. A full belly was what she needed.

"If she shifts, one of you is gonna have to knock her out," the woman insisted.

"I'm not gonna knock her out, Talla. She'll kill me before I even take a swing," Tongo said, backing away from snarls and growls.

"No one's going to knock her out." The green-eyed hero glared back at his companions. "She just needs to eat first."

He released her from his tight hold, and Katariya pounced on her meal. With ravenous need, she tore into the flesh, ripping through the mini bones and many scales.

The fish curbed the immediate need, but she could still feel an insatiable longing for something. For meat, for a kill, for more blood. Her beast grew restless.

As if the chill on her skin wasn't a strong enough indicator, her brain finally registered that the scraps of clothing she wore barely covered her body.

She had allowed a stranger, although handsome, to hold and caress her. In the moment, his gentle touch had been a source of comfort for her vulnerability, but now, as she crawled around in the dirt, savagely picking apart a carcass, Katariya felt raw and exposed.

With blood, guts, and fish juices pouring down her bare chest, her eyes flashed to that of a big cat's murderous gaze. Inspecting her new prey, she bounced around, searching for the weakest link.

The woman, Talla, was of the same weight and stature as Tongo. Bulky, muscular, boorish. Same nose with curly hair and misty gray eyes. Siblings perhaps? Twins?

There was tension in the air as their eyes nervously dashed between her and the hero, waiting for his next command. Their focus on the handsome stranger made it obvious he was their leader.

Commanding, threatening, dominant. His frame was almost twice the size of his companions, but that would not dissuade her lioness from the pursuit.

"Amos will not like it if we hurt her," her hero said, watching her hesitantly as she crawled around the ground, picking at the last patch of flesh dangling from the fish corpse.

Katariya's entire world busted at the seams, like a rockslide barreling down the mountains. She hadn't heard her brother's name spoken so freely in years. Not only did his name resonate with her, but her lioness knew of Amos as life and love. Her family. Her pride.

They would take her to him. Her beast would demand it.

"I don't like the look of this, Romelo. She looks ready to attack," Tongo said.

A weakness, a weak link, prey. Katariya's eyes flashed to the bright specks of gold of her inner beast. With a steely determination, her mind raced with the feel of her beast's fur beneath her fingertips.

As a surge of power flushed through her, the light descended from the heavens to caress her human form.

Suddenly, the ruggedly handsome stranger came barreling toward her as she heard his deep rumble.

"I'm really sorry about this, Wild Kat."

A massive fist collided with the side of her face, and Katariya was met with darkness.

CHAPTER 27

YOUR BUFFALO ARE WILD AND I WANT THEM
TO STAY. BUT IT'S BUFFALO WILD DOWN
HERE. BUFFALO WILD! IN THE WILDEST WAY!
- DEIDRE HAVRELOCK, BUFFALO WILD

Had she died and gone to heaven? The blinding light was back again. The beams were bright enough to induce a rattling headache, and a sharp pang of nausea made her slip into a void. Except this time, she could hear the whirling sound of wind, the voice of chirping songbirds, and the loud, thunderous clap of what she could only describe as a thousand hooves thudding against the tough soil.

Tied around her mouth was a tan cloth secured so tightly Katariya couldn't make a sound. Her hands and feet were tied together, and the only movements she could make were from the unsteady bounce of the wagon rocking side to side.

When she finally found the strength to open her eyes, Katariya was instantly stunned. For miles on end, a massive herd of shifters ran in a blur, their musky smell tainting the air.

United, was a herd filled with buffalo, zebras, wildebeests and all different subspecies of antelope. Intermixed between them were dozens of painted dogs, cheetahs, spotted leopards, panthers and more.

Katariya had been placed on her side, and from that angle, she could see the wide-open plains of the Outlands filled to the brim with shifters. Their hooves pounded in the dirt, stirring up a billowing cloud of dust in their wake. It was a sight that could only be described as magical and majestic.

It was everything Katariya and Amos had imagined, but so much more. A massive herd, moving together as a collective unit. The way their goddesses had intended.

Running next to her was a buffalo with a smiling young girl saddled around the animal's back. The girl's strawberry-kissed hair flowed in the breeze as they weaved through the herd.

The plains seemed to go on forever, but from what she knew about the Outland clans, they were nomads, moving day by day through the grasslands. Without the protection of the mountain, the Animalia shifters were constantly in danger of poachers and threatening tribes. They were always moving for safety, but they also were more in touch with their Animalia spirit, with little to no restrictions on how often they remained in their animal forms.

The beast inside of Katariya was angrily trying to release itself by attempting to scratch its way out. Dirt, sweat, and tears stained her skin, and there was a lump in her throat from a lack of water.

Strapped and tied down, Katariya couldn't shift without the use of all of her limbs. Her beast was raging, and the snarls that mumbled around the cloth did nothing but earn her a worried look from her uncle.

"Hey, you're awake," Ram said cautiously.

With slow movements, he lifted his arm to wave at someone in the distance.

Katariya snarled, and her normally fearless uncle looked at her with concern.

Ram's signal drew the attention of a buffalo running behind them. They had thick, powerful frames and dark brown fur with a set of horns on each side of their head. *Lion killers.* That was what they used to be before the Animalia gift. Lions, who were desperate for a kill, would resort to attacking the massive herbivores. A dangerous game, but necessary for survival.

At a weight of nearly two thousand pounds, a buffalo had the sheer force to trample and break every bone in a lion's body. One minor mistake during a hunt would leave the animal immobile, forced to die a slow, painful death.

The massive beast sped forward, and the wagon followed him, veering away from the herd. They moved through crowds of rhinos, giraffes, tigers, maned wolves, and more. The sounds of feet pounding, hooves stomping, and paws bashing were accompanied by brays, whinnies, and roars.

At the end of the herd, they came to an abrupt halt. The buffalo transformed back into a human, revealing that the massive beast was the woman who had been with her green-eyed hero and the look-alike male.

At nearly six feet tall, the female captor towered over Katariya and probably a lot of men, too. She had short curly brown hair, shaved down with tattooed designs decorating the sides of her exposed skin. Her facial features were soft, but her muscles were as fit as King Cairo's top warriors.

Without a word, the captor climbed into the wagon and searched through a crate sitting behind Ram. From the crate, she pulled out a small vial filled with a light blue colored liquid. Untying the rope, the buffalo woman yanked the cloth from Katariya's mouth.

Immediately upon release, Katariya tried to scream, but no words came off of her sandpaper tongue. The captor took the opportunity to force some of the blue liquid down her open mouth, and with a pinch against her nose, she was forced to swallow.

As wild as her beast was made out to be, Katariya was suddenly complacent. There was a bubbling anger lingering beneath her, but mostly, her spirit felt drained. Her captor seemed hesitant as she stared at the empty vial, but she then returned it to the satchel and pulled out a canteen of water.

Lifting the bottle of water to her mouth, Katariya drank every single drop that her captor allowed. When she could finally make use of her voice, she cleared her throat in a garbled cough and screamed, "Who are you and where the hell are you taking me?"

The captor raised her eyebrow at her quipped remark.

"Watch your tone. You're the captive, so I'm the one who gets to ask the questions. I'm Talla, and this is the Mufiki Tribe, one of the largest tribes in the Outlands."

Talla handed the canteen to Ram to take a drink.

"Our leader is taking you to the Sandstone king."

Katariya's uncle guzzled the water down, half of the canteen drenched on his chest. He didn't bother to smell the liquid for poison or question the buffalo woman's demands.

"Who—who is the Sandstone king?" Katariya asked, holding her breath as she waited for the answer.

His name was on the tip of Talla's tongue; Katariya could almost hear it. Despite feeling calmer with the liquid, she was still growing impatient. Any shifter would. A slightly inhuman snarl threatened Talla.

Rolling her eyes, the buffalo uncapped the mysterious elixir. "I think you are forgetting that you are the one strapped down, not me."

She shook her head in an attempt to calm down her beast, but instead let out a simpering plea, "Tell me, please. Who is the king of Sandstone?"

Before she was knocked out, she could vaguely recall the green-eyed shifter's deep, resounding voice as he uttered her nickname. There was familiarity there, not enough that Katariya thought she might have met him before, but as though *he* knew *her* beyond the title of Tulamund's future princess.

This tribe had the answers she needed; Katariya was sure of it.

"If you keep drinking this elixir," Talla said, holding up another vial, "I will tell you. If you don't, well, I'll be forced to knock you out again."

"Yes, fine. Whatever you want. Just tell me."

Katariya knew it wasn't smart to drink an unknown concoction of herbs, but she was desperate to hear the truth. Her beast felt as though they were traveling in the right direction. A light dust clung to the air as they moved further east. In a few days' time, she would be in Sandstone, back to her brother, reconnected with her lioness's pride.

"Open," Talla grunted, holding the bottle above Katariya's head.

She took a sip.

"More."

Talla's eyebrows shot up, and her lips formed a thin line of challenge.

Katariya contorted her face in disgust as the putrid taste hit her tongue. Knowing Talla had refused to answer her question twice now, she changed her tactics.

"No, no more until you tell me. Who is your leader?"

"Chief's name is Romelo; he's a buffalo shifter, like me." Talla gave her a wonky smirk, and Katariya rolled her eyes.

Whatever the woman had given her, she could feel her limbs settling. The stress lines on her face dissipated, and her tongue dangled from the side of her mouth.

"What did you give me?"

The words fumbled out of her mouth like vomit. Disjointed and garbled.

"Just a mild sedative. It will keep the beast calm until we reach your brother."

Her eyes grew soft and beady as Katariya remained hopeful. "Amos."

His name came out sounding nothing like it was actually pronounced, but Talla understood her.

Talla's hardened expression softened as she gazed down at Katariya, her eyes fluttering from the loopy stupor caused by the elixir.

"Yes, Amos. Amos Abara, the new king of Sandstone."

Katariya was stunned into silence. The effects of the elixir dulled her senses, but no matter how foggy her mind was, she heard Talla loud and clear.

Her eyes shot toward Ram. The bear didn't appear surprised at all. He already knew the missing pieces. He was willingly traveling with the Mufiki tribe. There was nothing securing his wrists, nothing bound to his feet.

"What's gonna happen to us—"

"We'll have to kill you."

Talla let out a snarl that slowly pulled into a drawn-out cackle at the sight of Katariya's fear.

"Oh, goddess." Talla laughed louder. "I can't—I can't. Did you see her face? Did you?"

Their captor turned toward Ram, who rolled his eyes and groaned.

When she finally calmed down, Talla said, "Don't fret. I'm sorry, but that was too good. You Tulamund shifters don't know how to take a joke."

Making sure Katariya's ties were tight, Talla patted her back and said, "Don't worry. We'll get you back to your brother."

Amos. Her kindred spirit.

"Drink this, and when you wake up, we'll be halfway there."

Talla lifted the elixir to her lips once more.

As the sedative settled, Katariya drifted into the space of the in-between. There she was, running alongside the Mufiki tribe with a golden mane blowing in the wind beside her. It was a lion who could keep up with her lioness, weaving through a united herd of Animalia shifters.

When Katariya woke, she found herself nestled inside a tent with her legs and arms bound together. The scraps of ripped clothing had been replaced by the bright indigo blue of her ceremonial dress.

In front of her was a cooked meal, still steaming as though someone had just dropped it off just moments before. Out of the tent, there was the faint sound of voices, and although her shifter abilities should have allowed her to hear, the elixir running through her system had dulled her senses.

Her beast crawled into a crevice in the back of her mind, watching idly with a flick of her swishing tail. Her lioness was angry but complacent. Frozen, unable to protect Katariya from any threats. She felt cornered.

Ram could not be found anywhere, but her bow, sword, and satchel sat by the tent's entrance. Her knife had been lost in the disaster at the tavern.

Her arms were tied in front of her, and if she tried, she could probably maneuver her hands enough to take a drink from the canteen, but she wasn't confident that she could eat this way. She stared at the food with longing, but there was also a lingering distrust in her captors.

Even though they promised her safety and baited her with talk of her brother, their actions did not convince Katariya that they were on her side. They were strangers, members of an Outland tribe, who had taken her as their captive.

Inching across the floor, she grabbed onto the ends of an arrow, shuffling it around in her hands. She used the pointed end to try to cut through the rope, but even the slightest movement caused the conversation outside the tent to come to a halt.

Barging through the slit in the tent was her rugged, green-eyed hero.

"I'd be happy to take those off, but only if you promise not to attack me." His deep, rumbling spooked her, making Katariya drop the weapon.

Attempting to look innocent, she gave him a disinterested look as he eyed her suspiciously.

He took a seat, and Katariya made no sudden movements, allowing him to scoot beside her. Taking her hands in his, he took his time slicing through the ties with a small knife. He stared into her hazel eyes, and his rough voice somehow became even raspier.

"I'm Romelo. It's nice to finally meet you."

Katariya didn't bother with her own introduction. He already knew who she was.

Instead, she asked, "What is in the tiny bottles that you've been giving me?"

The rope fell, but neither of them made any sudden movements.

"Blue lotus. The shifters in Sandstone use it to mellow out the beast. It keeps you from shifting while it remains in the system. We use it as a sedative, but sometimes it can have unique effects on the body."

Katariya had heard of the herb before. It was often used to aid in slumber, but it had other-worldly properties said to allow the mind to travel to and from the heavens.

"Is the bottle on the table the same as what I drank earlier?" The glass bottle sat in the corner of the room, but it was a darker shade of blue than the substance she was forced to drink earlier.

"Yeah, the blue lotus, combined with valerian root, will put you in a deep slumber."

Katariya bit her tongue, resisting the urge to tell him that she already knew the plant's effects.

"How long have I been asleep?"

From inside the tent, the only clues she had that it was evening were the lantern's light and the gentle chirp of crickets in the distance.

"Almost two weeks," he said nonchalantly, as though it was expected—as though it was no big deal that she had been in a psychoactive induced slumber for two whole weeks.

"You can't just keep me asleep for two weeks!" Katariya screamed, backing up on her heels.

She wobbled in this stance, but it made her feel less vulnerable than sitting on the ground. Her feet were planted firmly in place, ready to launch herself forward if necessary. If needed, she would rip his ear off, or remove a finger or two.

Ignoring her outburst, Romelo grabbed the plate of food and said, "You need to eat, or you will get sick."

Her stomach growled as she glanced down at the food. The hesitancy left her body the more she smelled the tempting aromas of the spiced fish.

Garlic, pepper, dillweed, paprika and a pinch of... ginger.

"And how do I know that you aren't trying to drug me again?" Katariya raised her eyebrows at him as he pushed the food closer.

"Because, Kat, we can't just keep you knocked out for another week. Talla has already given you way more than recommended, and having too much of the elixir can have the opposite effect."

Romelo rolled his eyes, as though he was tired of her questions. Picking up a fork, he held it out for her.

"You know, I could use that as a weapon." She glared at him.

Her beast wasn't active, but that didn't mean Katariya wasn't angry. She'd take the fork and stab him in the eye if need be.

"I'd like to see you try," he chuckled.

Hours ago—well it was weeks ago now—she would have cowered in fear, running like an antelope at the sight of her enemies in the tavern. Now, with the power and confidence of a lioness, she had no desire to back down.

Katariya was the beast that the entire kingdom of Tulamund feared. Countless stories and fables depicted her as a savage, bloodthirsty animal. Inside her mind, her lioness licked her lips, biding time before she could unleash her inner strength.

Realizing that without the drugs, her beast would take control, she let out a huff and allowed her nose to smell the meal.

If she ended up killing her captors, she would have an even harder time finding Amos. She'd bide her time, take as little of the blue lotus elixir as they would allow, and soon she would be reunited with her brother.

The fish was no longer steaming hot, but it was delicious. The carrots were glazed with salt and honey, and a small piece of bread complemented the dish. She ate the food in silence, surprised that a land filled with brutes and scoundrels took the time to perfectly season their meals.

Romelo watched Katariya with unwavering eyes, studying her as she swallowed each bite. With a mouthful of food, she was excused from talking and, in return, she studied him with the same peculiar gaze.

In the lantern's glowing light, her hero was just as handsome as she had seen him the night of her shift. Nearly seven feet tall, big-boned, but not chubby, Romelo was much larger than her uncle but smaller than Bron. In the light, Katariya could see tattoos of symbols and markings covering his arms, trailing along the side of his ribs and hips and all the way down to the middle of his calves.

Without her gift, Katariya would have trembled in his presence, but as a lioness, she could only picture him as someone to devour.

She tried to turn her attention back to the food, but his watchful gaze never shifted, causing her breath to quicken.

"It's rude to stare, you know," she seethed, not caring to bother with any manners.

Romelo chucked in disbelief as he said, "Sorry, it's just unbelievable that someone like you is the princess when you don't even have the basic manners to chew with your mouth closed."

Katariya rolled her eyes.

"Yeah, well, you and the rest of Tulamund have had that question on their mind ever since the prophecy was declared."

Unfazed by his comment, she continued to shovel a mouth full of food down her throat, and he laughed again.

It only furthered her frustration. "Obviously, you know who I am. The woman shifter, Tall—Talla, said that you are the leader of the Mufiki tribe, but what I need to know is how Amos plays into all of this."

"Yes, I am one of many shifters on the council that is under the leadership of the Sandstone king. I'm in charge of over a thousand shifters who live just south of the river."

Her eyes widened in surprise.

"A *thousand* buffalo?"

The antelope tribe only had a hundred members and were one of the largest tribes living within Tulamund behind the apes, who remained unified among their subspecies.

The sight of the massive herd of shifters spread out across the plains was awe-inspiring. But a thousand? That was unbelievable.

"No, that's not exactly right. We have about six hundred buffalo, a hundred different carnivores, and three hundred other herbivore species."

His explanation left her dumbfounded. "But how? How do you lead an Animalia shifter who is not of your own species?"

"How is it that your father was the leader of the antelope, not just the leader of the impalas?" Romelo retorted, his expression giving her pause.

"Well, our numbers are smaller, and most antelopes share the same abilities, needs, and desires. We are more unified together."

"It is the same here. The Mufiki tribe, like most tribes in the Outlands, runs together and takes care of one another. It doesn't matter the spirit you carry; there is always a home among the endless plains."

Katariya wouldn't be convinced until she saw the truth for herself. Until then, she would regard the men and women of the Outlands with suspicion, and she would move cautiously. This, like everything else that had happened so far, had gone against everything she had ever known.

"And Amos? My brother? He is the Sandstone king."

Romelo nodded softly.

"Yes, Amos Abara is our king, but we can continue this discussion later. Your uncle is waiting."

She hadn't tasted the elixir in her food, but she could feel the effects as her beast settled into the back of her mind, licking her light golden paws with a sandpaper tongue. Calm and complacent. The perfect prisoner for her captors.

If she was going to find Amos, Katariya would need to be mindful of how much of the elixir she drank. She needed to stay alert. While being passed out for two weeks wasn't ideal, it only meant that she was already halfway to Sandstone. Soon to be reunited with Amos.

Romelo rose from his seated position, putting a few feet of distance between them. He rummaged around in a crate before he came back to her with an extended hand.

She was skeptical of his kind gesture, and he let out a laugh.

"Come on. I'll take you to your uncle, show you around, and you can see for yourself what the tribes in the Outlands are really like."

Promise of seeing her uncle combined with her curiosity had Katariya accepting his help. Taking Romelo's hand, she allowed him to guide her out of the tent.

CHAPTER 28

IT'S BETTER TO BE A LION FOR A
DAY THAN A SHEEP ALL YOUR LIFE.
- ELIZABETH KENNY, AND THEY SHALL WALK

When they stepped out of the tent, Katariya expected a flurry of judgmental stares and wide, curious eyes. Instead, she was met with the pulsing rhythm of the drums and wood instruments, the delicious aromas of sweet pastries and mulled wine, accompanied by the joyful movements of shifters dancing.

The herd of animals was too large to be contained by the warmth of a single fire. In the dark, the swirling circles of dancers were illuminated by the flickering flames that lit up the vast plains. The surrounding shifters and animals moved in unison, creating a symphony of sound and sight that left her in awe.

While her senses were dull from the elixir, her nose was strong enough to decipher some of the Animalia scents.

There was a panther girl leaning into a buffalo man's warm embrace, her laughter mingled with his own as two small children circled them, mimicking the movements of the dancers in a not-so-graceful manner.

On the opposite side of the fire, there was a buffalo woman wedged in between a bushbuck antelope man and a cheetah woman. The three shifters held one another in a warm embrace.

Katariya felt her cheeks burn, though she could not look away from the love that radiated from each unique couple or group. In Tulamund, such behaviors could cause risk for exile, yet as she beheld their passionate moment, she felt nothing but a sense of freedom.

As they weaved through the herd, the shifters and animals they encountered acknowledged Romelo with a respectful nod or a hearty pat on the shoulder. He smiled warmly at each shifter as they passed, calling them by name and taking the time to ask them personal questions about their day, family, or thoughts on the ongoing celebration.

The commodity of the event was celebrated with a magnitude that was a thousand times greater than that of the antelope tribe. In fact, it was a million times more inviting than the disparity at the king's palace.

"What exactly are you all celebrating?" Katariya asked as a group of men clinked their glasses in a toast.

She felt the weight of Romelo's watchful eyes studying her. Despite her attempts to ignore him, her curiosity was too strong for her not to ask the questions that burned inside.

"The gift of our mother creator. In Tulamund, you celebrate for a day. Celebrations in the Mufiki tribe last for a month," Romelo answered.

A group of women came fluttering through the crowd with plates of pastries, and Romelo snagged two puffed pieces of sweet bread drizzled with a smooth vanilla glaze.

Biting into it, she moaned around the sugary treat and asked, "A whole month of this?"

He seemed to enjoy the pastry just as much as she did. Licking his fingers clean, he said, "That's right. Our newest shifters travel west to transform in the water that is the closest to the heavens. Then we run together as a herd to the east. It's a month-long trip from the mountains to Sandstone. It gives the new shifters time to practice using their new legs, and the rest of the tribe joins in support."

Katariya was taken aback by the foreignness of the experience because the "savages" of the Outlands were nothing like she had known them to be. She was taught to expect a scene of horror, but instead was met with the gentle melody of laughter and song.

"Come along. We have much to see before the night is over."

Romelo led Katariya through the throng of shifters until they reached a less-crowded part of the field. Moving around the towering bonfire, a group of young men and women fought in a synchronized formation. Their spears and swords swung in time with the rhythm of a battle song.

Katariya was enraptured by the sound of their feet thundering against the ground, their weapons and bodies moving in perfect harmony. The older shifters in the front moved with grace, leading the young boys and girls in the combative dance. While some dancers were newly transformed Animalia, many of the others were small children eagerly following along.

Romelo's eyes moved slowly up the line of shifters, settling on a small girl with the same dark hair and distinctive almond-shaped eyes as the buffalo leader. With a confidence beyond her years, the young girl moved her weapon as though she had been practicing since birth.

To Katariya, it was a dream come true to watch not only women but also young girls hone their fighting skills. Her last sparring partner had been Amos. The scarecrows served as practice targets, but there was only so much she could learn from an enemy that couldn't put up a fight.

Romelo pointed to the group, a soft smile on each of their faces, and said, "Go. Join them. Your brother mentioned you are no stranger to a sword, and you are a new shifter, after all. Have some fun. Celebrate. You've earned it."

Shaking her head, completely out of her element, Katariya replied, "Oh no, I couldn't. I've never used a spear before."

"I promise you, it will be fun. I'm gonna go grab your uncle, but you should dance a little. Celebrate and get to know some of our young girls. Maybe they'll inspire you... or maybe you'll inspire them."

Katariya observed the dancers warily. The motion of their spears swinging in their arms was reminiscent of a sword slashing through the air. The young shifters, equally split between boys and girls, were unfazed by their mistakes, gleefully laughing no matter how many times they dropped their weapon or how amateur their form looked.

In the middle of the shifters, Talla emerged with a heavy weapon placed at her side. With her skin glistening in sweat, the commander spotted the apprehension in Katariya's expression, and she taunted with a sly smile, "Scared, *princess*?"

"No, but despite my title, I am not the best dancer, especially not with a sharp weapon in hand." Katariya frowned and gestured to the powerful pounding movements of the warriors.

"It's less about the dance and more about the strength you possess. Just watch Romelo's sister, Kove. She's new but has been making great strides with her formation," Talla said, guiding her to the middle of the dance circle. "Follow me. Let the lioness's power guide you. Her spirit will know exactly what to do."

Katariya cast a hopeful glance at Romelo, praying he could save her from the humiliation, but all he offered her was a hopeless smile and a wink as he stepped away into the flickering light of the fire.

Standing in the middle of the circle, she moved in line beside Kove. The movements of the shifters created a rhythmic wave of energy that danced through her trembling muscles.

With a deep sigh, Katariya tried to move, but her body remained frozen. Missing the first step had caused the young girl to step into her, but instead of being annoyed or angry, she offered Katariya a sympathetic smile.

"Left foot first. Then right. Then two more to the left." Kove motioned toward her feet.

Talla returned with a wooden spear, and Katariya stared at the weapon, hoping the girl would also teach her the hand movements.

Kove had her own small spear, which reminded Katariya of the days when she had wished for a child-sized bow. Here in the Outlands, women were celebrated warriors, and the moment a child expressed their desire to learn to fight, they were handed a weapon and taught the skills to do so. It sounded so deadly, but this little girl didn't seem like she was anyone to be feared.

Talla led the group with deep, throaty chants. The change in the drum's tempo was a directional symbol guiding the dancers into the next movements.

Kove moved at snail speed to show Katariya where she needed to place her hands on the spear to create fluid movements. The weapon weighed less than her sword, and she found that the arm motions were easier than the foot placements.

As soon as Katariya started feeling confident in her steps, the beat grew faster. She could no longer keep up. Tumbling into the girl next to her, she fell into the row of shifters, causing everyone to topple over like a ripple in a pond.

Katariya waited for mocking comments to spew from her fellow dancers, but she was only answered with a wave of laughter.

"Oh, goddess, I'm so sorry," Katariya apologized, reaching down to help Kove regain her footing.

Kove had a wide smile and flushed cheeks from the fast, strenuous movements, but her eyes were soft.

"It's okay. I fell twice on the first night. I even nicked Raina here," she said, nudging a girl with thick, curly black hair.

Raina shared a friendly smile and pointed to a lengthy mark that ran up the side of her arm. The wound was scarred but starting to fade.

"Did that hurt?" Katariya asked, puzzled.

"Ehh... my cheetah took care of the healing process. The mark will never fully go away, but at least it's a fierce battle scar." Raina chuckled deeply before she went to join the rest of the shifters in the next dance sequence.

When the dance was finally over, the music continued to play but softened to a sweet melody. A signal that the night was coming to an end.

Placing their weapons in a heaping pile, the little warriors and new shifters turned to their loved ones with open arms. After proud hugs and sweet kisses, the children were guided back to their tents while the new shifters transformed into their Animalia spirits. The group took off, trotting into the thick grasses, and quickly disappeared into the camouflaged darkness.

A straggler of the group, Raina, stopped to ask, giggling, "Are you coming? We're all headed down the river for a night swim before bed."

Katariya pivoted toward Romelo and her mind filled with the threat of her beast. For the duration of the dance, her obligations, troubles, and the perilous situation of her beast's insanity had been forgotten.

With a polite smile, she declined the invitation. "Next time, perhaps. I believe Romelo is waiting for me."

Raina looked up at their leader. Every few seconds, his jade green eyes would momentarily stray from the conversation he was having with her uncle to stare directly into Katariya's hooded gaze.

From here, she could see Ram in the middle of a conversation with Talla's look-alike, Tongo. He appeared to be joyfully laughing with an amber bottle in one hand and a roll of tobacco hanging from the corner of his mouth. He was not only unharmed but also happily gorging himself on a tray filled with meats, cheese, and pastries.

It surprised her how quick and easy it was to immerse themselves in the tribe's grand celebration. Never did she feel as welcomed into a tribe as she did with this massive herd of shifters.

"Ahh, yeah—no, I understand. You shouldn't leave him waiting. I'll see you around," Raina said, and with a blink of an eye, she was ripping off her tan cloth and tumbling into her cheetah form.

Katariya turned to catch Kove and Romelo in an endearing moment. A tight hug and a little sister staring in awe at her beloved brother. It was the same look she used to give Amos, as though his golden eyes held all the right answers.

Katariya trudged up to the siblings, desperately trying to push away the sweat-soaked curls that clung to her forehead.

"Did you have fun?" Kove asked, her face glistening just as much as Katariya's forehead.

"Yes, thank you for your help! You were exceptional out there."

The compliment was truthful. For someone so young, the girl had a level of confidence that she couldn't fathom.

"Did you hear that, Melo? Even the lioness thinks I'm great. Does that mean I can go on the next scouting trip?" Kove's mossy eyes sparkled with hope.

"I heard her. You are talented for your age, but you still have many years of practice before you are ready for battle." Romelo gave his younger sister a disapproving look, one that didn't seem to faze the little fighter.

Spirited, she replied, "You'll see. This time next year, I'll be next in line for commander!"

"For commander?" Katariya tried to stifle a giggle. "I look forward to leadership under the finest warrior."

"Alright, Wild Kat. Don't go filling her head. It's big enough already." Romelo rolled his eyes before nudging his little sister forward. "Say goodnight, Kove."

Kove's bottom lip pouted. "But—but the other girls are running by the river."

"Oh no, warriors do not pout. Mama wanted you in bed an hour ago, but I knew you'd be able to help our newest friend. If you are up any later, Mama will have both our heads."

Hardening her face, the young girl held her head up high. With a deep sigh, she smiled at Katariya and said, "It was nice meeting you." Kove's eyes were hopeful as she asked, "Do you—do you think I could see your bow tomorrow? I've heard you got one and I've never seen one up close."

Katariya's eyes widened as she eagerly nodded in agreement.

Romelo's voice boomed, "Absolutely not. There's no need to involve yourself with poacher weapons."

Frozen, she watched as the buffalo leader's eyes flashed to a brighter green, and a huff of anger escaped his widened nostrils.

"But—"

"No buts, Kove. It's time for bed."

His voice rose to that of a leader commanding his tribe. The mouthy little warrior shut her mouth and waited for her brother's direction.

With their entire focus on Romelo, he continued, "Katariya, go on, go sit with your uncle. I will return to you once I get my sister off to bed."

When he was a few feet away, the aura of his commands dissipated, and Katariya called out a sweet goodnight. "I'll see you tomorrow, Kove. Maybe we can have ourselves a quick spar in the morning!"

As the young girl spun on her heel, her wispy black hair flew in all directions, and she smiled at Katariya with bright, wide eyes.

"I can't wait!"

Katariya moved toward a small group of men and women. They laughed together and drank from goblets filled with mulled wine. Pastries passed between them, and her uncle sat in the middle, stuffing his face with the same sweet bread that Katariya tried earlier.

Feeling out of place, she shuffled back and forth on her feet. With the dampness of the sweat, her dress clung to her body, forcing her to take a moment to adjust the straps hanging down her arm.

Noticing her struggles, Tongo's booming voice said, "It would be a lot easier if you just wore our clothing, or better yet, why don't you just walk around in nothing at all?"

His eyes raked her form with a devious grin accompanied by a lustrous wink.

"I promise you, no one would mind."

The men in the group could not suppress their laughter, while the women's eyes flickered with anger. With a loud thud, Talla's hand smacked the back of Tongo's head.

"Hey! What the hell?" he groaned, rubbing the back of his aching skull.

"Brother, you should know better than to make comments about women like that. Would you dare speak to the other commanders that way?"

The women in the circle gave him a pointed look and a knowing smile, begging for another slip so they could put the buffalo in his place.

"No, they'd kick my rump for saying anything like that."

"Exactly. Just because she's a Tulamund girl doesn't mean she has to put up with your crass mouth."

Talla pinched his side, and he squealed like a hollering chimpanzee. With fury, the warrior rose from his seat and threw himself at his twin sister, wrestling her to the ground.

Talla let him have the upper hand for a few seconds before she flipped him onto his back, her sword flush against his neck.

"I don't know why you still try," Talla said with a victorious smile.

"Oh, come on. One more, but this time without the weapon," Tongo begged for another chance.

"Oh, I like this girl," Ram said, leaning toward the fight. Never taking his eyes off of the tussle, her uncle held out the sweet bread and groaned around a giant bite.

"Kid, you gotta try this. It's to die for."

Eagerly taking the bread from his hands, Katariya said, "I had some earlier, but all this dancing has worked up an appetite. Did you see me, Ram? Did you see the kids? All of it." She gestured toward both everything and nothing at the same time. "This celebration. These people. How did we not know?"

Ram shuffled between shoveling down pastries, taking big sips of wine, and drawing out a cloud of smoke from his rolled tobacco stick.

It took a minute before his mouth was empty and, with a mumbled reply, he said, "I don't know, kid. I'm not so sure about that one." He pointed toward Talla, who had her brother pinned down in a headlock. "She was a bit too eager to torture us, but this, the food alone, is enough for me to feel like we've been missin' out."

Katariya couldn't agree more. It made her wonder how many other lies the kingdom of Tulamund had been told about the shifters in the Outlands. If the Mufiki tribe, who was filled with love and compassion, was working with the shifters of Sandstone, how bad could the savage beasts really be?

Joining the circle, she took a seat on the wooden stump next to her uncle. The glow of fiery embers waned as the night drew to a close. No one bothered to feed the fire, just like no one seemed to give Katariya any special treatment or attention. Whether they didn't know who she was or had mixed feelings about her presence, they spared her from the curious whispers.

Being unnoticed suddenly felt like a calmness in the storm. After spending years subjected to the wishes and wills of everyone but herself, she didn't mind the lack of interest. She was an average girl with average looks, and the whispers of a wind didn't make her anything great, nothing more than normal. It wasn't crushing or soul-wrenching. No, not at all. It was freeing.

CHAPTER 29

FIREFLIES ARE STARS THAT COULD
NOT JOURNEY TO THE SKY.
- MICHAEL BASSEY JOHNSON, SONG OF A NATURE
LOVER

After getting pinned for the fifth time, Tongo tapped out with the excuse of a leg cramp. He brushed it off by downing a drink and spent twenty minutes complaining about an old injury that was holding him back.

Uncle Ram was already immersed in the group, sharing war stories and comparing weapons. The circle of commanders was a mix of herbivores and carnivores, and despite the differences in the Animalia's size and behaviors, everyone treated each other the same. Banter flowed between them, and private jokes bounced around.

An hour later, Romelo found Katariya moaning around a savory fish pastry. "Those are some of my favorites. I swear you can't have too many."

Startled by the boom in his voice, she choked on her last bite with a dry cough. Beads of sweat had pooled above his brow, and when she focused, Katariya could hear the rapid thump of his racing heart.

"Did you run here?" she asked.

"Yeah, Kove was too excited to sleep. She demanded a warrior story, and I felt as if I had already kept you waiting long enough."

When he was attentive to Kove, Katariya felt an appreciation for him she hadn't expected. He reminded her of Amos, but he surely didn't look like him.

Most of her lioness's abilities were toned down from the blue lotus, but she felt waves of desire being in the presence of the buffalo leader. Her beast had more primal urges than she had on her own, and staring at the ruler, who led a thousand unified carnivores and herbivores, sparked an interest in her.

"How about we take a quick walk before bed? I can answer any questions you may have about the journey." He nodded in the direction of an empty field.

Katariya was tired, but her curiosity outweighed any fatigue. The evening had revealed many truths, but she had failed to catch up to the true task at hand. Immediately, she had been thrown into their celebration, and although they were welcoming, there was so much uncertainty about her future.

How did they meet her brother? What were their intentions? What was their plan to control her beast?

Turning toward Ram, she asked, "Care to join us?"

The bear's eyes moved between her and Romelo. He gave her a slight shrug and said, "Nah, you two go ahead."

Katariya's brows raised. "Not too concerned about my safety, are you?"

His eyes glazed over, flickering with guilt. Her words were more sensitive than she had meant for them to be, and her mind flashed to the horrid scene at the tavern.

"Nah, kid, I'm more concerned than ever, but the second you stepped into the water, that was the end of my expertise." He took another swig from the amber bottle, and his eyes narrowed. "That spirit of yours is rumblin' within. I can see it behind your eyes, and whatever they are giving you, that blue stuff, that seems to be workin' just fine. As much as I hate to say it, we've got no choice but to trust 'em."

Her ever-changing hazel eyes flickered with the spirit of the lioness. The beast inside her was somehow still complacent, but he was right. There was no way she could return to the kingdom.

Anything and everything she knew about her old life was gone. She had a beast roaring inside her that needed to be dealt with, and the shifters living in the Outlands had the answer she needed.

Even if they weren't actually working with her brother, what choice did she have?

There was a gnawing hunger deep inside her core that was momentarily satisfied, but without the elixir, she was sure her lioness would see her uncle as their next meal.

Rising from the stump, Ram pulled her into a half hug. It was the most affection she had ever received from the grouchy bear, but it was a comfort that she hadn't realized she had been missing over the past few days.

When Ram pulled away, he gave Romelo a pointed look that was laced with his expectations on how the buffalo should treat his niece.

With a grumble, he said, "I'll see you at the tent."

Sending the group a casual wave, Romelo led Katariya away from the Mufiki tribe's camp.

Out of the commotion and into the waning light of the campfires, the night sky lit up above them. The music stopped, but she could hear the faint sound of laughter, and the chirps of crickets growing louder in the suppressed noise of the celebration.

They walked in silence, mulling over the possibilities of the unknown until a cluster of lightning bugs danced around them, illuminating the path.

Reaching out, she pointed her finger at a flashing bug. The insect crawled into her hand, tickling its way up her arm.

"Have you ever caught lightning bugs?" Katariya asked, breaking the silence.

"Oh? You mean fireflies?" Romelo came to a halt. "Not since I was a child."

"You don't catch them with Kove?"

The slow, flickering glow of the lightning bugs was a beacon guiding the insects to their mates. As she watched them fly through the night sky, Katariya found herself wishing there was a similar beacon guiding her back to Amos.

"I've supervised trips away from the herd to catch a few, but no, it's been a long time since I've caught one myself."

He stared at her with wonder, as if she was something completely out of the ordinary.

"It's one of the simplest acts of childhood joy. They're everywhere, lighting our path just as much as the moon and the stars." She let go of the bug, letting it flutter away.

Romelo stepped forward to grab the insect, but the minuscule creature had a mind of its own and landed on the tip of his nose. The sensation of the bug's little legs tickled his skin, causing him to let out a rumbling sneeze, blowing the creature into the night sky.

They looked at the bug spiraling through the air, then looked at one another. There was a soft glow on his face and a painful stretch in her cheeks.

There was excitement and a sliver of joy that caused Katariya to burst into laughter. A full-bellied laugh that had her keeling over, pulling both of them down into the tall grass.

As they collapsed, a layer of dust lifted, coating their lunges. The unexpected fit of coughs had them laughing again, rolling around in the grass until they settled beside one another, staring at the twinkle of dancing bugs and many stars.

When the air had settled into a quiet hush, Romelo was the one to break the silence.

"Can you tell me about Tulamund? Your brother barely talks about it."

Katariya hesitated for a second, thinking about everyone who wanted to hurt her because of her lioness's spirit. As angered as she was at the king, she couldn't deny the beauty of her home.

Breathlessly, she said, "It's magnificent, really. The waterfall rains down from the heavens, and everything is lush and green along the river. You can get anywhere in the city through the light rapids, and it's even faster after a heavy rain."

"Different from the greenery here?" he asked, his deep, rumbling voice smooth with curiosity.

"Yes, oh my, you can grow anything in Tulamund. Nearly every tree and bush bears fruit, and everywhere, even the highest mountains, are vibrant and filled with life."

"It sounds like a great place to grow up."

His voice drifted away as though he were picturing it just as vividly as she could remember.

"It is. There are different species, too. The Mufiki have so many species of antelope, plenty of carnivores, but no apes," she said, recalling the way the herd moved as one.

There was a blend of shifters, but the tree dwellers were absent from the herd.

"The plains don't appeal to them like the trees in Tulamund do. The rocky bends of Sandstone call to a few apes, but I expect many of their spirits long to be born within your city."

"I've only really known one gorilla, and all he talked about was bananas. I doubt the fruit would even grow here," she replied, thinking of how quickly bananas would brown under the sun's direct rays.

"No, no bananas here."

Katariya turned her head to the side, her cheek brushing against the rough grass.

"I don't think I've ever had one," Romelo admitted.

His crooked nose crinkled his piercing, and his eyes furrowed as his mind searched for a memory that wasn't there.

"Well, they aren't the sweetest fruit, but they will fill you up. My Ma always liked to feed us bananas when we were having stomach problems. They do a lot for muscle cramps and wonders for an upset stomach," she said with confidence.

"You seem to know a lot about the benefits of our food."

As Romelo glanced back, a soft smile spread across his lips when he noticed her eyes on him.

Normally, Katariya would have been embarrassed, but as he studied her features, she felt herself warming under his heated gaze. Inside, her beast was purring, comforted by the soft jade glow.

"It's the antelope way of life. My siblings and I had a good thing going. Dreams of running the shop ourselves. My sister, Sade, can tell you anything and everything about each herb. Amos was mostly in charge of the harvest, and while I can tell you a little bit about the health benefits, I was more confident in the flavors. I can't tell you how many tea and spice blends I have crafted over the years."

He nodded. "Our way of life has always been nomadic, but the introduction of different methods of farming has been beneficial. I never thought I'd see the day where there was a successful harvest in the desert."

The mention of Amos and the work he was doing in Sandstone piqued her interest, but once Katariya started on the topic, she would never stop.

"Can you tell me about Amos?"

How was it he could conquer his beast? What was their plan for maintaining Katariya's lioness when the effects of the blue lotus wore off? She wanted to know their strategy, but on a deeper level, she wanted to know everything about Amos. She cared little for his accomplishments of war, but rather she wanted to know her brother's friendships, his loves, his passions.

Romelo's voice was like a gentle breeze as he spoke.

"What do you want to know?"

"I—" She didn't know where to start. "I want to know everything."

He pondered her words and said, "I found him chained up inside a cave, just days after the storms ended."

"Chained up?" Her voice wavered.

"Tulamund's king left him that way. Unable to transform and without food or water. Left for dead."

King Cairo claimed he had given her brother an opportunity to live but chaining him up proved otherwise. It wasn't the king's mercy that spared Amos's life, but rather it was Romelo and the Mufiki tribe who, by fate, happened upon him mere hours before his death.

"How did you know that the blue lotus and valerian root would work?"

"We hoped. At first it was just the valerian root, but with your brother's efforts, he found that blue lotus worked in similar ways. It took almost a full year before Amos found a blend to ease his cravings."

"What I don't understand is how he became the leader of Sandstone. I was taught lies about the tribes of the Outlands. I see that now, but I have also seen men come back from war mutilated by a crazed animal. How did he cure their raging beasts?"

Sandstone had always been so far away that she had never worried about the threats herself, but Katariya knew the stories. The damage that Malau caused in Scout and Tatu's tavern was tame compared to the bodies that returned to Tulamund after a long battle. The hyena may have lost an arm, but the savages of Sandstone were known to devour their victims. Even with the power of her lioness, Katariya still feared the Sandstone shifters.

"When his beast roared, it controlled those who had been lost to their animals for many years." Romelo sucked in a deep breath that exhaled into a wordless sigh. "It was amazing, really. Shifters who'd been stuck as their animals for decades suddenly transformed back into their human bodies. It took a while to make the cure, but once we had enough, we could distribute it among the herds. In just two years, your brother has made a drastic change in desert life."

Katariya never imagined Amos to rule over the savages, but all he ever wanted was to make a difference. He was a leader, and amid his own suffering, he created a miracle.

"What's he like now? Has he found himself a wife? A child?" So much time had passed, anything was possible.

"No, not at all. He doesn't have the time." Romelo rolled to his side, facing Katariya. "He was seeing a wolf girl for a while—a little black minx. Oh boy, she was *trouble*."

Amos had always been the center of attention, and he had a particular fondness for strong-willed women. It was no shock that Amos found someone who shared his passionate spirit, but the exact words Romelo used rattled her mind.

"You said, *was*. What happened?"

"I don't know." Romelo shrugged his shoulders. "They used a little fun to let off some steam."

Katariya crinkled his nose and he snickered. "Even with the blue lotus, he was a bit of a hothead the first season."

"I'm sorry—I—I think I'm just a bit shocked." Katariya laughed in disbelief. "I can't seem to imagine a world in which the goddesses hadn't chosen me to marry the prince."

He subtly nodded. "Things are different here. Mating season brings us together, sometimes not by choice, but by nature. We huddle through the winter, mate through the spring, and by summer, some of us stay bonded, while others go their separate ways."

"And the man earlier with the two women?" Katariya's cheeks reddened at the memory of the intimate moment.

"That could be just about anyone."

His words made her eyes widen even more.

"I'm talking about the bushbuck hanging out near my tent," she admitted, her face turning a deep, beet red.

"Like I said, that could be anyone." He shrugged. "There is no judgment here. I know they call us savages. They say we are lost to the beast, but no, we are one with our animals."

Katariya couldn't imagine loving anyone other than Prince Zahir. Their fates had been intertwined since her birth.

The thought of having a crush—of kissing anyone other than him, had never crossed her mind before. She knew what her obligations and duties were to him—to her family—to the kingdom. Yet when the moment unfolded, she savored the heat that burned inside her as their lips met.

As she looked at Romelo, heat warming her cheeks, she wondered if the feeling was a product of her own desire, or had it been brought on by the desire of the beast?

She asked a question that she wasn't sure she, nor her lioness, wanted to know the answer to. "And you? A man who guides a thousand shifters. How many mates do you have?"

"None that have been serious. Like your brother, there is too much pressure and not enough time. Helping him save those who are lost to the spirit has been enough for now. That is where my heart is."

Slowly, a soft smile escaped her lips, one that did not go unnoticed by the tribe leader. Trying to hide her excitement, she pried, "But surely you have entertained the idea of your future."

With sparkling eyes, Romelo assured her, "As leader of the Mufiki tribe, I can only hope that the title will be passed down to my son, but only if he has earned it. We battle for the right. There is no push for legacy among the Outland tribes. If I am fortunate to find a woman I love, then I'd say I only picture one—one woman. With more wives come more children, and as much as I love Kove, she is a handful. I couldn't imagine multiple, especially not at the same time."

"Oh goddess—I didn't even think about that."

"Yeah," he chuckled. "One of my commanders, Dreynor, has twenty-three children all under the age of the gift. The poor man has to weave four tents together to fit them all in."

Horrified by the idea, she shook her head, then turned to the side to face him. "Oh, no. That is not the life for me."

"Yeah. Me either," he whispered.

His own jades danced around the features of her face. They weren't children. He wouldn't point out her freckles or her frizzled, unruly curls, but adults had their own way of judgment through pointed looks and crinkled noses.

Staring at one another, she found that his face softened just as much as hers did. When she took in his piercing, his crooked nose, and the scar running through his left brow, she saw a fighter, a leader, a brave older brother and son. His outer form was ridged from a lifetime of hardship and war, but in his softening irises she saw a man who loved his sister, was proud of his tribe's culture and cared deeply for her brother.

He was handsome, ruggedly so. Much different from the prince, but handsome, nonetheless.

Her breath caught in her chest as Romelo's gaze dropped to their hands. Her fingertips fell inches short of touching his own, and they trembled as if they were desperate to move closer.

Clearing his throat, he said, "What about you? If you weren't expected to marry the prince, what would you do?"

Katariya paused, taking a moment to consider the idea.

"I've never thought of my heart loving another. My only concern the past few years has been finding Amos. Sure, I've enjoyed the company of the prince, but would I still pick him, if given the choice? I—I'm not really sure."

"And when you say enjoyed the company of the prince? Does that mean you kissed him, kitten?" he asked with a devious smile.

The nickname made her feel delicate and dainty—*womanly*. It made her heart flutter and her palms sweat.

"Yes. The prince and I had a few—heated moments."

"And have you ever thought about kissing anyone else?"

His eyebrows rose in curiosity. He dropped his hand down, his fingertips lightly grazing hers before pulling them away.

Not until today, but she didn't dare utter the words aloud. His jades flashed to a look of desire, longing, and wonder.

"I don't know—I have a lot of new feelings and changes. Even with my beast, I still feel—"

She turned to look at the night sky.

"Still feel what?" Romelo's hand grasped hers, weaving his fingers through the crevices of her own.

Heat flared through her, and the word slipped from her lips in a breathless moan, trailing off the tip of her tongue.

"Desire."

Katariya had spent hours staring at her reflection in the water's surface, in sheets of metal, and in crystal edges. She created little patterns, constellations in the dots that scattered across her face. As his eyes darted around, with a look of inquisition, she wondered if he too had found a formation, much like one does when they were gazing at the night sky.

"Am I tempting you, kitten? Does your beast wish to prey upon me? I am the largest in my tribe, but I'm not so sure your lioness could take me down."

He was taunting her, searching for a reaction. She could handle his playful dance, but she could not ignore the call of his scent. A hint of nutmeg, bathed in orange.

Overwhelmed by his aroma, Katariya pounced. She pinned him to the ground beneath her, similar to the experience in the palace gardens, except this time, she was the one on top. Katariya was the one in control.

Romelo's body, although three times as large as hers, succumbed to the onslaught of her wandering hands as they molded against his form. She was lost to the passion, lost to the mindlessness of the heated moment.

The elixir she was taking was supposed to keep her beast under control, however, when he moved closer to kiss her, the lion pushed its way through her mind. The wild cat was ready to remind him that she was the huntress, and he was prey.

In an instant, her body was tearing through her dress, and in place of her human form was the lioness, weighing down her victim. To her surprise, her beast did not attack.

Romelo's eyes were sunken, but he did not have the scent of fear or the visible tremble that came with the anticipation of death. His response wasn't what the beast expected, nor what she craved.

With a low growl, her lioness dug its paws into his chest while taking a slow lick of a tongue against his throat. Her actions caused her victim to whimper, but the sound was coated with desire and settled in with the biting pain of her deadly claws.

In the most intoxicating moan, Romelo said, "I need you to come back, kitten. I don't think we are ready for this."

Katariya laughed in the back of the beast's mind while her lioness stared at him in confusion, teetering in and out of control. He wasn't scared. Not an ounce of fear rippled through his bones.

As her eyes flashed from the light golden brown of her beast to the ever-changing hazel of her human body, Romelo saw the opportunity to reach Katariya through her animal.

"Come back to me, Wild Kat."

The childhood nickname forced Katariya to the front of her mind, allowing her to move past her beast. With a few grunts of pain, accompanied by the retching sounds of bones crunching, Katariya found herself naked, cradled in Romelo's arms.

"Thanks for coming back. Until we get your dosages sorted out, I'm afraid that this thing between us, whatever it may be, is going to have to wait."

He let out a gentle laugh, despite the fact that he had almost been ripped apart by her beast.

A pang of guilt hit Katariya. Marrying the prince was no longer an option, but her heart swelled with the thought of him. One moment she could picture Zahir and the caramel glow of his eyes and in the next breath, she was shivering as Romelo ran a hand up and down her arm.

After a few moments, he released her, and she used the remnants of her clothing to cover up.

"I'm sorry—" they both said at the same time.

He stared at her with bewilderment. "You're sorry? Why are you sorry?"

"I shouldn't have done that. I am bound to the prince, my fate commanded by the king and sanctified by the goddesses!" Katariya backed away.

"You don't have to—"

"Romelo, I could have gotten you killed!" she yelled, walking toward the camp.

Saying it out loud did nothing to calm her spirit. Here she was again, just seconds away from crumbling under the beast's power.

Romelo didn't hesitate to storm after her. "No, no. You can't apologize for that. It's not your fault. I am well aware of how overwhelming it is for new shifters, and I have witnessed your brother's own struggles firsthand. I shouldn't have—"

"No, you don't understand." Katariya spun around to face him. "I don't even know you, and I'm throwing myself at you. This isn't me."

With a look of pity that only fueled her anger, he shook his head and said, "No, this one's on me. I should have known better than to spark interest in your beast."

Reaching up to tuck a curl behind her ear, his hand grazed her cheekbone. He shook his head in disbelief, as if his hands had acted of their own accord, and instantly let them rest at his sides. Without breaking eye contact, Romelo moved to create space between them.

"I know it doesn't feel like freedom yet, but I promise you, soon you will be reunited with your brother, and he can help you gain full control of your lioness."

"I want to believe you, but the king will come looking for me. Whether he finds the truth of my lioness or not, he will come for me. Everything Amos has worked for will be ruined."

He shook his head and inched closer. "We'll take it one day at a time. Your brother and his followers have the support of the Mufiki tribe and many other tribes who reside in the Outlands. The king does not stand a chance against us all. You feel the weight on your shoulders now, but let the universe take care of it. Trust that everything will be alright."

Katariya felt powerless, but if Amos had mastered the gift, then he could help her do the same.

She was determined to fulfill her destiny. She would fight for her lioness's pride, for the choice of free will, and for the shifters that her brother rescued from the grips of their wild beasts. Katariya would settle for nothing less than the greatness she deserved.

Her future was crafted from her parents, her past, and the whispers of the wild that came from a prophecy in the wind. Taking the foundations of what good graces the goddesses had already given her, she would mend them into own dreams, wishes, wills, and desires.

"Kat—are you okay?"

His words broke her out of her revelations.

"I'm sorry, I'm fine. I just—I shouldn't have touched you."

They were walking side by side, his frame towering over her.

"It was my fault. I was taunting the beast, but I don't regret it. I have never had someone rile my spirit in such a way." He chuckled softly, jade eyes gleaming down at her.

"Oh, and how about the part where I almost clawed through your chest and into your heart?" Katariya asked, playfully nudging her shoulder into his side.

"Oh well, you have to know from my reaction that your claws were the best part." He winked and strutted away, leaving her to pick up her dropped jaw and chase after him.

On their way back, she bombarded him with endless questions about the Outlands, the Mufiki tribe, Sandstone, and her long-lost brother. After the seventh or eighth question, she started to sound like Malau, so she let the stillness of the night settle around them as they walked to their tents.

CHAPTER 30

Do not fight a lion if you are not one yourself.
- African Proverb

Over the course of a week, Katariya developed a new routine. Early in the mornings, she collected wood and brush for fires, stirred pots, and washed linens. In the afternoons, she practiced fighting with Talla, and when she could track down her uncle, Katariya would find him eating, sleeping, or swindling a shifter for a shiny ring or a sharp weapon. In the evenings, they sang songs, played games, and danced. They danced so much that Katariya had to give herself foot massages in order to survive the long days of travel.

She spent most of her free time with Kove and Raina, but every few nights, Romelo would accompany the girls on a peaceful walk back to the tents. They would share stories, and Kove would stare with a childlike wonder that Katariya wasn't sure she ever had.

The elixir helped sate the lioness, but she felt herself growing restless. Impatient more than anything, knowing she was just days away from seeing her brother.

This morning started like any other, with the sound of clinking glassware stirring her from a semi-restful slumber. Ram was already gone, but Talla stood in the corner of the tent preparing another dose of the blue lotus flower.

The tiniest rustle of Katariya's blanket had Talla spinning around with a not so quiet exclamation.

"Good, you're finally awake. Romelo sent most of the herd to ride ahead, but we should be able to catch up to them if we leave soon. I'm gonna need you up and ready in ten minutes."

Katariya wiped the sleep away from the corner of her eyes.

"How long have I been sleeping?"

"A while, but it's fine. Chief wanted an early start to the day, so he sent a team of scouts ahead. We'll take up the rear and catch up in no time."

Talla poured hot water on the top of the herbs and gave Katariya a pointed glare.

"When the elixir is done brewing, meet me outside. Your uncle's already bugging the elders for more sweet bread, but I'll make sure he comes to help you take down the tent."

Without waiting for Katariya's reply, Talla exited. Beside the seeping elixir lay the Mufiki tribe's traditional cloth apparel, two small wraps used to cover up her intimate areas. Despite her initial reservations, Katariya realized by day two that the thin clothes were necessary when the shifters transformed into their animal spirits multiple times throughout the day.

All at once, multiple screams erupted from the field. Katariya's growing familiarity with her lioness's abilities allowed her to hear the quick rustle of tents and blankets, the urgent commands to arm the fighters, and the grunts from Mufiki warriors as they transformed into their Animalia spirits. Without a second thought, Katariya grabbed her bow and the remaining arrows and exited the tent.

The scene outside was just as chaotic as it sounded. Mufiki tribe members frantically ran with weapons in hand and panic in their eyes. Tents were pulled down, wagons were filled, and those yet to receive their Animalia gifts distanced themselves from the action.

"Attack! We're under attack!"

Talla came running, eyes darting back and forth as she yelled commands to the warriors.

Katariya didn't know where to go. She didn't know what to do, but she clenched her bow and waited for direction.

Talla grabbed Katariya by the arm. "Princess, you need to go. Follow the children!"

Katariya scoffed. "Absolutely not. I'm not a child anymore. I have my gift, and I want to help."

The female warrior rolled her eyes. "Yes, I understand the need to feel heroic, but you can't shift."

"No, but I have my bow and arrow. I'm a skilled archer, I swear!"

Talla wasn't listening to her, busy directing the crowd to either safety or toward the battle. Katariya tried to follow one of the warriors but was yanked back by Talla's firm hold.

As Katariya spun around, she tumbled backward, falling into the tent. A loud crash emerged from inside.

Talla's eyes widened, and she groaned. "Please tell me you already took the elixir."

Katariya's face said it all.

"No, no, no, this is so reckless."

Talla dropped her weapons and took Katariya by the arms.

"Look, Princess, the king's warriors are here. They are looking for you. Get on a wagon and leave with the rest of the herd. We have more than enough fighters to take them on. Leave now, before the action awakens your beast. Leave before you hurt someone."

Katariya felt powerless to help. Unwanted and a danger to the rest of the tribe. It was becoming hard to ignore the distant panicked screams, the deep grunts of warriors, and the snarls and brays. It was too much. Too bright outside. Too loud. Was Talla right? Would her beast truly hurt someone?

Talla pushed Katariya into the crowd. The stampede of shifters forced her to follow them to safety. Traveling away from the fight, she bumped shoulder to shoulder with the herd until she reached the wagons filled with children.

Surrounding the wagons, young men and women who were younger than her stood guard with spears in hand. Katariya looked on with jealousy, embarrassed to sit among children when she could be fighting alongside the other shifters.

When she chose the lioness, she chose power over fear, but was she actually ready to fight? Could she take the life of another? The beast inside her stirred, excited by the idea of a battle, but if someone struck her, would it be enough to spark the fire that would ignite her lioness?

Accidentally killing a member of the Mufiki tribe was not something Katariya could live with. So instead of running to join the battle, she turned to one of the many crying children and tried to calm them down.

As soon as they moved, the buffalo pulling the wagon let out a painful grunt. The dreadful sound curdled into a shriek, and the wagon fell backward. An arrow wedged deep inside the buffalo's shoulder forced the shifter back into his human form.

Panic ensued as the children dove for cover, finding shelter behind the wagons and jagged rocks. Katariya moved to go with them but hesitated as she saw a blur of movement on the hillside.

One of the king's warriors, camouflaged by the dense rock and brush, shot arrows into the crowd. A tiny figure barreled toward the warrior, but he was too busy making sure no wagons could escape to notice the attacker.

Faint notes of citrus filled the air, similar to the scent she associated with Romelo. Hoping off the wagon, Katariya crouched down, shuffling closer toward the hill.

From the vista, she could see Romelo's fearless little sister advancing on the warrior. Taking her chances, Katariya shot an arrow and held her breath as it flew across the battlefield.

A miss, but still worth it.

The warrior looked across the field, searching for another archer. The Mufiki tribe didn't use bows, and Katariya could tell he hadn't expected the attack.

With the warrior distracted, Kove closed the distance, using a forceful blow to stab her spear into his right shoulder. His cries echoed off the hillside, and Katariya ran to join the fight.

The attacker took some damage, but the hit was not enough to slay the warrior. Enraged by the pain, the man abruptly transformed into a snarling leopard.

Surprised, but determined, Kove readied her spear.

As brave as the girl wanted to be, Katariya could see the fear in her eyes as the wild cat stalked his prey. With full focus, she drew back her bow, and with the intention of saving the girl, Katariya took the life of another. A gasp left both of the girls' mouths as the leopard fell to the ground.

Katariya took no time to feel remorse. She needed to get them to safety. Ripping out the arrow, she took Kove by the arm and barreled down the hill and away from the fight.

"What were you thinking?" Katariya yelled.

"I just wanted to help. You've seen me fight! I am just as good as the older girls," Kove wailed, stumbling down the hill.

There was no time to argue; more of the king's warriors had noticed the hillside battle. No longer thinking like the princess of Tulamund, Katariya moved at the speed of a Mufiki tribe shifter.

"Kove, go! You need to get out of here!" she yelled, witnessing the gruesome sight of shifters fighting below.

Carnivores bashed into the necks of herbivores. Herbivores stomped their hooves into their opponents' chests. The clash of swords, the deep grunts of pain, and shrills of the scared children merged to mimic the sound of death.

With her adrenaline spiked, Katariya's beast ached to be released. Her lioness wanted to challenge the shifters who frightened the young Mufiki girl, but getting Kove to safety outweighed her desire to shed blood.

Most of the children had already escaped, protected by a strong group of Mufiki fighters. The wagons were loaded, and many of the others were already on the route to safety. Katariya needed to get across the cleaning and get Kove onto a wagon.

"Stay low and stay alert," Katariya demanded.

The command of her lioness was on the tip of her tongue. The young girl's rattling fear slithered away and was replaced by the need to comply with Katariya's wishes. The mouthy, brave girl followed her with no hesitation.

Crouching low, Kove held her spear up as they moved through the grasses. They would receive no relief. Running toward them was a group of Tulamund warriors, swords in their hands, ready to take on a fight. The warriors paused as though they recognized Katariya, but still, they continued their advance.

Katariya didn't want more bloodshed on her hands, but as Kove peered from behind her, their faces changed as though they saw the little girl as a threat.

Would they hurt a child? They didn't hesitate to shoot at a wagon filled with women and children.

The risk of death weighed heavily on Katariya's shoulders. Positioning her stance, she pulled back her bowstring and shot down her enemies, but the more arrows she released, the closer the warriors seemed to get, their battle cries echoing around her.

Pushing Kove backward, Katariya pleaded, "I'm running out of arrows. I need you to run as fast as you can. Head to the clearing and get on a wagon."

"No—I can fight! You saw what I did. I can fight. I swear!"

Kove's words were courageous, but her voice trembled with a mixture of fear that was masked by her adrenaline. Katariya felt the same.

"Kove, please. I know you want to help, but the younger kids need you. They need someone to help them feel brave. I will be right behind you. I promise."

Kove's eyes were conflicted, darting back and forth between the two scenes. In the distance, wagons were already on the move, directing everyone to safety.

"Fine. I'll go protect them."

The brave little warrior sounded hopeful as she ran away from Katariya and listened to the command.

CHAPTER 31

AND THE MOMENT YOU ARE UNAFRAID OF
THE CROWD, YOU ARE NO LONGER A SHEEP,
YOU BECOME A LION. A GREAT ROAR ARISES
IN YOUR HEART, THE ROAR OF FREEDOM.
- OSHO, COURAGE: THE JOY OF LIVING
DANGEROUSLY

With her last arrows, Katariya helped the young girl get to safety, but as soon as Kove was out of eyesight, a loud shriek wailed from behind the rocky bend.

"Get off of me!"

Prince Zahir held Kove in a deadly grip.

"Where is the princess? Where is Katariya?" Zahir yelled, shaking her. "You smell just like her."

There were too many scents and too much commotion to focus on a particular smell. Even her own beast searched for the familiar scent of juniper berries and could barely distinguish his smell from Kove's notes of citrus.

The brave little warrior was not a complacent child. She kicked and screamed and tried her best to bite his arms, but she was no match for the prince.

"You scent me because I am here, Zahir. Let her go." Katariya's command raged from deep inside her beast.

"Little cub," Zahir whispered, releasing Kove.

He was dressed in gold armor with a sword strapped to his waist belt. His hair was braided, and his skin glistened in the sun's bright rays. Despite his initiated attack, Katariya could feel his aura mix with hers. A pull between their beasts that she didn't entirely understand.

With an aura that matched her own, there was no doubt that the prince was a powerful leader and a ferocious carnivore, but did the jaguar match the strength of her lioness?

"Katariya—Oh thank goddess, I found you. Are you okay? Have they harmed you?"

Zahir had been careless when he let Kove go. Distracted, he failed to see the fearless girl reaching for her spear.

"Kove—don't!"

It was too late. The girl's spear was out of her hand, flying toward Zahir.

With the speed of a wild cat, the prince turned, grasping the handle of the spear moments before the jagged edge stabbed his neck. Turning, he stalked toward the child, casting a shadow over her small frame.

"Kove, go find your brother!" Katariya yelled.

Picking up a rock, Katariya threw it at Zahir's shoulder, and his orange-hued eyes flashed red. If he was going to get mad, she'd provoke his anger at her, not Kove.

The child's wide eyes darted back and forth between them. For once, the ruthless child was smart enough to know when her battle was lost and sprinted in the opposite direction.

"Did you know that blue lotus flowers can control the rage?" Katariya asked in an attempt to break the tension.

Startled by her abruptness, Zahir stared at her as though she had two heads. His breathing slowed before it turned into a chuckled sigh.

"It's not uncontrollable rage. I almost got hit with a spear by a child. *A child*. They have children fighting their own battles. I don't need an herb to calm down my beast. I need this madness to end. I need to take you home."

"Home? That palace is not home." Katariya shook her head. "Tulamund can't be home for me anymore, not with what I have become."

"Tulamund is your home, and the palace will soon feel like it, too. I don't understand why you are here. I know the pressures of my father more than anyone, but why would you run away from your duty? From the prophecy? From me?"

His voice broke as the angry orange of his eyes settled into a caramel brown.

"You fled, but I will not allow my father to consider it as treason. You can come back. Come back to me. To Sade. To your parents. It's not too late, Katariya."

Zahir tried to close the distance between them, but she pushed her last arrow against his chest.

"Don't come any closer."

He ignored her warnings as he walked forward until the arrow dug into the exposed skin between his armor.

"Just tell me why? Why are you fighting among the savages? Have they already tainted your good heart?"

"They aren't savages, Zahir. The shifters here might differ from the tribes in Tulamund, but they are not bloodthirsty beasts. There is no disparity between the carnivores and herbivores. The herd is one. It's beautiful, really. Everything that I hated about Tulamund does not exist here."

"But they are unruly beasts! You have seen my warriors return from war, torn apart until you can't even identify their faces. How can you tell me they aren't savages?"

"They aren't. Not anymore. The blue lotus. It helps calms the beast, and Amos—"

"So, this is about your brother." He shook his head. "I told you I had a plan. When I become king, I will allow him to return to our kingdom."

"That's not what I want, and it's not what my brother needs. He has been cured by the flower, and the Sandstone shifters are freed from the rage of their beasts. He saved them, Zahir. He saved their spirits."

Zahir looked as though he refused to believe her.

"No—you are confused. There is no way to help the savages. We spare the wicked by sending them to Sandstone, but there is no saving them from losing their minds."

"There is a way to save them. I promise you. I have taken the elixir myself, and I know it works."

Her eyes searched his own in desperation, pleading for him to reason with the truth.

"You needed medicine to calm your beast? What—what are you?" He wrinkled his nose as he tried to scent her. "What have you become?"

Her mouth fell open as she tried to find the right words. If he found out the truth, would he care enough to let her go? Would he defy his father's wishes, or would he kill her upon confession?

They had spent their entire lives dancing around their duty and obligation to one another. When they were alone, there was a fire that pulled them together, much like the fates had determined. Their kiss was passionate, but was the heated moment enough for him to go against the throne? Could he turn against his father and his duty to protect his city from their greatest known threat?

"I need the medicine, Zahir. I can't—"

He pressed even closer to the arrow, barely wincing as it pushed into his skin.

"Katariya, just tell me. I promise I won't—"

He tried to plead, but his promise was cut short as Uncle Ram barreled into the prince, knocking him backward. Unprepared for the attack, Zahir scrambled to remove his armor. It took longer than the Mufiki's cloth wraps, but in moments, he was free to transform into his jaguar.

His beast was comparable in size to his father, but the rosettes that decorated his tawny fur were dense in the center of his forehead. The pattern created the shape of an upside triangle or a loose depiction of a heart. He was as glorious as Katariya always thought he would be.

The bear and the jaguar circled one another in a dance before they descended into a clashing battle. Ram used his excessive weight and powerful stance to ram into the jaguar. Zahir took a different approach, jumping through the air, paws and jaws stretched wide. His claws raked through her uncle's thick brown fur.

"No! Stop! Zahir, please!" Katariya wailed.

A pained grunt escaped the bear, but Ram continued to fight. Katariya didn't want to see either of them killed, but if she transformed, she wasn't confident that her beast wouldn't kill them both.

With the angry snarls of Zahir's jaguar, his beast drew his claws into the bear's back, pinning him down.

Katariya yelled her protests, but it did nothing to stop the jaguar from sinking his teeth into the bear's shoulder.

A loud roar stole the rest of her uncle's resilience. Beaten and broken, the animal shifted, and the jaguar stood over her uncle, watching the shifter struggle.

"Leave him alone!" Katariya yelled, but Zahir was too blinded by rage to see reason.

A combination of the blood, anger, and fear fumbled into a burning chaos. Red flashed over her eyes, a fire that she never felt before. She didn't just see red; she saw blood.

With great might, Katariya's lioness let out a ground rumbling roar. The commotion of the battle came to a halt, and Prince Zahir stood frozen in the middle of his next attack.

Advancing on the jaguar, her lioness pounced, using her claws to throw the spotted beast off of her uncle. Her lioness didn't instill the same fear as her brother's lion, but it's not the lion who makes the kill but the pride of lionesses.

The force of the throw snapped the jaguar out of her control. Their eyes danced as the two impossibly large wild cats studied each other's movements.

The humans inside them saw one another underneath the fur and sharp, pointed teeth. The soft touches, heated gazes, and the obligations they had for one another lingered between them, but there was loss and longing mirrored in their expressions.

No matter how much he thought of her as his, Zahir could not keep her. He could not change the outcome of her goddess-given gift.

The shifters of Tulamund would never let the lions back into the city. They would never accept her for who she truly was, and because of that, he needed to make a decision.

Fight her now and end it all, or let her go and face the wrath of his father.

Without breaking eye contact, Zahir transformed again and studied the wild cat. Disbelief was written across his face, but he could scent her. He knew her spirit.

"Katariya—how?"

As he closed the distance, she failed to hear the swoosh of an arrow flying through the air. The tipped stone head landed deep within the shoulder of her four-legged beast.

"No, oh goddess, no."

Zahir did not hesitate. He ran to Katariya despite his fear and pulled her into his arms.

Battling between the dark spots that flashed across her eyes, Katariya teetered between the here and now, the in-between and the afterlife. She was so close to a mended heart. So close to her brother and yet, the arrow, the very thing that brought Katariya and Amos together, was wedged inside her shoulder, inches from her heart.

She could barely find the energy to open her eyes, but through the small slits, she could see Zahir's orange-hued gaze. The irises dazzled with a warmth that she hadn't noticed before.

A distinct, booming voice yelled from behind Zahir, followed by the sound of shuffling feet and heavy breathing.

"What have I done? I saw the lioness and I—" The elephant wailed, running to the prince's side. "My princess, I'm so sorry. Oh goddess, please forgive me."

Katariya let out a surprised, airy gasp. *Bron.* Bron shot her with an arrow.

The smell of her own blood mixed with the metallic smell of Ram's and the other shifters fighting nearby. Even through the pain and overpowering smell, she could still make out the wafting scent of sweet oranges.

"Get off of her," Romelo yelled, his voice roaring with a command that made her feverish body tremble.

All at once, Katariya felt a wave of hot and cold. The sweat on her face dripped into her eyes and she blinked over and over again to get rid of the salty burn.

Zahir did not ease the tight grip he had on her. Instead, the buffalo leader's words caused him to pull her closer.

The sight of the elephant should have been enough to dissuade the buffalo from his pursuit, but the Mufiki leader was ruthless. His fist collided into Bron's stonewalled chest, and the two shifters hit one another until they were bloody and bruised.

"Make them stop—please make them stop," Katariya begged, but her words were lost, floating between the void of love and loss.

Zahir's eyebrows furrowed, and his plump lips froze in a tight line. He stared right at her, but he wasn't *seeing* her.

"Romelo! Please stop!"

The sound of her voice was enough to make the buffalo leader cease his fight. Soft jades met her hazel eyes. With his attention on her, Romelo failed to see Bron's fist crash against his face with a sickening crunch.

"Zahir." No response. "Zahir!" Flash of fiery orange.

Despite her condition, Zahir let the shock and disbelief take control, and he pushed her away. She tumbled onto the dirt ground, wincing as the arrow pushed deeper. His arms remained open as though he wanted to pull her back, but he remained frozen.

The prince's coldness was enough to make Bron and Romelo stop fighting. The buffalo leader moved to aid her, but Katariya held up a hand and snarled at him to keep him at a distance.

A hush fell over the crowd as they watched the intense stare down between Tulamund's jaguar prince and the former princess. The space between them was delicate. A single wrong move could set off the fury that simmered.

With the arrow stuck in her shoulder, Katariya wouldn't be able to shift, but if she removed it, her beast would emerge to heal the wound and combust in a fit of rage. The wild cat flickered behind her eyes, and every time Katariya took a deep breath, the snarl of her animal spirit echoed in her mind, thrumming against her eardrums.

If Prince Zahir took Katariya's life, the battle between the Outlands and the kingdom of Tulamund would never end. Amos would avenge her death, and he would hold himself accountable. Katariya was familiar with guilt, but she never stopped believing that her brother was still alive. Her death would destroy him.

Wincing with every step, Katariya closed the distance until the feathered end of the arrow pressed against Zahir's chest. "Are you going to kill me?"

The prince's eyes sank. The weight of her words pulled him out of his rage.

"Do it, Zahir. I am what your king fears. Kill me and end this now!"

Desperate sobs escaped her lips, and every staggered breath made her quiver. The weight of his body pressed against the arrow and pulsed against the tight muscle. A push or a fall forward would wedge the arrow straight into her heart.

"What—I can't kill you, Katariya." His eyes never strayed from hers.

"All I have to do is fall forward, and we can end this now." She wrapped her hand around the end of the arrow and placed the other on his chest, using him as support. "But I know you won't let that happen, Zahir. Your heart will not allow it."

"The prophecy binds you to me." He placed his hand over hers and his eyes flashed red. "Why would the goddesses deceive us this way?"

The prophecy was simple. *Protect the children of the night. Secure their tribe and stake their claim.*

Despite what the king and his priestess made it out to be, the decree held a completely new meaning to her. Katariya and Amos had a pride, an entire kingdom of shifters to save from the same madness they were burdened with.

The shuddering pain from the whisper of death was enough for Katariya to see that Zahir needed to make a choice. Would he let her go, or did the loyalty to his father outweigh his feelings for her? If she could change the prince's heart, Katariya and Amos would change so many lives. A new era.

"The prophecy is not a lie. It was your father who bound us together through marriage, but it was the goddesses who intertwined our lives for you to see reason."

"See reason? How am I to see reason when you are a lioness? Two hundred years ago, your beasts killed almost half of Tulamund. How am I to let you go when your brother has created an army that is destined to destroy us?"

Zahir was careful not to move despite the rage that burned inside. His shoulders slowly dropped as he reeled in his wild spirit, his eyes slowly transforming into a caramel glow.

Katariya needed him to see the truth.

"There is an elixir, a medicine that has changed the lives of the Animalia in Sandstone. I have taken it myself, and it works, Zahir. I am myself when the medicine runs through my veins. There is hope. Hope for my brother. Hope for me, but you have to let me go."

Standing made the blood rush to her head and caused Katariya to wobble forward. She took shallow breaths as her lungs grazed against the arrow, and his expression changed to deep concern.

With a shaky hand, her fingertips trailed against his cheekbone. In his eyes, she could see the mischievous boy she used to loathe, but even now, she couldn't bring herself to hate him.

"You are bound to me." She lowered her hand to his heart. "Our souls intertwined so that the lions could live."

His body grew rigid.

"You can't be serious. You always had a fire that drew me in, but I never thought you would become the very thing my father seeks to destroy."

"Our kiss was real, Zahir. Despite the fact that your father exiled my brother, I still see the good in you. The boy who helped spare my brother's life. You've been lost, jaded by the fear of your father, but I need you to hear my truths. I can live a normal life, but I need to be with the Outland tribes. I need to be with my brother."

Her sentiments settled his rage, and his touch turned into a tender hold. Reaching out, Katariya placed his hand on the arrow's long stem. Her life now resting in his hands.

"If I wasn't the child of greatness, your father would have never taken pity on my brother." She cupped his cheek. "Without the prophecy, you would have never cared for me. We never would have been able to care for one another. It might be a sick joke to the goddesses to mess with our hearts, but they wove our paths together so that you could see past my beast and into my soul. You know me, Zahir. We may never be together, but you will always be in my heart."

Her words created a spark, and his lips crashed against her own. It was thunderous, like lightning crackling at the peak of a storm. A fusion of pain, love, and loss combined into one heated kiss. A promise and a goodbye.

When Zahir pulled away, he searched her eyes for the fire he sought to return with him, but the fire was dwindling every second they wasted not attending to her wounds.

"Take care of Sade for me," Katariya whispered, turning to meet the stark blue eyes of Bron. The enormous man nodded, tears pooling at the corners of his eyes.

The spirit of the lioness was desperate to heal her dying flesh, but without the blue lotus, she was an uncontrollable nightmare. All of the king's warriors would be subject to her wrath, and anyone who made it out alive would run back to King Cairo to report on her destruction. Katariya knew of the king's ambition to eliminate Amos and his army, and she would not challenge that threat.

Katariya grew more and more desperate as her eyelids drooped with her waning consciousness.

"Romelo, tell Amos I love him. Don't—don't let him lose himself because of me."

Romelo's jade eyes dropped at the weight of the words laced with her last wishes.

Refusing to believe this was where her journey ended, Romelo barked at Zahir. "We need to bind her hands and pull out the arrow. If we get it out now, we may avoid infection. We'll give her an extra dose of the lotus, and hopefully the induced slumber will keep her alive until we make it back to her brother."

Romelo reached for Katariya, but the prince's arms only tightened around her.

"No—she's mine," Zahir snarled, flashing his teeth. "Just pull it out now. Let her shift. The lioness will heal her."

Fire and possession blazed in his intense gaze.

"Without the elixir, her beast will kill you," Romelo said.

Zahir's hands were still placed on the arrow. One quick pull or push could define her fate.

"So, give it to her! Give her the medicine."

Zahir shook in her arms, tears streaming down his face.

"We need more than just the elixir. We can't save her like this. We need to get the arrow out and get her to Sandstone as soon as possible. That is the only option." Romelo's eyes were sullen, and his voice was strained.

With her chest wheezing between every other word, Katariya croaked, "Let me go—or see me die."

With reluctance, Zahir carefully passed Katariya into Romelo's arms. His hand softly grazed her cheek as he took one more look at the girl he thought was destined to be his.

Katariya's eyes darted between the two men. The rich caramel of Zahir's bright eyes against his dark skin and the warm glow of Romelo's jade stones against his copper flesh. The carnivore and the herbivore. Two separate parts of herself, staring back at her with love and fear.

Closing her eyes, Katariya let the goddesses decide her fate. The prince made his decision. He chose her over his father, but it was now up to the Mufiki tribe to use her brother's elixirs to heal her wounds.

"Ropes. I need ropes," Romelo yelled.

Her hands were tightly bound. The bite of the ropes was numbing compared to the excruciating pain of the arrow as Romelo pulled it out of her tender flesh.

A low roar erupted from inside, followed by stifled chuffs. Katariya's eyes sparkled with dark spots that burst into a blinding light.

CHAPTER 32

REMEMBER WHO YOU ARE.
- MUFASA, DISNEY'S THE LION KING

An abyss. A void. The in-between the light and dark that could either consume her or spit her back into the world's impending chaos.

Katariya's lioness ran with purpose. Her claws tore into the dirt, and wind rippled through the tall grasses.

Was this the afterlife?

Prowling through a herd of wildebeest, the lioness bumped into a patch of hippos and flustered the feathers of ostriches. There was a gleaming light that covered her furred form and welcomed her into oblivion.

"It wasn't supposed to be this way."

Whipping her head to the side, Katariya looked for the source of the pulsing voice, yet all the creatures in the area remained oblivious to her presence.

"I should have fought harder."

Fought harder? Katariya had given the fight her all. She exuded a warrior's strength, and her actions were a testament to her might. It wasn't her lioness who triumphed above all, but rather it was Katariya who held the bow and arrow.

"I've got you all patched up. It's up to you now."

The voice was close to her, yet so far away.

Familiar, but changed.

It felt almost impossible to leave the plains and the ever-changing world that flashed around her. It was every-thing but somehow not enough. The good that outweighed the bad, like thunderstorms and a belly aching, full of sweets. A treasure and a curse.

The clinking sound of glass pulled her away from the abyss, but as soon as she was away, darkness closed around her, teetering back and forth.

"You made it this far. You can't give up."

Reemerging into the light, Katariya's lioness resurfaced in front of a rippling body of water. A current that matched that of an ocean, going on as far as the eye could see. Waves lapped the shoreline, but the shore lacked the dry sand and salty air. The mysterious body of water held an energy of a living essence, glowing like luminescent plankton.

Out of the shadows, a herd of antelope and a pride of lions materialized with huffing snouts and inquisitive gazes.

"You cannot give up, child."

The spirit's voice was a cadence that echoed around her, not quite human nor fully animal. The vibrations were a velvet glove, wrapping her in a quilt of bumps and chills.

"Who are you?"

Katariya tried to use her words, but they came out in a low roar that rumbled through her. The sound was foreign, but the spirits understood.

Stepping from the large herd was the elder gazelle, her nose adorned with a thin strip of white. The marking was reminiscent of the ancestor whose painting hung in her family's entry hall. Powerful hooves with a graceful frame, always on the move, never stagnant. Observant and focused. Agile and noble.

Standing beside the gazelle was a lioness with dark, golden fur. This spirit was someone she recognized, someone from her past—a person who would follow her in this life and every life after.

"We are those who guide you from beyond, and we have been lucky enough to bear witness to your tribulations. Katariya, spirit of the lioness, you never let the world weaken you. You have appreciated the worth of your ancestors from the realm of the living and the lands beyond. Only the great can take the words of our goddess and forge their own destiny. As a loved one says to you now, *it's up to you*. Breathe new life into something forgotten and rekindle the ambition. Wake up, Katariya. Wake up and rise above."

A Clink. A Crash. Her eyes fluttered open.

Awakening from the comatose slumber, she shook her stiff limbs, and they crackled as she regained mobility. The rattle of clinking glass and metal instruments came to a stop.

"Kat."

Her name sounded breathless out of his mouth. His voice had dropped an octave, and she couldn't tell if it was from the surprise of the reunion or if his voice had changed since she'd last heard it.

She was laid out on a cot in a small room filled with vials of roots and seeds, jars of herbs, and pots filled with seeping elixirs. There was an aromatic blend of lemongrass wafting from a simmering pot steaming over the fire.

Her shoulder ached, but there was no longer an arrow sticking out of her chest. The wound was already sewn tight. A protective layer of cloth lay over the gash, and there was a slight burn from the wet healing mixture lying underneath it.

The air grew heavy with the weight of their shared memories. Their gazes mirrored, and their bodies were still as if all of the missed time was suspended between them.

His curly chestnut hair was a wild, chaotic mane, but she imagined hers looked just as unruly. They were accustomed to braids, but there was something special about the way he looked when his hair was loose and free. He was the same person, yet his features seemed to have shifted with the desert heat and the acceptance of his Animalia gift.

His light golden skin kissed by the sun was now three shades darker. The freckles decorating his body had increased, covering every inch of his face, much like ones she had been born with.

When his shock subsided, his face transformed into a radiant smile with wide cheeks pushed up against his eyes. The sight of his beaming, toothy grin sent a wave of warmth through her. A feeling of comfort and control.

Inside, her lioness beamed, and a glow enveloped her beastly form. Katariya wasn't sure if they had given her something stronger than the blue lotus, or if her lioness felt settled with her pride. That was what the animal recognized him as.

Her pride, her family. Amos was here.

After years of being apart, Katariya's entire world was crashing, but this time, it collided with the fate she most desired. Amos threw his arms around her, and a fountain of tears stained his kaftan.

"Why are you crying? Did I hurt you?" Amos exclaimed.

He tried to pull away, but Kat grabbed his shoulders and pulled him back to her. The force of the pull caused him to graze her wound, but she held back her pain, only slightly wincing.

The pain was worth it. Without the comfort of his embrace, she was certain her brother would dissipate into the void.

Amos tried to wipe her tears away, but the more he attempted to soothe her, the faster the tears fell.

"It's okay. You're safe now. I'm here, Kat. I'm really here."

Every word vibrated through her.

"I just can't believe it, being here, *with you.*"

Kat's words were laced with disbelief and rough like sandstone. The dryness of her throat extended down her chest and caused her to break into a fit of hacking coughs. Immediately, Amos rushed to aid her, lifting a cup of tea to her pale, chapped lips.

As the warm liquid traveled down her throat, it caused the wound to pulse into a tremble of pain. Kat tried to hold back a reaction, but it did not go unnoticed by the person, who even after all this time, knew her better than anyone.

Pulling back the blanket, Amos carefully slipped the cloth away from her wound, exposing a row of dark, irritated stitches. His brow crinkled as he inspected the gash.

"Did you patch me up yourself?" Kat asked, studying his movements.

Chaotically, Amos sifted through cabinets and drawers. Jars, roots, and whole flower stems littered the counter, evidence of his apothecaries' constant work.

"No, I wish I was that skilled. Talla did it before she stitched up Uncle Ram."

Oh goddess. Ram. How could she have forgotten the injured bear?

"How—how is he? Is he okay? He has to be okay. I didn't mean for any of this to happen. No one else needed to be hurt. Oh goddess, please tell me he's alright," she rambled as more tears fell.

"Hey, hey, no more crying, Wild Kat. He'll be okay. No worse off than you are."

"And Romelo? Kove?" Her heart stopped, feeling as though it had skipped a beat.

"They are both fine. Kove is excited to see you, but Melo has her distracted working with Talla in the healing center."

Although his apothecary was unorganized and messy, he worked at speeds that resembled their mother. It was a confidence that could only be instilled from years of practice.

Yarrow, calendula, andiroba. The makings of a healing balm.

"Deaths. How many deaths?" Katariya held her breath.

"Very few casualties. Anyone not being healed by Talla has already been healed by their spirit. The Mufiki tribe has suffered worse losses at the hands of King Cairo."

Amos dabbed a light green substance over a warm, damp cloth. Placing the cloth over the wound, Kat gasped as the sting from the medicine seeped through her stitches. A new influx of pain wrapped around her aching guilt.

Amos gently wiped her nose as if she were a child in need of care. His actions made her mind flash back to a memory she thought she no longer had. A flashback of her in the arms of her three-year-old brother. His arms wrapped around her like a fortress, ready to sacrifice his life for hers. They were three years apart in age and had spent three years apart from one another but being together felt as though no time had passed between them.

"What are you thinking about?" Amos asked, his light golden eyes sparkling above her.

"You. *Us*." She paused. "Do you remember living here before? Do you remember our birth parents?"

The air stilled, as though he were trying to find the right words to say. Mindfully, he said, "When Pa brought us home, I could barely speak. I wouldn't eat. I wanted nothing to do with the antelope tribe. In my mind, we were here."

His eyes glanced around the room as though he were searching for the same scattered memory that haunted her.

"I—I could still feel her warm hugs, still hear her voice as an echo. I even sang her lullabies to you every night until Ma taught me the ones she would sing to Sade."

Amos wrapped her wound with tenderness, the gauze crinkling as he worked. When he was done, he laid the cloth and vial on the small table before taking her hand in his.

In his eyes, there was a gloss of pain, but it was distant. Nostalgia of the past that would be forgiven but never forgotten.

"I was an angry child, Kat. Nasty and spiteful until the day your prophecy was declared."

"The prophecy—"

She tried to speak, but her voice was still dry and weathered. To relieve her from another coughing fit, Amos held the teacup to her lips.

When her throat was soothed, she asked, "How did the prophecy change things?"

Amos stared into her eyes, his hand never leaving hers.

"The prophecy gave me hope. Our birth mother always said you were destined for greatness. 'Protect her, Amos; protect her with your life, and she will light your path. With your help, your sister will achieve greatness.' Those were her words: not mine, not the king's, not some prophecy declared by an old priestess."

A mudslide of emotions came tumbling down, but she wasn't sad. Kat felt a flutter of hope in her chest that was almost as optimistic as the gleam in her brother's eyes.

Over the past few weeks, Kat had reworked the prophecy's meaning many times. She grappled with the notion that she could determine her own destiny, regardless of the decree from the goddesses, regardless of King Cairo's demands.

Instead, the prophecy came from the faint whisper of a spirit from the great beyond. The spirit of her mother called with a cadence of a promise; her bones and flesh became one with the ground and soil, but her soul was alive with a whisper in the wild winds.

Without breaking eye contact, Amos grabbed her face with both hands, his eyes piercing into her shattered soul.

"We suffered for a reason. Everything that happened to us. From growing up in the antelope tribe, exile, and our forced time apart. It was all for a reason."

Kat stared wide-eyed at her brother, unsure if the words coming out of his mouth were how he truly felt, or if they were the start of a terribly morbid joke.

A reason. They suffered for a reason. Was he seeking penance, or was he still troubled by the lion's ruthless intent?

"How can you say that? How can you be so sure when we were robbed of our parents? Taken from the life that both of us have always longed for."

His voice rose with irritation. "We were loved, Kat. Above all circumstances and above all the bad things that could have happened to two lost children, the goddesses spared us. They gave us two loving shifters who went to the end of the world to protect us. Answer this. How many carnivores are brought up in herbivore tribes?"

"Not many," she answered, her eyebrows knitting together.

"From the start of our lives, Ma and Pa taught us to care for the land. From the trees and bushes to the ants and bees." He pulled his hands away, yet his eyes still held hers, undiminished in their intensity. "We learned from the best healer in the kingdom. It's Mama's herbs and spices that have calmed my beast. It is the antelope tribe that will save Sandstone."

CHAPTER 33

BELIEVE IN YOURSELF, AND THERE WILL
COME A DAY WHEN OTHERS WILL HAVE

NO CHOICE BUT TO BELIEVE WITH YOU.
- MUFASA, DISNEY'S THE LION KING

Taking the steaming pot off of the fire, Amos poured the boiling water into a glass container filled with a spectrum of herbs. The seeping liquid caused the blend to mix, filling the air with a medley of aromatic flavors. Kat sat in silence and studied him as he moved around the workstation. His intentions were reminiscent of their mother, but his movements were clunky with his lack of experience.

"How did you know the herbs would work?" Kat asked, taking in a deep waft of cinnamon.

"I didn't." Amos shook his head. "The Mufiki tribe has been using valerian root for centuries. It started there, but when I realized the herb made my beast agitated, I knew we had to find something that could last long term."

Romelo had told her the same thing. Valerian root was not a lasting solution because it numbed the body and soul, crushing the animal's spirit.

"Some shifters in Sandstone stopped transforming decades ago, but without their beasts the spirit dies. That was our birth parents' fate. Whether we witnessed them as children or thirty years later, they would have suffered. Lost to the madness of the mind." Amos turned away from his task to look at her. "We are Animalia. Our souls were split in two to help forge a better world, but we can't do that if our souls can't align with the beast."

"So what do you use if you can't use the blue lotus or valerian root?"

"I'm glad you asked." He smiled, adding three blue petals to the hot liquid.

"I wish it were as easy as a single herb, but the cure differs for everyone." Amos walked toward her, holding a mortar filled with ground herbs that wafted a delectable scent.

A woodsy, silky spice wrapped around the bitter essence of lemon and nectar-like nuances of the blue flowers. It called to her, crackling a fire under her scrunched nose. The lioness inside let out a small chuff, reveling in the savory aroma.

"Why does it smell sooooo good?"

She watched as Amos took the pestle and ground up a strip of dried lemongrass.

"It smells good to *you*. Not to everyone." He poured the paste into a thin cloth. "Every blend we make is uniquely designed for each Animalia. Every scent that calls to you creates the perfect blend to calm the senses."

"Everyone has a tea tailored to them, and anyone who says they don't like tea is a liar." Her words were breathless as the echo of their antelope mother's voice moved through her.

"Exactly, as Ma always used to say," Amos replied with a soft chuckle, his eyes glistening as though he, too, could hear her voice.

"Taste this. Tell me what you think." He held up the cup, guiding Kat to take a sip. Even with a burning tongue, she could taste an explosion of flavor that enveloped her body. It called to not only her senses but also called to her beast. Miraculously, completely settled, the beast inside of her purred.

"So, tell me? Did I get it right?"

Amos's voice was full of anticipation.

The blue lotus flower was subtle, but it was there. It was the key to calming the senses, but this tea was so much more. The earthy citrus of lemongrass was unmistakable. Once Sade introduced her to the herb, Kat had added it to every cup. It wasn't pungent, but its slight flavor could bring together almost any cup of tea.

The warm, woodsy scent of cinnamon wrapped the blend in a cocoon. Cinnamon wasn't her favorite, but it made her think of Amos and the hours he spent chopping the branches from the trees. He would tell her and Sade stories while they took their knives and cut back the thick bark layer by layer until they reached the rich center.

Butterfly pea flower was Sade's favorite. She loved to watch the color of her tea shift from a vibrant blue to a vivid purple with the added mix of citrus. Every day her older sister watched the color change with curiosity, as though she hadn't seen the magic a hundred times before. Just thinking about the gleam in Sade's eyes made her smile.

"It's almost perfect, but I think it might be better if you added—" She swept her tongue over her teeth and deciphered the missing ingredients. "Juniper berries. The edible ones, that is."

"Not a fan of poison?" Amos chuckled, turning back to his spice rack.

Kat laughed back, but the movement made her wince. "No, not at all. I already escaped death once. I don't think I can risk it again."

Dried sprigs of eucalyptus and cloves of garlic hung from the ceiling, and each shelf was overrun with an elixir seeping with different herbs, spices, and roots.

"You do all of this by yourself?" Kat asked, watching him stir in the berries.

"No, Talla helps a lot, but I'm hoping once you get settled here and get used to your strength and extra senses, that you might want to help. You were always better at crafting teas than I was."

Amos threw open the cabinet doors, grumbling softly to himself. His mumblings weren't beastly but were the sounds of a frustrated man unable to find anything in his many unlabeled and unorganized jars and vials.

"Of course! I'd love to help, but we are sorting through all of this first." She gave him a sharp, pointed look.

"Hey now, I've been busy! It isn't easy being a king. It's my job to stay on top of this. To be a leader and restore this lifeless desert. You know they don't even have crawdads? I'm dying out here." Amos wiped his brow and perked up when he found the jar he was looking for.

Kat emitted a short, low chuckle before her expression became serious. "No one is faulting you, Amos. It's truly amazing what you are doing for these shifters."

Amos carefully walked back to Kat, trying not to spill the nearly overflowing cup of tea.

"Like I said, everything happens for a reason. We were meant to be here. We were meant to help these shifters."

Taking a spot next to Kat on the bed, Amos carefully blew on the tea as though she was too fragile to do so herself. As childlike as the behavior was, Kat couldn't deny that she missed his comfort and diligent care.

While she would miss the antelope tribe, Kat knew they would be happy together. A small but powerful pride uniting the Animalia shifters to their lost souls.

When the ingredients settled into the blend, Amos lifted the cup to her lips once more, and she swallowed the liquid in three large gulps. The flavor of the tea reminded her of home, but home wasn't a place; it was a feeling. A perfect blend of all her favorite memories merged into one.

A soft purr not only vibrated through her lioness, but it also rumbled through her chest. Amos's face was filled with as much warmth as her own, and the same rumble reverberated through him.

Lifting her hand, Amos placed her palm over his chest.

"You feel that, Kat? We're home. It means we're home."

They took a few moments to hold one another, careful not to brush against her wound. As they reconnected, their souls exchanged purrs of joy and contentment.

Amos's eyes danced and his golden gaze reflected his excitement as he asked, "Are you ready to heal the rest of the way?"

He wasn't really asking if she was ready to heal. That was a senseless question because, of course, she no longer wished to suffer. What he was really asking was if she felt confident enough to shift. He wanted to know if her beast was stable.

"I think I'm ready. Once I shift, can I see everyone? I need to make sure Ram's okay."

"Of course. They are already waiting for you."

Kat was so eager to see her new friends and her uncle that she sprang ahead only to be halted by a stabbing ache and a deep, painful grunt.

"Hey, slow it down. I'll carry you there." Amos tightened the robe that had been loosely spread over her shoulders.

He carried her through the halls of the sandstone cave that was carved out from the mountainous slabs of stone. They walked until they reached a gigantic dome filled with dozens of shifters hanging flowers and herbs to dry.

In a unified formation, much like they would on her family farm, the Animalia shifters in Sandstone sifted through different seeds, peeled fruits, and stripped herbs from their stems.

A natural light shone through the dark cavern from a hollowed-out center at the top. It lit up the dome and sparkled against the red, orange, and yellow lines that patterned the sandstone.

Kat searched for the shifters she knew but couldn't see them in the colorful crowd. Moving into the center of the room, the sound of the workers' conversations died down and were replaced with hushed whispers as they caught sight of the two siblings.

Through the whispers, she could hear the grumbles of her uncle pushing his way through the dense crowd, dragging a chair behind him.

As soon as she settled into the seat, Ram dropped to his knees, careless with the gashes on his lower stomach, shoulder, and back. Placing her hand in his, Kat felt the tension leave his body, and a tiny bit of her own melted away.

"You scared me there for a second, kid."

Ram's grumbling voice was laced with deep concern. He took the time to scan her body for further injury, careful not to irritate her wounded chest when he lifted her arms and inspected the damage. When he was satisfied, his dark eyes melted into a muddy brown.

"Is everyone okay? The tribe? Kove? Romelo, Talla—Tongo?" Her worries tumbled out of her lips.

"They are all fine. Your prince made good on his promise." He gestured his hand toward the group standing in the far corner.

Even from a distance, Kat could see Romelo's jade eyes observing her. His arm was placed around his younger sister, who waved at her with excitement. Tongo and Talla stood next to them. Their support was tangible, written across the smiles and the gleam in their matching eyes.

Kat let out a sigh. The trapped air felt as though it was being sucked out of her body, leaving her with a sense of relief.

With a wave of his hand, Amos's voice rumbled like a thunderclap, drawing the attention of every shifter in the room.

"Animalia of the Outlands, Animalia of Sandstone! I ask that you welcome my sister, Katariya! Welcome her as she is, not for where she comes from. Welcome her as you have welcomed me. As her brother, I ask for your support, your wisdom, and your love in guiding this new Animalia. Join us as she opens her heart and soul to her lioness."

As Kat looked inside her soul, she heard a low growl emanating from her beast as its golden eyes gleamed. Instinctively, she looked at Amos, her biggest supporter, her brother, her best friend. His golden cinnamon eyes, a mirror of her lioness's, glowed with the same supportive look they shared during her archery lessons.

The crowd clapped and cheered, accompanying the sound of trumpets, brays, roars, and chuffs. They viewed her brother as their savior, and they stared at her with hopeful expressions, as though she were an extension of him.

"Can you help?"

Ram nodded, shrugging the robe from Kat's shoulders. Slowly rising to her feet, she used Ram's good arm as support.

Closing her eyes to the new world around her, she willed the shift to happen. Bones cracked and skin shed with an intensity that was far more painful than anything she had experienced so far. Her aching body contorted around her open chest wound, using the extra strength and magic of the lioness's spirit to fully heal her.

As her paws pounded on the ground, the lioness let out a soft chuff, wriggling her bushy tail and sharpening her nails on the rough stone. In moments, Amos was pulling off his own robe and, with a glow of light, he transformed with ease.

Taking his place was a lion. A thick chestnut mane flowed down his beast's neck, and his golden eyes shimmered with a rich, vibrant glow. As they looked out at the crowd, the two siblings could see nothing but supportive smiles and celebratory cheers.

Amos's beast scraped his claws on the sandstone floor, grounding his animal spirit in this world. As soon as he was settled in his new body, his beast let out a loud roar, echoing a single word that caused the crowd to return his sentiment.

A unified cadence called out to the heavens and beyond. Here, she would welcome a new *Pride*.

ACKNOWLEDGMENTS

Family. A family can look a lot of different ways and have different meanings and emotions tied to it. Family can mean love. Family can mean togetherness. Sometimes it can be overwhelming.

For me, family is everything. I am incredibly grateful to have two parents who have loved and supported me through every aspect of my life. I want to thank my mom for being my number one fan and my dad for always taking the time to involve himself in my interests, like watching Disney's *The Lion King* with me every New Year's Eve.

Somewhat similar to Katariya, I come from a blended family. Although my half-siblings and I are six years apart in age, I have always felt great comfort in the memories where we all lived in the same house together. Despite the time and miles between us, their love for me has never been questioned. I know that no matter what, they will stand by me.

Family can also be found in friendships, and in that, I thank my best friends for weaving themselves into my heart and into my family.

When I fell in love with my husband, I also fell in love with his family. My sister-in-law was a major help in the publication of this novel, and I can't wait to expand the Kingdom of Animalia Series with her by my side.

My most gracious thanks go to my husband. You are my best friend, and I couldn't have written this book without your love and support. *I love you forever and a day.*

The last special thanks goes to every animal I have had over the years. The love that animals have for you shows no bounds, and on the darkest of days, a vibrating purr or a wet kiss on the face is the only thing needed to turn the day around. You, too, are family.

It was a long time coming, but it feels fantastic to have this book out of my mind and on paper. I hope to continue writing with the same fevered ambition as I did while working on this novel.

Thank you again to all of my family and friends who supported and continue to support me along this journey! Every like, share, and compliment has been a motivator, and I can't wait to see what happens next!

GLOSSARY

Many of the animals mentioned in *A Whisper in the Wild: Kingdom of Animalia* are threatened, vulnerable, or endangered species. This means that these animals face different levels of extinction risks caused by overhunting, overharvesting, habitat loss, pollution, and more. During her writing process, Author Allysa Salena dedicated over 50 hours to watching animal documentaries and reading educational journals. Recognizing the platform, Allysa wants to educate the book's readers on animal and wildlife conservation.

On the next page readers can find a list of each species featured in *A Whisper in the Wild*, as well as their conservation status.

Lion - Status: *Vulnerable.* Lions are the most sociable of all big cat species. They live in groups called prides, which can comprise anywhere from 2 to 30 members. They have yellow-gold coats with brown tufts on the end of their tails. Male lions have shaggy manes that range in color from blond to reddish-brown to black. From prophecies, legends, and scriptures, lions have been dubbed as the king of the Jungle. Today, they have a population of 20,000-25,000 remaining.

Impala Antelope - Status: *Low Risk.* Habitat fragmentation and poaching threaten Impala safety. The Impala Antelope is 1 of 91 species of antelope, most of which are native to Africa. They have reddish brown fur with white under their belly. Male impalas have slender, ringed horns. They live in herds from 15 to 100 antelopes. In the wild, they are the primary source of food for carnivorous animals such as lions, cheetahs, leopards, hyenas, and painted dogs.

Jaguar - Status: *Near Threatened.* Jaguars have the largest jaws out of the entire big cat family. They have tawny colored coats with bold, black rosettes spotted across their bodies. They are found in South America and live in 18 different countries. Jaguars are strong swimmers and climbers and require a large territory to ensure survival.

Elephant - Status: *Endangered.* Massive gray mammals, weighing 4-7 tons, with large ears and a trunk made from pure muscle. They use the extra appendage to uproot trees, pick apart fruits, and to both drink and bathe. Between

2002-2011, Elephant populations declined by 62%. Today, there are 415,000 Elephants in the world. As the largest mammal on earth, they require large territories due to their migratory behaviors. Their homes are threatened and destroyed by human settlements, agricultural developments, and infrastructures such as roads, canals, and fences.

Gorilla - *Critically Endangered.* Gorillas share 98 percent of their DNA with humans, and they are smart enough to learn sign language and use tools. They are powerful animals with thick chests and wide shoulders, and other than their faces, hands, and feet, they are covered in thick black fur. Despite being 4 times stronger than humans, they are considered shy, gentle giants. Today, there are estimated to be less than 200,000 Gorillas remaining in the wild today.

Brown Bear - Status: *Least Concern.* In the United States, Brown Bears are called Grizzly Bears, while there is a subspecies known as Kodiak Bear, which is comparable in size to the Polar Bear. They have shaggy brown fur and can weigh up to 1,600 pounds. They can stand on two feet and communicate with one another through scratch marks left on trees. Today, there are estimated to be 110,000 Brown Bears.

African Buffalo - Status: *Near Threatened.* The African buffalo is the only type of animal that is a member of the buffalo and cattle family. They have dark brown to black-gray fur and can weigh up to almost 2,000 pounds. They have thick, broad horns expanding from the middle of their foreheads. These buffalo run in herds that can exceed over 1,000. Today, there are about 900,000 African buffalo, and 75% live in protected areas.

Okapi - Status: *Endangered*. Okapis are known as the "forest giraffe" and are one of the oldest mammals on Earth, yet they have only been known to scientists since the early 20th century. They are a shy and elusive species that are a huge part of indigenous culture. They have brown bodies with white legs and black and brown stripes. The stripes can act as a camouflage, mimicking the sun through the dense forest and act as guidance for their young to follow them through thick brush. Today, there are estimated between 10,000 to 20,000 Okapi remaining in the wild.

Hyena - Status: *Near Threatened*. Hyenas are dog-like carnivores found in Asia and Africa and are known scavengers. They have hunched backs with thick brown fur and, depending on the subspecies, they can have black spots or black stripes. In *A Whisper in the Wild*, and throughout many other films and books, hyenas have been portrayed as the villains. Despite their depiction in media, they play a crucial role in maintaining ecological balance. As scavengers they help prevent the spread of diseases and help keep the prey population under control. Human-wildlife conflicts are a major threat to hyenas, as they often prey on farmers' livestock. Along with encroaching on their land, they are often seen as pests by farmers and are poisoned as a result. There are between 5,000-14,000 hyenas left today.

Baird Tapir - Status: *Endangered*. Tapirs are large mammals that look like wild hogs with an anteater snout but are more closely related to horses and rhinos. They are endangered due to populations declining by over 50% in the past 3 generations and are projected to further decline by another 50% in the next 3 generations. Today, there are less than 5,500 Baird tapirs, while the Malay Tapirs have less than 2,500 remaining.

Capybara - Status: *Least Concern*. Capybaras are the largest rodents on Earth. They can weigh over 100 pounds and grow to be 4 feet tall. They have coarse brown fur and partially webbed feet that allow them to be excellent swimmers. Despite commonly being used for meat and leather, they are at low risk because of high breeding success.

Wild boar, *Least Concern*. **Oxen,** *Not Endangered*. **Zebra,** *Near Threatened*. **Ostrich,** *Least Concerned*. **Hippopotamus,** *Vulnerable*. **Sloth,** *Critically Endangered*. **Rhinoceros,** *Critically Endangered*. **Tiger,** *Endangered*. **Leopard,** *Critically Endangered*. **Cheetah,** *Endangered*. **Maned Wolf,** *Near Threatened*. **Giant Anteater,** *Vulnerable*. **Aardvark,** *Least Concern*. **Painted Dogs,** *Endangered*. **Chimpanzees,** *Endangered*. **Orangutan,** *Critically Endangered*. **Wildebeest,** *Least Concern*. **Crocodile,** *Vulnerable*. **Panther, *Vulnerable.* **Snow Leopard,** *Vulnerable.* **Bonobos,** *Endangered.*

LC	**Least Concern**
NT	**Near Threatened**
VU	**Vulnerable**
EN	**Endangered**
CR	**Critically Endangered**
EW	**Extinct in the Wild**
EX	**Extinct**

Author Allysa Salena kindly asks that you take the time to research the Wildlife Warriors, World Wildlife Fund, National Wildlife Federation, and Endangered Species Coalition. Through these organizations, you can learn more about different animal species and what you can do to help.

Even if you don't believe that you directly affect the species listed above, you will find that there are animals at risk in every state, country, and continent.

To reduce your impact, try these recommendations from the Endangered Species Coalition:

1.) Create a wildlife habitat in your own backyard, such as bird feeders and baths, bee fountains, nesting boxes, and other covered areas.

2.) Plant native vegetation in your yard or garden (avoid invasive species and non-native plants).

3.) Minimize the use of herbicides and pesticides as well as the overuse of fertilizer.

4.) Place decals on cars to deter bird collisions (millions of birds die every year from collisions).

5.) Slow down when driving (350 million animals are killed by traffic each year in the US alone).

6.) Never purchase products from endangered species like ivory, coral, and tortoise shells (Always buy exotic plants and animals from reputable stores).

7.) Reduce your water use in the home and garden (Do not dump paint, oil, antifreeze, or other chemicals, which pollute the water and can harm people and wildlife).

8.) DON'T LITTER (Hold on to your trash until you see a bin).

9.) As always, try your best to REDUCE, REUSE, RECYCLE.